"A sweet tale of the coziest kind! Mix a little chocolate with a dash of murder and a pinch of deception, and you get *Candy Apple Dead*, a new mystery that is sweet, deadly, and highly entertaining . . . A lively, fast-paced story of sweet and sour."
—*The Best Reviews*

"A promising new mystery series. Abby is a wonderful new character . . . Anyone with even a minor sweet tooth will enjoy the various descriptions and recipes included here."
—*The Romance Readers Connection*

"Small-town intrigue, a juicy conflict or two, and some fun characters are the highlights of this story, which launches what will probably be an exceedingly popular new series. Carter has a very accessible style—and is equally talented at inducing sugar cravings in the reader. Dieters beware!"
—*Romantic Times*

"Delightful start to a new mystery series featuring a feisty heroine . . . An engaging, entertaining tale . . . Abby is a sensible, believable heroine. She's strong, yet vulnerable, and definitely feisty! The story moves along at a quick pace . . . And the Divine Almond Toffee . . . yummy!"—*Fresh Fiction*

"A delicious whodunit full of interesting, well-developed characters. I can't wait for the next installment!"
—*Affaire de Coeur* (four and a half stars)

"An exciting one-sitting amateur-sleuth tale . . . Readers will appreciate [Abby's] spunk and desire to insure justice occurs."
—*Midwest Book Review*

A Candy Shop Mystery

Goody Goody Gunshots

Sammi Carter

BERKLEY PRIME CRIME, NEW YORK

THE BERKLEY PUBLISHING GROUP
Published by the Penguin Group
Penguin Group (USA) Inc.
375 Hudson Street, New York, New York 10014, USA

Penguin Group (Canada), 90 Eglinton Avenue East, Suite 700, Toronto, Ontario M4P 2Y3, Canada
(a division of Pearson Penguin Canada Inc.)
Penguin Books Ltd., 80 Strand, London WC2R 0RL, England
Penguin Group Ireland, 25 St. Stephen's Green, Dublin 2, Ireland (a division of Penguin Books Ltd.)
Penguin Group (Australia), 250 Camberwell Road, Camberwell, Victoria 3124, Australia
(a division of Pearson Australia Group Pty. Ltd.)
Penguin Books India Pvt. Ltd., 11 Community Centre, Panchsheel Park, New Delhi—110 017, India
Penguin Group (NZ), 67 Apollo Drive, Rosedale, North Shore 0632, New Zealand
(a division of Pearson New Zealand Ltd.)
Penguin Books (South Africa) (Pty.) Ltd., 24 Sturdee Avenue, Rosebank, Johannesburg 2196,
South Africa

Penguin Books Ltd., Registered Offices: 80 Strand, London WC2R 0RL, England

This is a work of fiction. Names, characters, places, and incidents either are the product of the author's imagination or are used fictitiously, and any resemblance to actual persons, living or dead, business establishments, events, or locales is entirely coincidental. The publisher does not have any control over and does not assume any responsibility for author or third-party websites or their content.

PUBLISHER'S NOTE: The recipes contained in this book are to be followed exactly as written. The publisher is not responsible for your specific health or allergy needs that may require medical supervision. The publisher is not responsible for any adverse reactions to the recipes contained in this book.

GOODY GOODY GUNSHOTS

A Berkley Prime Crime Book / published by arrangement with the author

PRINTING HISTORY
Berkley Prime Crime mass-market edition / September 2008

Copyright © 2008 by The Berkley Publishing Group.
Cover illustration by Jeff Crosby.
Cover design by Steven Ferlauto.
Interior text design by Kristin del Rosario.

ISBN: 978-0-425-22332-1

BERKLEY® PRIME CRIME
Berkley Prime Crime Books are published by The Berkley Publishing Group,
a division of Penguin Group (USA) Inc.,
375 Hudson Street, New York, New York 10014.
BERKLEY PRIME CRIME and the BERKLEY PRIME CRIME design are trademarks
belonging to Penguin Group (USA) Inc.

PRINTED IN THE UNITED STATES OF AMERICA

10 9 8 7 6 5 4 3 2 1

Chapter 1

A chill November wind howled outside the windows of my car as I pulled into the drive outside my brother's old farmhouse. Lights spilled from the windows, making the house look warm and welcoming, and I allowed myself a moment's regret that I wouldn't be going inside. In the distance, the Colorado Rockies formed a protective barrier around the valley and the town of Paradise. I could see their snow-covered spines arching upward in the moonlight to meet the night sky.

Trees towered over the two-story house, and even from where I sat I could hear the branches scratching the walls of the old house. Dry leaves and bits of dirt scuttled across the gravel driveway. A cool gust of wind filled the car as the back doors opened and my nephews, Brody and Caleb, spilled happily out into the storm. Each clutched a small tin of their favorite candy under one arm. With a wave, nine-year-old Caleb raced up the driveway and disappeared into the kitchen. His older brother Brody hung back for a minute.

My sister-in-law, Elizabeth, appeared in the kitchen window and peered out into the darkness. I flashed my lights, hoping she'd realize that Brody was still with me.

A gust of wind swept a lock of Brody's dark blond hair into his eyes. Looking far too serious for a twelve-year-old, he reached back into the car for his basketball, and I was struck by his resemblance to my brother. When he suddenly grinned, the resemblance grew even stronger. "So, have you thought about it?"

He was like his father in more than just looks. Neither of them had any patience, and once they got their teeth into something, they didn't let go. Elizabeth said it was a trait all of us Shaws shared, but I couldn't see it in myself.

Since Wyatt had to work late and Elizabeth had had a conflicting engagement, I'd gone with the boys to their Youth League basketball game that evening. Frankly, I'd jumped at the chance. I'd lived away for most of their lives, and I welcomed every opportunity I could find to bond with them now.

Once there, they'd talked me into sitting on the bench in the empty assistant coach's spot to keep the team from forfeiting the game. It wasn't until the game was over and the three of us were eating pizza and chugging Cokes that my sneaky little nephews revealed their true reason for asking me to come with them tonight.

I motioned for Brody to get in out of the wind. "You only asked me about being assistant coach an hour ago. I haven't had time to think about it."

"If you think about it too much, you might say no," Brody said impatiently. "Please? We need you there."

I laughed and shifted into park. "So your nefarious plan is to lock me into a promise before I can say no? Nice try, but I know better than to think you *need* me. I'd be about as useless when it comes to coaching a team as your dad would be in the candy shop."

Brody's smile faded. "That's not true. Dad said you used to play on a team and everything."

"That was many years ago. I've forgotten everything I used to know." His little face registered such disappointment, I looked away before it could influence me. I'm a sucker when it comes to Wyatt's four kids, and they all know it. "In case you didn't notice, I didn't do anything tonight."

"You don't have to *do* anything," Brody insisted. "Coach knows plenty. We just need another grown-up there, or we can't play anymore."

I made the mistake of looking at Brody, and a powerful auntlike instinct urged me to say yes. Unfortunately, I had half a dozen good reasons for saying no. "Don't you think Coach Hendrix would rather have an assistant coach who knows something about the game?"

"He doesn't care. Honest! He likes doing everything himself."

I laughed, knowing that what he said was probably true. Kerry Hendrix was a bit of a control freak. I didn't want to give Brody false hope, but that aunt thing poked at me again and made me ask, "How often do you guys practice?"

"Mostly once a week." Brody shifted his weight around, and his gaze dropped to his hands. "Sometimes two. And then there are the games. We usually play once or twice a week."

"You'd need me three or four days *every week*?"

"Yeah, but only for a couple of hours, and it's after work. Mostly."

Four days a week probably didn't sound like much to a kid, but I'd only inherited Divinity a couple of years earlier, and I was barely keeping up with the candy shop's demands as it was. With just two of us working sales, and one of me hand-making the majority of the candy we sold, when did I have time to do anything extra?

I knew I should say no. I *had* to say no. But then I looked at Brody's little face again, and my resolve dissolved like sugar in hot water. I'm such a sucker. For the past two years, I'd been searching for some way to connect with the boys. Now one had landed in my lap. How could I turn my back on it? But I also had responsibilities, obligations to Karen and to the shop. How could I say yes?

Knowing I'd cave in if I stayed there even a minute longer, I made myself say, "I don't know, Brody. I'm going to have to think about it."

"But we have to prove to the league that we have another coach in two days. If we don't, we can't play this season."

"I understand that," I said, "but I'm not sure I can commit to something that's going to take so much time. I have to consider what's best for the shop."

"Can't Karen take care of the store while you're gone?"

Karen was my cousin and assistant manager of Divinity. Actually, she knew more about the candy-making business than I did, but I was learning. "Karen and I are barely keeping our heads above water the way things are right now," I told Brody. "If I disappear four times a week, the whole thing might go under."

Disappointment flashed across his face, but he tried to look brave. "Okay."

I felt like a weasel. "I'm not saying no," I said, backpedaling so I wouldn't have to see his little chin quiver. "I'll still come out here tomorrow and talk to Coach Hendrix like I said I would."

"Yeah, but you probably *will* say no."

"I might," I said honestly, "but not because I don't want to help out. You know that, don't you?"

"Yeah." He swept his gaze across my face quickly and got out of the car again. "I gotta go. Mom's waiting for me."

He scuffed his feet as he crossed the yard and dragged himself onto the back porch. I'd let him down, but what other choice could I have made?

Feeling lower than pond scum, I watched until he was safely inside, then put the Jetta into reverse and backed out of the yard. Newcomers to the area sometimes find the closeness of the mountains intimidating. Some even become claustrophobic. But for those of us born in the heart of the Rockies, these peaks are a comforting presence, and I needed their comfort tonight. Even with a storm looming, their solid, steady presence made me feel as if everything would be all right. I wanted to believe that, but I wasn't so sure.

Lost in thought, I reached the main road and turned toward town. The storm was gaining strength, and wind buffeted the car as I maneuvered along the twisting two-lane highway that separates my brother's house from town. Every few minutes a handful of raindrops hit my windshield—just enough to blur my vision, but never enough to swipe away with the wipers.

I forgot all about the blinking red light the county had recently installed at Hammond Junction until I was almost upon it. I'm still not sure what actually pulled me out of my reverie enough to hit the brakes, but as I did, I caught a movement out of the corner of my eye and a short, dirty man in a trench coat and knit cap stumbled onto the highway in front of my car.

I jammed my foot hard onto the brake and shouted, "Hey! Watch out!" but my windows were up, and I don't think he heard me. My tires bit on the gravel that was scattered over the highway's surface, and I skidded sideways, straight toward the man who stood in the glow of my headlights, his eyes wide with shock.

At the last second, my tires found something solid, and the car jerked out of its spin. The man's eyes met mine, and I realized that the shock on his face had been replaced by a look of terror. Smudges of dirt and grime covered his face, and it looked as if he hadn't shaved in days. He stretched one trembling hand toward me.

I sat frozen, unable to move, while my heart slammed against my rib cage and my mouth grew dry from a mixture of fear and anger. What in the hell was wrong with him, darting into the road like that? I could have killed him! Did he even realize how close I'd come to hitting him?

Anger was just what I needed to get my brain in gear. I fumbled for the window control on my armrest, ready to yell at the idiot who'd almost gotten himself killed. But before I could get the window down, he jerked upright and lurched away from my car toward the other side of the highway. He ran awkwardly, dragging one foot slightly as he moved.

Had he limped before, or had I hit him? I could have sworn that I hadn't, but what if I was wrong? Anger changed to guilt in the blink of an eye. I didn't want a lawsuit to blindside me later, so I grabbed the door handle.

"Hey!" I shouted again.

Whether he couldn't hear me over the wind or chose to ignore me, he kept running.

I thought about going after him, but something about the deserted road, the rising wind, and the shadows on the sides of the street stopped me. He'd be okay, I told myself. I'd probably frightened him as much as he'd frightened me, that's all.

Giving a thin laugh, I reached for the gearshift. At the

same moment, a loud bang sounded just outside my car, followed by a second, and then a third. The man in the trench-coat jerked backwards with each shot, and then, while I watched too stunned to move, dropped to the ground like a rag doll.

Chapter 2

Thirty minutes after I left it, I pulled back into my brother's driveway. I'd tried calling both Wyatt and the police from my cell as I drove, but the storm must have been playing havoc with the signal—it's not even all that reliable in good weather. That's one of the bad things about living in the mountains, I guess, but it's a small price to pay for the scenery and the lifestyle.

I left the car running and pounded onto the porch, helped along by a gust of wind. I rang the doorbell out of courtesy, but turned the knob to let myself inside at the same time. "Wyatt? Where are you? It's me, Abby."

Footsteps sounded overhead, and boards creaked under my brother's weight as he came down the stairs. "Abby? What the hell's wrong with you? You're making enough noise to wake the dead."

I hurried down the hall and met him at the bottom of the stairs. He's five years older than me, a wall of solid muscle from working hard his whole life. If it weren't for the liberal streaks of gray in his hair and the wrinkles etched into his weathered skin, he might have been able to pass for much younger. Sometimes when I look at him, I see Grandpa Hanks scowling out of his deep brown eyes. Tonight, even with irritation written all over his face, I saw the big brother who once threatened to toss a couple of boys into a ditch for bothering me, and that's the one I needed.

He scratched at the T-shirt covering his chest, and I realized he was wearing nothing else but a pair of boxers. "What is it?" he demanded. "Don't tell me you have a flat tire, because I'm not going out in the middle of the night to change it for you."

Okay, so he's not exactly a knight in shining armor. He's big, and he's tough, and he's nicer than he acts most of the time. "My tires are fine." I glanced up the stairs to make sure none of his kids were listening, then snagged his arm and drew him a few feet away just to be sure. "Go get dressed, while I call the police. I just saw a man get shot, and I need you to come with me."

I started toward the kitchen phone, but Wyatt caught my arm and stopped me in my tracks. "Whoa, whoa, whoa. Wait a second. You saw *what*?"

"Keep your voice down," I warned in a whisper. "I don't want the kids to hear us." Then, because he was obviously losing patience, I said again, "I just saw a man get shot out at Hammond Junction. I don't know who he was, but somebody shot him right in front of me."

"Are you kidding?"

"Do I look like I'm kidding?" I pulled my arm out of his grip and waved him back toward the stairs. "Get dressed," I said again. "I'm going to call the police. I'll tell you everything I can on the way."

"You want me to go with you to a place where a man just got murdered? Are you nuts?"

"I'm going to have to show the police where it happened," I explained, trying hard to hang on to my patience. "I'd kind of like to have somebody with me while I wait. Besides, he might still be alive, so *hurry*. What's wrong with you, anyway?"

"What's wrong with *me*?" Wyatt barked a laugh. "Some guy's out there shooting people, and you want me to drive you back there so *we* can get shot?"

"I want you to drive me out there so we can make sure the poor man who already got shot gets medical attention if he's still alive. Whoever shot him isn't going to hang around waiting to get caught. He's probably long gone by now."

"You don't know that for sure."

"Would you hang around?" I marched into the kitchen,

grabbed the phone, and punched in the number for the police. Wyatt trailed after me, still scratching. Before he could say something dumb like claiming he *would* hang around the scene of a shooting, Justin Cole picked up the dispatch phone at the police station.

I breathed a sigh of relief. I'd met Justin a few times, and I liked him. I filled him in on the crime I'd witnessed, and he promised to send someone to investigate right away. I promised to meet the officers on the scene and started to hang up, but at the last minute I asked Justin to let Pine Jawarski know what was going on.

Jawarski's a friend. Some might even say he's more than a friend, but if you ask the two of us, we'll both tell you that hasn't been established yet. He's also a detective with the Paradise Police, and if I had to go back out to Hammond Junction in the middle of the night, I wanted him there.

With the phone call out of the way, I turned back to my conversation with Wyatt because, of course, he hadn't moved an inch the whole time I was on the phone. He's stubborn like that. "Let's say you just shot somebody," I said, still trying to hang on to my patience. "What would you do? Hang out in the bushes waiting for the police to show up, or hightail it to someplace safe?"

I don't know what Wyatt would have said to that, because Elizabeth chose that moment to join us. She was dressed for bed in a pair of flannel pajama pants and one of Wyatt's T-shirts. Her sandy red hair hung loose to her shoulders, and her hazel eyes were dark with concern. "What's this about a shooting?"

Apparently, Wyatt and I hadn't done a very good job of keeping our voices down.

Wyatt jerked his head toward me. "Abby says she saw somebody get shot out at Hammond Junction. She wants me to go back there with her to make sure the guy's okay and wait for the police."

The concern in Elizabeth's eyes deepened. "He was shot? Are you sure?"

"I heard the shots and saw him go down."

"But he's not dead?"

"I didn't wait around to find out," I explained. "My first instinct was to get out of there and call the police."

"Good instincts." Oblivious to the need for a quick response, she dragged a chair from the table and sank into it. "Do you know who it was?"

I shook my head. "I only saw him for a minute. I don't think it's someone I know, but I may have seen him around town. I didn't see who shot him. Whoever it was must have been hiding in the trees on the side of the road. I didn't even know he was there until I heard the gunshots."

Elizabeth gave a shudder and turned her gaze toward my brother. "You can't let her go back there alone."

"I don't want her to go at all," Wyatt snarled. "Seems to me the smart thing would be to let the police come here to talk to her."

"Wyatt—"

"No, Elizabeth. I mean it. If I go with her, it will only encourage her."

"Wyatt."

My brother jerked one hand through the air and glared at his wife. "She doesn't need to be there, Lizzie. You know what she's like. If I go back there with her now, the next thing we know, she'll be up to her eyeballs in it."

"Hey!" I said, "I'm right here in the room, remember? And just for the record, I have no intention of getting up to my eyeballs in anything."

Wyatt snorted a laugh. "Yeah. Right. That's what you say now."

"And that's what I'll say when the police meet us at the junction. No matter what you think, I'm not running around looking for trouble. Like I said, I don't even know who the guy was."

"Yeah, but you'll find out," Wyatt predicted, "and then you'll figure out some reason you need to get yourself wrapped up in the middle of it. And the next thing you know, you'll be in some kind of trouble, and then guess who you'll call."

Jerk. Just because that's what had happened a couple of

times in the past . . . I glared at him and patted my pockets, trying to figure out where I'd put my keys. "Fine. Don't come with me then. I'll go by myself. I've already been here too long."

"Abby, wait!" Looking stern and maternal, Elizabeth glared at her husband. "You can't let her go back out there by herself, Wyatt. She's your sister."

He growled low in his throat and turned away.

"Don't push him," I insisted. "I'll be fine. I've been hanging around here so long, the police are probably there already." I gave Elizabeth a brief hug, promised to call when I was home safe, and let myself out onto the back porch. I'd just settled behind the steering wheel of the Jetta when I saw Wyatt come out the front door, his hunting rifle in one hand.

He'd pulled on a pair of jeans and some boots, and he motioned for me to get out of my car and into his truck. Irritated as I was with him, I was also relieved. He put the rifle on its rack in the back window and climbed into the driver's seat, while I hoisted myself into the passenger's seat.

With a pointed look at me, he started the truck, gunned the engine a couple of times to show me how annoyed he was, and shifted into reverse. "Damn pain in my ass," he muttered as he backed the truck around the Jetta.

"Yeah, maybe," I snarled back, "but at least we're even. It's no joyride having you for a brother, either."

I couldn't be sure, but I thought I saw his lips twitch. He blusters and bluffs a lot, but like I said before, underneath it all, he's got a good heart. It's just that sometimes you have to dig really deep to find it.

We carried on only desultory conversation as we covered the distance to the junction. There just wasn't a whole lot we hadn't said.

When we finally reached the junction, Wyatt pulled to the side of the road just before the flashing red stoplight. Now that we were here, I was more nervous than I'd expected to be. I felt like there were eyes watching me from the side of the road, and I had no way of knowing whether the feeling was real or imaginary.

Wyatt jumped from the truck and grabbed the rifle, looking like a page right out of history as he stood there with the rifle held firmly across his chest. "So? Where is he?"

I came around the front of the truck to stand by him and scanned the opposite side of the road quickly. I pinpointed the spot where the man fell easily enough, but where I expected to see a body, I found only gravel and dry grass. "He should be right over there," I said when I realized Wyatt was waiting for an answer.

"Where?"

"There. He fell just a little to the right of that rock."

"You're sure?"

"I'm positive. My car was stopped right about there," I said, indicating a spot just this side of the traffic light. "He fell almost directly across from me, there." I started across the highway, determined to figure out where he'd gone. "He must have been alert enough to drag himself out of harm's way."

Wyatt followed me and peered down at the ground where the man's body should have been. "You're sure he was shot?"

Fear was rapidly giving way to anger. I rounded on my brother and shouted, "How many times are you going to ask me that? *Of course* I'm sure. I wouldn't have come to get you if I weren't. The gunman fired three shots, and the guy went down like a bag of rocks *right there*."

Wyatt kept his eyes locked on the ground in front of him. "Then where's the blood?"

"What?"

"If he was shot, there should be blood. There isn't."

I looked again, but I didn't need to. I knew he was right. There was no body, no blood. In fact, there was no sign that anything had gone wrong here at all.

Chapter 3

Wyatt and I didn't say much to each other while we waited for the police to arrive. We'd climbed back into the truck where at least we had a couple of locked doors between us and whoever else might be out there. He sat slouched down on his tailbone, his head tilted back against the seat, eyes closed—or nearly so. He might look lazy and unconcerned, but I know my brother, and I knew he was aware of everything around him.

I couldn't tell whether he believed me about the shooting or not. Not that it mattered. I knew what I'd seen. Wind buffeted the truck, and cold air seeped inside from a crack somewhere. I could feel it brushing my neck every few minutes, but I refused to ask Wyatt to turn on the truck's heater. No way I was going to let him think I was a sissy, and besides, he has strict rules against idling any motor vehicle for more than a minute or two. Something about fuel residue condensing inside the engine.

Anyway, I had my rising fury to keep me warm. If this was some kind of joke, it wasn't funny. What if the boys had been with me? What if I hadn't been the one driving? What if one of Wyatt's twin daughters had been behind the wheel? Danielle and Dara both had new driver's licenses and drove every chance they got.

After what seemed like forever, sirens sounded in the distance and grew steadily closer. A few minutes later, Wyatt and I were bathed in the surreal flashing of red and blue bubble lights.

Wyatt sat up and cut a glance at me. "Well, come on. Let's get this over with."

I opened the truck's door, battled with the wind for a few seconds, and jumped to the pavement as Jawarski's truck pulled up behind the patrol car. He glanced around quickly, spotted us standing there, and strode along the edge of the highway toward me.

Jawarski and I might not have been able to figure out what's going on between the two of us, but when the chips are down, there's nobody I'd rather see. Knowing that I've started to rely on him to some degree bothers me a little, but I'm learning to cope.

We made eye contact while the first cop on the scene got my story, but Jawarski made no effort to interfere with the process. He listened while I talked, made an occasional note in the notebook he keeps in his shirt pocket, and glanced at Wyatt several times, apparently trying to figure out what my brother thought about what I was saying.

That annoyed me, but it didn't surprise me. Wyatt and Jawarski knew each other only slightly, but they'd immediately formed a mutual admiration society—something that both pleased and annoyed me at the same time. Wyatt hadn't ever liked my ex-husband, Roger, and it turned out he'd been right. I appreciated the fact that he approved of Jawarski. I just didn't like it when they teamed up against me.

It wasn't until the uniformed officers had drifted away to search for evidence that Jawarski said anything to me at all. Keeping his voice low, he looked me square in the eye and asked, "You okay?"

I nodded. "I'm fine. I was pretty shaken up when it first happened, but I'm calmer now. More angry than anything else."

"So tell me again," he said, slipping easily from friend to cop in the bat of an eye, "you were driving home from Wyatt's, and what happened?"

I told my story again, while Jawarski made a few more notes. It's irritating to answer the same questions over and over again, but I was an attorney in my previous life, so I know about interrogation techniques, and I understood why the police do what they do.

When I finished, he nodded slowly. In his best cop voice, he asked, "You're *sure* that's what you saw?"

"Of course I'm sure." He looked at Wyatt over the top of my head, and I felt the slim hold I'd been managing to keep on my patience slipping. "Would you stop looking at Wyatt? He wasn't here. *I* was. I know it's hard to believe, but I'm not making things up, and I'm not overreacting."

Jawarski hadn't exactly been smiling, but his expression sobered immediately. "I never said you were making it up, Abby, but you have to admit it's a little strange that we can't find any sign of foul play. If the guy was shot the way you say he was, seems like we'd find *something*."

"That's what I think," Wyatt said. "There'd be blood, signs of a struggle . . ." As if he was suddenly an expert in crime scene investigation.

I growled at both of them and headed once again toward the place the body should have been. "Maybe the guy with the limp was standing farther from the side of the road than I thought at first."

Jawarski grabbed my arm and hauled me back to stand beside him like I was nothing more substantial than a rag doll. "Just stop right there, Abby. My guys'll do the searching. They don't need your help. Besides, if there *is* evidence in that patch of weeds, I don't want you destroying it."

When he's not playing cop, I like the fact that Jawarski's bigger and stronger than I am. Just about any woman packing more pounds than she likes would feel the same way. But he *was* working, and I resented being manhandled. I jerked my arm away and put a few more inches between us. "You're going to have them search, even though you don't believe me?"

"Lighten up, Sis," Wyatt snapped. "He never said he didn't believe you."

"Not in so many words, but I can see it in his eyes. Are you humoring me, Jawarski?"

"I wouldn't waste taxpayer dollars," he said, as if that was supposed to make me feel better. "I'm just suggesting that maybe someone was pulling a joke," Jawarski said. "Is that possible?"

"Some joke, pretending to shoot someone in the chest." I leaned against the bed of Wyatt's truck and thought over the chain of events again. "It's possible, I suppose," I admitted grudgingly, "but who'd do something like that? And you didn't see the look on that poor man's face. He was terrified of something."

"Okay, then," Jawarski conceded. "Tell me more about him."

I sighed in frustration. "I've told you everything I remember. He looked short for a man. I'm guessing maybe five four. He was dirty, and his clothes looked like he'd pulled them out of a garbage can."

"What about his hair color?"

"Dark. Eyes the same. If he had any distinguishing marks or scars, I couldn't see them under all the dirt."

"You're sure the limp was real?" Wyatt asked.

"I can't be one hundred percent certain, but yeah, I think it was."

"And you're sure he wasn't limping because of the run-in with your car," Jawarski said.

I shook my head again. "No. I've been over and over that since it happened. I didn't hit him, but I came close. I'm sure the limp wasn't caused by me."

"And you didn't see the shooter at all," Jawarski said.

"I didn't see the shooter at all."

"If you had to guess, where would you say the shots came from?"

I closed my eyes, relived the moment for the hundredth time since it happened, and pointed toward a grove of trees on my right. "If I had to guess, I'd say the shooter was hiding in there."

"You didn't see or hear anything unusual?"

"I didn't hear anything, see anything, smell, taste, or feel anything unusual. I didn't even realize there was anyone else around until I heard the shots."

"And when you heard the shots? What happened then?"

Even though I understood why he asked, the questions were starting to wear on me. I kneaded my forehead with my fingertips and went over the same ground for the umpteenth time. "He was running in that direction," I said, indicating a tangle of brush across the street. "I heard the shots, and he sort of stopped and then dropped. He just crumpled to the ground like a bundle of old rags."

Jawarski looked as if he was about to say something else, but one of the officers who'd been looking through the trees shouted, "Got some tire tracks over here, Detective," and whatever Jawarski had been thinking was immediately forgotten.

I jumped as if I'd been poked with a cattle prod and started toward the officer. Jawarski and his long legs passed me as if I was standing still, and Wyatt was only half a step behind him.

Hoping that someone had finally found proof that I wasn't hallucinating, I kicked myself into high gear and pushed through an opening in the trees I hadn't noticed before. I stopped on the edge of a clearing about twenty feet square, and I could tell immediately that it had been flattened by more than one set of tires. "Anything?"

Jawarski crouched to look at the prints the officer pointed out to him but shook his head as he stood again. "There've been cars here recently, but it's impossible to tell how recently. We haven't had rain in weeks."

"But they could be fresh," I prodded.

"They could be." Jawarski tucked his notebook into his breast pocket and put a hand on my elbow. "We'll check them out, but I don't think they're going to tell us anything. There are probably a thousand vehicles around here with tires like those."

"So now what?"

Jawarski shook his head slowly. "We'll keep checking, Abby, but I wouldn't worry too much. If the man you saw had actually been shot, there would be signs of foul play. Whatever you saw, it wasn't murder."

I chewed my thumbnail and tried to figure out what I'd missed. I *knew* I'd seen the limping man get shot. There was no question in my mind. But I also knew that Jawarski was right; there wasn't one shred of evidence to prove it.

Chapter 4

"They found nothing at all?" my cousin Karen asked the next morning. Not surprisingly, I hadn't slept well the night before, and she'd noticed something was wrong with me the instant I stepped into the shop. After making coffee and pouring two cups, she sat me down at one of the wrought-iron tables in the shop and pumped me for information.

"Are you *sure* you saw the guy get shot?" She asked, brushing a lock of auburn hair from her eyes.

"I'm positive. Why does everybody keep asking me that?"

Karen, ever practical, shrugged, scowled at something on the opposite wall, and stood again. "Because there's no sign that it happened." Quick as a whip, she darted behind the counter, grabbed a handful of handmade candy sticks, and headed back to the nook where we'd set up the display of old-fashioned candies.

I couldn't just sit there while Karen worked, so I carried my coffee behind the counter and glanced out the kitchen door to make sure Max, my Doberman pinscher, was still curled in a sunny spot. The dog had spent his formative years as the inventory retrieval specialist for a friend's clothing business. When Brandon died, I took Max in, but the poor dog's life had been forever altered when he moved from a clothing store to a candy shop.

Health codes prevented me from letting him hang out in our shop, but he didn't mind spending time outside when the weather was good. Unfortunately, he made no effort to hide his unhappiness when it wasn't. Luckily, last night's storm had blown itself out, and the day had dawned sunny and warm, so Max seemed content.

I had no idea what I'd do when the weather turned really cold. During the worst of the previous winter I'd sometimes let Max stay in the rooms on the second floor of our building. Recently, though, I'd wiped out most of my bank account repairing and renovating that space. We'd added a small service kitchen, replaced windows, repaired walls, and created a space large enough to host parties and meetings. I was pleased with the results, so I wasn't willing to leave a lonely Doberman alone up there.

Through the front window, I saw the people of Paradise going about their business. Marshall Ames on his way to his restaurant. Carma Moran walking toward Once Upon a Crime, the bookstore around the corner. Kim-Ly Trang setting out signs to advertise a sale at 415, her boutique across the street from Divinity.

I sliced the Chocolate Sour Cream Coffee Cake I'd made the day before while Karen restocked empty spots left on our display shelves from yesterday's business. If the folks at my old law firm could have seen me now, searching for recipes in magazines, books, and online to supplement the list Aunt Grace had left me—and enjoying it—they'd have fallen over in disbelief.

"The guy jumped into the road right in front of me," I said, resisting the urge to help myself to a small piece. I'd already baked a test cake and together, Karen and I, along with a few friends, had pronounced it edible. I'd probably gained two pounds from that alone. Karen had been blessed with some mutant gene that allowed her to eat everything in sight and never gain an ounce. Standing next to her usually left me feeling like a lump, so I tried not to overindulge—most of the time.

"At first I thought I'd hit him," I went on, "but then he ran off, and I realized I hadn't. The shots came just as he reached the other side of the road. I was absolutely positive that he was at least hit."

"But Jawarski said there was no blood?"

"Not a drop." I dusted each piece of cake with confectioners sugar, then carefully inserted one into a small gold-edged Divinity gift box. "I stayed there for more than an hour. I looked everywhere, Wyatt looked and the police, too. None of us could find anything."

With the displays stocked, Karen pulled the cash drawer from the small safe in our office and wedged it into the old-fashioned register on the glass counter. "He must not have been hit," she said with a scowl. "Otherwise, there would have been some sign of it."

Frustrated, I closed the first cake box and set it aside. "I *know* that. Jawarski and Wyatt pointed that out at least half a dozen times last night. There doesn't seem to be any explanation for what happened, but that doesn't change the facts. I know what I saw."

"Maybe he only pretended to be shot," Karen offered.

"Why would he do that?"

Karen lifted a shoulder and shut the cash register drawer. "Maybe he and the other guy were working together, trying to get you out of your car for some reason."

I gaped at her, not because she'd come up with the suggestion, but because I hadn't thought of it myself. "Of course! They must have been counting on me to get out of the car and check on the guy after he went down."

"And once you did . . ." Karen only shrugged again, but I figured we were both thinking the same thing. I could have been hurt or killed last night, and if I'd been a kinder, gentler soul, I might have been.

With a shudder, I scooped another piece of cake into its box. "I don't like the sound of this," I said. "If these guys are hanging around Paradise, they could try it again." And next time they *might* get one of my nieces or even Elizabeth. I didn't think Elizabeth would be lured out of her car, but I wasn't so sure about Danielle and Dana.

"That's true," Karen said, "but now that the police know, I'm sure they'll keep their eyes open."

"I wouldn't count on that," I mumbled. "I'm pretty sure Jawarski thinks I exaggerated what I saw."

"Even if that's true," Karen said, "what can we do about it? We don't *know* that's what those men were doing last night."

"No," I admitted reluctantly, "but we could find out. All we'd have to do is find the guy with the limp and make him talk."

Karen stared at me as if I'd lost my mind. "Assuming we could find him, how would we make him talk? Threaten him with a lollipop stick?"

"No. But if we could just prove that he exists, Jawarski would have to believe me."

Karen laughed and pulled the key from its hook beneath the register. "Jawarski doesn't *have* to do anything, Abby," she said as she headed for the front door. "By the way, how did your evening with the boys go last night?"

Reluctantly, I abandoned the shooting, real or imagined, and moved on. "It was fine. Brody scored eight points, and Caleb actually pulled down a rebound. The whole team did well, as a matter of fact. They seem to like their coach."

"Really?" She looked surprised. "Didn't you say that Kerry Hendrix is coaching their team?"

I boxed up another piece of cake. "Yeah, why?"

"You probably don't remember him, do you?"

I shook my head. "He can't be more than thirty, can he? I think he was about ten when I left town, and I didn't pay a whole lot of attention to kids when I was eighteen and full of myself. Why, is something wrong with him?"

Karen laughed and returned the key to its hook. "I wouldn't say there's anything *wrong*. It's just that he seems a bit . . . intense to be coaching kids that young."

"He's kind of a control freak," I agreed, "but like I said, the kids seemed to like him."

"Well, that's good then." Karen tossed a smile at me and hurried off to the supply cupboard.

When she came back, I said, "Brody and Caleb asked if I would help with the team all season, but I don't know . . . I don't remember enough about the game, and I'm not exactly what you'd call athletic anymore."

Karen didn't even look surprised. "I heard that they need another adult on the roster, or the team will fold."

"That's what the boys said, but I don't think I'm the solution they're looking for." Now that I'd said that aloud, I knew how right I was. "Somebody else will step in, and I'll catch their games when I can."

Karen straightened several boxes on a shelf of one-pound Divinity cream-filled chocolates, but I couldn't help noticing that she was taking care not to look at me. "Don't you think the boys'll be disappointed?" she asked casually.

The image of Brody's face flashed through my head, but I ignored it. I'd find another way to bond with them—something that would actually work in my world. "They'll be more disappointed if I say yes. I don't remember enough about basketball to be an effective coach."

"You know enough," Karen said mildly. "It's really not about you and your skill level, it's about the boys."

"I don't know," I said hesitantly.

Karen finally made eye contact. "What's not to know, Abby? It's a Youth League team, not college ball. Who cares if you're not the greatest basketball player in town?"

I laughed, but I wasn't amused. "You need to work on your powers of persuasion," I said. "Even if I was interested, which I'm not, I'd just be window dressing. I'd probably end up embarrassing the boys."

Karen propped her hands on her hips, a sure sign that she was getting angry. "They asked you, didn't they? How often do you think kids actually ask an adult to step into their world? Do you have any idea how lucky you are? You should be grabbing this opportunity and running with it."

She had me there. Groaning, I slipped another piece of cake into its box and tucked in the flaps to hold it shut. "I know you're right, but you're forgetting one tiny thing: I don't have the time. If I were to agree, I'd be gone three or four evenings out of every seven. I can't be away from the store that much. You already have more than enough to do."

Karen stopped long enough to take a sip of coffee. "You could be if we were more organized." She lifted the cup again and mumbled something behind it I couldn't understand.

"What?"

She lowered the cup slowly. "I said, you could be gone more if we had some help around here."

I stopped working and stared at her. We'd had this discussion a dozen times in the past few months, and we never seemed to get anywhere with it. "I thought we'd agreed to wait."

"*You* agreed to wait," Karen said, locking eyes with me and gearing up for a fight. "I've never been convinced we should."

"Aren't you missing something?" I asked. "If we hire somebody because I'm gone, we aren't ahead. We're just paying more money for the same amount of work."

"It doesn't have to be that way," Karen said stubbornly. "If you focus on making the candy and let me hire somebody to help me with the sales floor, you could get everything done that you need to and still have time to spend with the boys."

"That sounds good in theory," I said grudgingly, "but there are just too many factors to consider."

Color crept into Karen's cheeks, more proof that she was becoming agitated. "Just how many chances do you think you're going to get with your family, Abby?"

"*Excuse* me?"

She stalked back to the supply cupboard, opened it, and slammed it shut without taking anything out. "I don't mean to be rude, but you lived away from here for most of those kids' lives. They hardly know you. Right now, all four of them want you to be part of their lives, but you can't keep turning your back on them or they won't want you anymore."

The air left my lungs in a *whoosh*, and resentment coiled up my spine. I desperately wanted to find some moral high ground, a place where I could look down on her and ask how she dared to say something so hurtful. Trouble was, I knew she was right. I didn't want to know it, but I did.

I'd left Paradise for college, met and married my husband while I was away, and spent the next twenty years living a life that had very little to do with the Hanks and the Shaws of Paradise, Colorado—and absolutely nothing to do with Divinity.

I'd been as shocked as anyone when the lawyers read Aunt Grace's will, but I was determined to show the world she hadn't been wrong to put her faith in me.

I picked up a piece of cake and tried to get it into its box, but I ended up jamming my thumb into it instead. Frustrated, I tossed it into the trash can. "Fine," I snarled. "Have it your way. I suppose you still feel the same way about who we should hire?"

To give her credit, Karen tried not to gloat about my change of heart. "I know some of the cousins have been a pain in your side since you came back, but I think hiring one of them makes the most sense. They're familiar with the business, and hiring outside the family will just make a lot of people angry."

I might have been ready to capitulate on the subject of my nephews, but the cousins were another matter entirely. I'd had nothing but trouble from my cousin Bea since I came back to Paradise, and there were others just waiting for me to screw up and prove that Aunt Grace should never have left Divinity to me.

I packed away the last slice of cake and carried the boxes to the end of the counter. "No matter what I do, I make the cousins angry. I'm not going to make business decisions based on their moods."

"Divinity is a family business."

"Divinity is *my* business," I reminded her. "Aunt Grace didn't leave it to all the cousins. She didn't set up some committee to run the show and make the decisions. And every time I let one of them in, it's trouble for me."

"The only two you've let in are Bea and me," Karen retorted. "You have a fifty percent success rate."

"And if I *do* hire one of the cousins, and it doesn't work out? How easy will it be for me to let her go? You think *that* won't cause bad feelings in the family?"

"Then what about Dana and Danielle? They're probably wanting to pick up some extra cash, and they'd be cheap labor."

I shook my head firmly. "They're both tied up with too

many extracurricular activities. Wyatt and Elizabeth want them to spend whatever free time they have studying. No, if I'm going to hire someone to work for me, I want it to be someone who . . . oh, I don't know . . . someone who acknowledges that I'm the boss and that I have the right to make decisions around here. I want someone who won't challenge me on every decision I do make."

"Then let me talk to Stephanie. She used to work here on weekends a few years ago. I know she'd be exactly what you want."

Of the whole, unreasonable bunch, my cousin Stephanie might actually have worked out all right, except for one thing. "I saw her a couple of days ago at the market. I guess you haven't heard that she's pregnant again?"

Karen's mouth fell open. "*Stephanie* is? But she's—"

"At least forty-two," I finished when words failed her. "Apparently the baby is as big a surprise to Stephanie and Kevin as it is to you. She's not having an easy time of it. I don't think she's a candidate."

"Hire Roz, then."

"Roz has decided that she's going to make her fortune selling Mary Kay. She predicts that she'll be driving a pink Cadillac around Paradise in two years."

Karen's brow furrowed in concentration. "Those would have been my top two choices, but give me a minute to think."

"This is exactly what I'm talking about, Karen. You just can't see it. If you worked for anyone else, you wouldn't push like this to get one of your relatives hired."

"They're your relatives, too."

All the more reason to keep them at arm's length when it came to business. "I'm not hiring from within the family," I said firmly. "End of discussion. You've convinced me to spend time with the boys; be happy with that. I'll put an ad in the paper tomorrow. Do you want to take care of interviewing the applicants, or should I?"

Thankfully, Karen recognized the olive branch I'd extended. She might not be happy with my decision, but she gave up the fight as the bell over the door tinkled to signal our

first customer. "I'll do it. God only knows what kind of 'help'
you'd stick me with."

I grinned as she slipped out from behind the counter to
greet Pearl Whitfield, one of our oldest and most loyal customers. And I wondered again what I'd do without her. I just
hoped I'd never have to find out.

Chapter 5

I spent the rest of the morning telling myself that it wouldn't do any good to keep rehashing the episode at Hammond Junction, and trying to keep busy in the kitchen. I pulled my favorite of Aunt Grace's saucepans from the overhead rack, then measured sugar, corn syrup, and vinegar into the pan and set the mixture over a low flame. When the sugar dissolved, I turned up the flame and hooked a candy thermometer to the pan. The temperature climbed steadily while I scrubbed down the granite counter, buttered a cookie sheet, and dug my kitchen shears from the drawer.

The thermometer finally reached 245 degrees, and I quickly stirred in butter and molasses. The heat in the kitchen had climbed, but even that didn't dispel the pleasure I found in the rich scent that filled the entire shop as the flavors came together. I left the candy on the flame, watching and stirring every few minutes, until it finally reached the hard-ball stage, then carried it to the workbench and poured the molten mixture into the pan I'd prepared earlier.

Every few minutes, Karen poked her head into the kitchen and made appreciative sounds—a habit of hers I find increasingly endearing. When you cook for a living, it's nice to know that someone is eagerly awaiting the results of your efforts. When I thought about how excited about candy we'd been as kids—and how many of us cousins there were—I decided Aunt Grace must have been on an emotional high most of the time.

I managed not to think about the previous night's encounter while I was actually cooking, but as soon as the mixture cooled enough to touch, my brain clicked into gear again while my fingers did the work. Hands buttered, I pulled and folded again and again, working air into the mixture so that the texture slowly changed, and the color morphed from molasses brown to a light, creamy tan.

With each pull, I went over another aspect of the near accident and shooting. Karen might be right about the limping man and his "assailant" working together, but the terror on his face had seemed so *real*. Was he just a good actor, or had he really been afraid? If so, what had he been afraid of? My car hurtling toward him or something else?

Karen left for lunch about the time I began snipping the thick rope of molasses candy into bite-sized pieces. I'd just finished wrapping the last piece in Divinity's distinctive gold-edged candy wrappers when she returned. By that time, I'd not only made myself tired of thinking, I'd also decided that I had to go back to Hammond Junction and see what I could find in the daylight.

I probably should have told Karen what I was planning, but I talked myself out of it by reasoning that it was daylight, and I'd have Max with me. Instead, I told her that I was going out to pick up a few supplies; then I tossed my apron over the back of a chair and hustled out of the shop.

Max was delighted to be let off his chain so early in the day, so I knew *he* wouldn't tell on me. Ten minutes later, we drove out of town on Motherlode Street, destination: Hammond Junction.

For years, the people who lived and worked in this part of the valley had come and gone without getting in each others' way. Everyone knew where Lloyd Casey was going to turn. Didn't matter if he was heading out to the pasture to check on his cattle or driving home at the end of the day. He didn't have to use his turn signal to alert us. And if he had a load of hay on, we all knew to go out around him. We just waited for the quick flash of his hand out his open window to tell us when.

Everyone knew that Marion Escott slowed to a crawl every time she approached someone's driveway because, as she was fond of reminding us, you just never knew. But bring in the tourists, who didn't know where the locals were going, and furthermore, didn't care, and suddenly the junction became a hazard.

The junction seemed far less sinister in the clear light of day than it had the night before, but I was still glad I'd brought Max with me. I drove through the light slowly, eyes peeled for flashes of anything unusual. After about a hundred feet, I made a U-turn, doubled back, and repeated the exercise going in the opposite direction. When I decided I'd never see anything from the car, I parked, hooked Max to his leash, and set out on foot.

I led Max to the intersection and let him sniff around for several minutes, hoping he'd reveal himself to be part bloodhound. He found plenty to interest him—everything from discarded gum wrappers to empty beer bottles—but nothing that looked like it might explain what had happened here the night before.

We checked the road in all four directions, both sides of the highway, but I still didn't find anything unusual. Even though a light autumn breeze rustled the leaves of the trees every now and then, sweat beaded on my nose and trickled down my back. The dry scent of dust, dormant through the long, hot summer we'd been through, tickled my nose so that when I wasn't wiping sweat from my forehead with my sleeve, I was fighting the effects of hay fever.

While I stomped up and down the road, sneezing and wiping my eyes, three cars inched up to the stoplight, then roared on past. I recognized Marion Escott, now well into her eighties and slower behind the wheel than she'd ever been, and Hank Weatherby, who'd been running cattle in the hills west of the junction for most of my life. The third vehicle—an SUV—was there and gone before I got a good look at it.

I searched thoroughly for more than an hour, then reluctantly admitted there wasn't anything to find. I still didn't know what had happened out there, but at least I knew for sure that I hadn't left a man bleeding to death. There was some consolation in that, I suppose.

Chapter 6

Now that I knew I hadn't witnessed a shooting, the anger that had been simmering all morning boiled to the surface. I wanted to know what *had* happened. Exactly. Had the whole thing been a setup?

After herding Max into the Jetta, I pulled up to the intersection once more and considered my options while I sat there, the only car in sight. It took a few minutes, but I finally registered the fact that if I could see Marion Escott's redbrick rambler from where I sat, she could see the intersection from there.

It was a long shot, but I turned right toward Marion's house anyway. Out here in the country, the shoulders on the highways were narrow to nonexistent, so I pulled into the driveway, taking care not to block her car. I poured water from a bottle into my emergency dog bowl (I keep both in the hatch at all times) and settled Max in the shade of a tree.

Marion opened the door while I was promising Max that I wouldn't be gone long and gave me a benevolent smile. "I heard rumors about you and that dog. Guess they were true."

She stood around five two, five three at most—a tiny woman who had once seemed much larger to me than she did now. A halo of white hair wreathed her elfin face, and her pale blue eyes gleamed with intelligence.

"Yeah," I said with a grin, "the rumors are true. I've given up men and gone to the dogs."

Chuckling, Marion stepped aside to let me enter. As I passed through to the cool indoors, she fixed me with a solid look that almost pinned me to the wall. "Well, now, Abigail, that's not the *only* rumor I hear about you. I have it on good authority that you've been seen around town in the company of a certain policeman."

Without waiting for me to respond, she led me into the living room, where I discovered that Marion wasn't the only thing that hadn't changed since I'd been here last. I swear the same crushed velvet sofa still sat in front of the long bay window, the same rocking chairs flanked the fireplace, the same pictures hung on the walls. Marion waved me toward one of the rocking chairs and settled herself in the other.

As she set the chair in motion, a bulky shadow moved in the hallway and startled me. A figure stepped into the light, and somehow, in the bulky, whiskered, potbellied man wearing a too-tight T-shirt and holey jeans I recognized Dwayne, Marion's youngest grandson.

I hadn't seen him since he was a kid heading toward puberty, all arms and legs and growing like a weed. I tried not to show my shock at the changes in him, but I'm not sure I succeeded.

He jerked his head at me, and I jerked mine back. I expected him to disappear once he'd satisfied his social obligations, but to my surprise, he dragged a chair from the kitchen into the hallway and straddled it so he could hear our conversation.

"So, tell me," Marion said, the rhythm of her chair uninterrupted, "What's going on with you and your policeman? Are things getting serious?"

Jawarski was *way* down on the list of things I wanted to talk about with Marion, but her expression was filled with such eagerness, I didn't have the heart to evade the question. "He's not *my* policeman," I said. "And no, things aren't exactly serious. We're friends."

"Friends." Marion leaned back in her chair and snorted softly. "Sounds like an excuse to me, girl, but have it your way. Suppose you tell me instead what brings you clear out here in the middle of the day?"

I tried hard to ignore Dwayne hulking in the hallway and to concentrate on Marion instead. Forcing a laugh, I said, "I take it you don't want to mess around with small talk?"

Marion wagged a hand in front of her face. "I'm too old to

mess around with conversation that doesn't mean anything. Now, what can I do for you? I don't suppose you have any of Divinity's caramels in the car with you. I'd just about sell my soul for a box of those."

I laughed again and shook my head. "Sorry, no." I thought Dwayne might offer to pick up a box for his grandmother, but he kept his big old mouth shut tight, so I said, "Tell you what. I can bring you a box next time I'm out this way."

"Well, don't go out of your way. I don't want to be a burden. Now, what's on your mind?"

"I'm wondering if you were home last night."

"Me?" Marion leaned her head against the back of her rocker. "Well, sure. I'm here most of the time, aren't I, Dwayne?" She turned her bird head in his direction, and he muttered something that sounded like he agreed with her. Satisfied, Marion turned back to me. "You see? Why do you ask?"

"I ran into a little trouble at the junction last night," I said, this time including Dwayne. "I wonder if either of you have noticed anything unusual out here in the past few days?"

Marion's smile faded. Dwayne just looked confused. "What kind of trouble?" he asked.

"Well, that's the thing," I admitted. "I'm really not sure. At first, I thought someone—a man with a limp—had been seriously hurt. Now I'm starting to think it may have been an attempt to hijack my car. Have either of you noticed any strangers hanging around in the past day or two?"

Dwayne shook his head slowly. "I don't think so. I've been staying with Grandma for a couple months now, but I'm not here all that much."

Marion gave him a fond smile. "And when he is here, he's out in that garage, working his fingers to the bone." She turned back to me and said, "You know me, Abby. I've never been one to encourage adult children to live at home. I think there's far too much of that going on these days. But sometimes, being with family is exactly what's called for."

The change of subject surprised me, and I didn't know how to respond, so I tried to gently steer us back. "I certainly know about that. That's why what happened last night concerns me. If it could happen to me, it could happen to any-one—even you."

Marion's brows knit in consternation. "Here in Paradise? What's going on in the world, anyway?" She slid another sugary glance at her grandson and lowered her voice to a stage whisper. "I guess it's a good thing Dwayne's here with me, isn't it? He's getting a divorce, you know. That wife of his . . ." She rolled her eyes expressively and mouthed, "sleeping around."

Afraid she might decide to share details I didn't want—and Dwayne surely wouldn't want me to hear—I tried again to steer the conversation back on track. "So, does that mean you haven't noticed anything out of the ordinary?"

Marion shook her head. "No, but then I wouldn't, would I? Like I said, Dwayne's out in the garage most all day long, and I don't drive at night much since my eyesight took a turn for the worse. I don't trust myself to see well enough."

"That must be frustrating," I said, "but you were out this morning. I was out at the junction as you were driving home."

"Well, I do go out sometimes in the day. I can't take Dwayne away from his work every time I need a gallon of milk. It's hard work starting up a new business."

Clearly, she wanted me to show an interest in Dwayne and his new enterprise, so I gave up the fight. "So, you've started your own business?" I asked, prompting him to do his part.

He lifted one shoulder as if to say it was no big deal, but the self-satisfied smile that tugged on his mouth told a differ-ent story. "I've been renovating furniture—secondhand stuff. Stuff people are willing to just throw away. There's a good market for refurbished goods these days."

"That's terrific," I said, hoping I sounded enthusiastic enough for Marion. "Considering how messed up the econ-omy has been the past few years, I'll bet lots of people are ea-ger to pick up quality furniture without having to pay a fortune to get it. I didn't realize you were a carpenter."

"I wouldn't go that far," Dwayne mumbled.

"There you go being too modest again," Marion scolded gently. "He took classes in carpentry, you know. Years ago, but he's always had a talent. His grandfather and I used to en-

courage him to do something with it, but he was more interested in lazing around with those no-good friends of his."

Color rushed into Dwayne's pudgy cheeks. "For God's
sake, Grandma. Do you mind?"

"Well, what's wrong with bragging a little? It's a grandma's right, especially since you never speak up for yourself."

Dwayne might have been a lump, but the misery in his
eyes touched something in me. I'd been embarrassed by relatives more than once, and I firmly believe that nobody should
have to endure that. "It sounds like you're doing well," I said.

He muttered again, and Marion started her chair moving
once more.

I tried one last time to get us back on track. "So neither of
you have seen anything unusual. Have you heard of anyone
else running into trouble of any kind? Maybe someone's
mentioned having a near accident or witnessing one?"

Marion glanced quickly at Dwayne, then shook her head.
"I haven't heard a thing. And if Dwayne had, he would have
told me, wouldn't you Dwayne?" He moved a thumb, which
apparently meant yes. "You said you almost ran over some
man. Do you know who he was?"

"No, but I wish I did. He was about five four, and it looked
like he had a pretty severe limp. Does that sound familiar?"

Marion gave that some thought but eventually shook her
head. "Paradise isn't what it used to be. There are strangers
around most of the time now, but I don't remember seeing
anyone with a limp. How about you, Dwayne?"

He wagged his head from side to side. "I haven't seen any
strangers since the end of summer."

"My cousin Karen thinks it might have been an attempted
carjacking or . . ." I couldn't bring myself to list the other,
much worse possibilities, ". . . or something."

Apparently, Dwayne didn't share my problem. "Or a kid-
naping?"

Marion gasped, and her eyes rounded in horror.

"It's possible," I admitted, wishing for his grandmother's
sake that Dwayne hadn't been quite so frank. "Although I
can't imagine why anyone would want to kidnap me. It's not
as if my family has money."

Dwayne lifted his head and looked straight at me for the first time. "There's other reasons to snatch somebody besides money, you know."

An involuntary shudder raced up my spine. I had no idea what to make of his comment. Was he warning me or just offering an observation? I'd known Dwayne most of my life, but we'd never been friends. He was just a kid who belonged to a casual friend of my mother's, not someone I knew well.

I shook off the uneasy feeling and kept a smile on my face, mostly because I didn't want him to think he'd frightened me. If that's even what he was trying to do. I wasn't sure what to think anymore.

Marion stopped rocking and glared at Dwayne. "That's a horrible thing to say, Dwayne. What on earth is wrong with you?"

He shrugged, and a sheepish look crossed his face that made him look all of ten years old. "It was just a thought, Grandma. I didn't mean anything by it. But you know it's true. There are all kinds of sick people running around in the world today."

"It might be true," Marion chided, "but that doesn't mean you have to say it. You probably frightened poor Abby half to death."

The irony of the situation wasn't lost on me. Here I was trying to protect Marion, and she was worried about protecting me. I smiled and shook my head. "I'm fine, Marion. Trust me, that thought crossed my mind long before Dwayne brought it up."

Marion sighed heavily. "What's wrong with the world these days? I just don't understand."

"I'm not sure anyone does." I stood, convinced there was nothing more either of them could tell me. "I hope I haven't frightened you by telling you about this, Marion."

"Me?" Marion looked surprised. "I'm not fragile, Abby, and I'm not as old as you think. Would you like me to keep my eyes open, just in case? I haven't noticed anyone suspicious lurking about yet, but I haven't been looking, either."

I could just imagine what Jawarski would say if I dragged an eighty-year-old woman into the middle of something potentially dangerous, so I shook my head quickly. "No, that's okay. I probably just overreacted. I'm sure it's nothing to worry about."

Marion struggled to her feet, for the first time showing signs that she was growing older. "If you say so, Abby."

I tried to duck the wave of guilt that hit me, but I didn't move quickly enough. I caught Dwayne's eye as I gave Marion a brief hug and tried to elicit a silent promise that he'd look after her. When I walked out the door a few minutes later, I tried hard to believe that he'd given me what I asked for, but all I'd really gotten from my visit was another person to worry about.

Chapter 7

By the time I was on the road and headed back to Divinity, I started to feel guilty about how long I'd left Karen alone at the shop. Deciding not to put off until tomorrow what I could do today, I detoured to the *Paradise Post* offices and placed a want ad for help with the sales counter at Divinity. Karen seemed pleased when I told her what I'd done, and the mood around Divinity was so relaxed, I spent the rest of the afternoon making lollipops for the upcoming holiday season.

It didn't take long for the entire shop to fill with the sweet scents of cooking sugar, cinnamon, wintergreen, piña colada, lemon, lime, and orange. By seven that night, I had row after row of gleaming red, yellow, orange, and green lollipops cooling on the granite countertop in the shape of turkeys, pumpkins, autumn leaves, and acorns. I was in the middle of giving myself an enthusiastic pat on the back for a good day's work when the phone rang.

I heard Karen answer. A few seconds later, she looked into the kitchen and said, "It's for you. Brody wants to know if you're already on your way."

On my way? My good mood faded as I remembered my promise to meet with Coach Hendrix tonight. What kind of aunt makes a promise one night and completely forgets about it by the next? Not a very good one.

Tossing my apron onto the table, I grabbed my keys and Max's leash before heading out the door. "Tell him I'm coming now!"

Thankfully, Max is always excited about the prospect of a ride in the car, so minutes later we were in what passes for traffic in Paradise, heading toward Wyatt's house. I still couldn't work up any enthusiasm about the prospect of assistant coaching the team, but with any luck at all, I'd convince the boys to change their minds and let me off the hook.

In too much of a hurry to feel nervous, I checked for oncoming traffic, realized I was alone on the highway, and gave my brakes little more than a token tap as I shot through the junction. Twenty minutes after leaving Divinity, Max and I parked beside a Jeep Cherokee I assumed belonged to Kerry Hendrix and loped up the front steps. It was a speed trial record, at least for me.

While I tried not to look as if I'd broken half a dozen laws getting there, Max concentrated on wagging the little stump of tail he has left. Caleb opened the door and beamed up at me as if I were the Easter Bunny. "She's here!" he shouted, and shoved open the screen door before turning away.

I found Wyatt, Elizabeth, and Kerry waiting in the living room. Elizabeth looked mildly bored, Wyatt looked mildly irritated, and Kerry looked as if he'd gladly tear something apart with his teeth.

He's a big guy, probably six one or two. Around thirty or so, clean-shaven, and in terrific shape. He sat on Wyatt's sofa, his back razor-straight.

Max made a beeline toward the boys and settled himself on the floor between them. I sat next to Elizabeth on the love seat. "Sorry I'm late. I lost track of time."

Kerry shot a look across the room, locking eyes with Wyatt as if to confirm something they'd been discussing before I arrived. When Wyatt didn't react, Kerry looked away and flicked a piece of lint from the starched knee of his khakis. "You know we're here to talk about the possibility of you stepping in as assistant coach of the boys' basketball team." His voice was tight and filled with disapproval, and that annoyed *me*.

For the boys' sake, I told myself to keep a civil expression on my face. "Yes, I know. I'm thrilled that they want me to be a part of the team."

Head bent, Kerry leaned forward, resting his elbows on his knees, and linking his hands together. He looked so solemn, he might have been finalizing negotiations for world peace instead of interviewing someone to sit on a bench in the recreation center a few nights a week.

"I'm sure you are," he said with a smile, but it looked as if the effort hurt him. "I'm also sure you understand why I'm a little concerned about this idea."

The perverse side of my nature rose its ugly head. I was there to talk the boys into changing their minds, but one look at Kerry Hendrix's smug face made me change *my* mind. Just knowing that he didn't want me as his assistant coach made me want the job with a passion.

I slid a glance at the boys to see if they were paying attention. They didn't seem to be, but kids can be tricky. I kept my tone even and my own smile pleasant as I said, "No, I'm not sure I do understand. What concerns do you have?"

Once again, Kerry glanced at Wyatt, but my brother had the good sense to keep his head down. "Experience, for one thing," Kerry said when he realized Wyatt wouldn't be helping him. "How much *do* you know about basketball?"

"I know enough. I played on one of the county teams when I was younger, and what I don't know I can learn. What's important here is that the boys *want* me to help coach the team."

"She has a point," Elizabeth said helpfully.

Wyatt mumbled something unintelligible, and Caleb looked up from Max. Caleb studied the four of us for a long moment, a kid trying to figure out why he felt tension coming from the adults in his life.

"We're talking about just two boys out of ten," Kerry said, lowering his voice a decibel or two. "I'm not sure it's fair to put the whole team at risk just because two of them want to bring their aunt on board."

"At risk of what?" Elizabeth asked.

Kerry looked at her as if she were slow-witted. "Of having a losing season."

If it hadn't been for Brody and Caleb, I would have told him what he could do with his team and walked out the door. "Why do you think they'll be at risk?" I asked. "Is it because I don't have enough experience, or because I'm a woman?"

To my surprise, a flush crept into Kerry's cheeks, but that was nothing compared to the fire in his eyes. "Don't put words in my mouth. All I'm saying is that I want the best assistant coach I can get for the team, and don't try to make it sound like there's something wrong with that."

"Maybe I misunderstood," I said, "but I thought the team was in danger of folding completely unless you found an assistant coach soon. I also thought that the concept of team sports for kids this age was more about cooperation and spirit than keeping track of who wins and loses." Not that I completely approved of that idea. As far as I'm concerned, there's nothing wrong with teaching kids how to compete and remain friends. But for the sake of winning the argument, I'd play along.

Kerry's eyes narrowed, and the corners of his thin mouth edged down, but he didn't say a word.

Wyatt leaned into the conversation for the first time. "Do you have someone else lined up for the job?"

"No," Kerry admitted after a long silence. "I don't."

"Then what's your problem?" I demanded. "You're up against the wire. You have someone willing to step in and make sure the team can play this year, and you're not sure I'm good enough. Even if I were a lump on a log, wouldn't that be better than having nobody at all?"

"She has you there," Wyatt said, moving the toothpick from one side of his mouth to the other. "You need somebody by tomorrow, don't you?"

"By tomorrow, yes." Kerry shifted uncomfortably on the sofa cushion and made an effort not to act like a complete slimeball. "Listen, Abby, I have no problem keeping your name on file, but if someone else with better qualifications steps forward before the deadline, I'll have no choice but to sign them on."

My smile turned brittle. I glanced at the boys again to remind myself why I was putting up with this guy at all. "Naturally."

Kerry stood and assumed a lock-kneed, clenched-butt stance as smug as the expression on his face. "If you *do* end up with the position, there will be some ground rules. Non-negotiable ground rules."

"I wouldn't expect it to be any other way." Not with him leading the team.

"You do things my way."

What a shock. "Understood."

"Fine." As if he and Wyatt had struck the deal, Kerry pumped my brother's hand, grabbed the jacket he'd tossed over the back of the sofa, and headed for the door. "I'll be in touch," he said, then disappeared out the door, leaving me to wonder whether I'd won that round or been soundly defeated.

Chapter 8

There's nothing quite like the smell of sweaty little boys. That's not really something I wanted to know, but knowledge is one of the perks that comes with being assistant coach on a Youth League basketball team.

On Saturday afternoon, three days after my meeting with Coach Hendrix, I sat on the coach's bench inside the city recreation center and watched Brody, Caleb, and eight other little boys run up and down the court, stop, aim, miss, and start all over again. The soles of their shoes squeaked on the heavily varnished floor, and their excited voices echoed in the cavernous space.

Coach Hendrix, annoyed at having to accept me as his second-in-command, had planted me on the bench twenty minutes earlier with strict instructions to make sure I had a clean towel and sports drink ready every time one of the boys came off the court. Otherwise, I guess I was free to file my nails.

For all the attention he paid to me, I might as well have been at Divinity, pulling my share of the weight on a busy weekend. So far, there had been no response to my want ad. I'd called Dana and Danielle to help Karen while I was away, and Elizabeth had reluctantly agreed to let them help out this time. But I still felt guilty for leaving Karen with the bulk of the work, especially since I had almost nothing to do at the gym.

For a while I watched people stride up and down the hallway as they traveled between the locker room and other parts of the recreation center. My parents had given me a gift certificate last Christmas for twenty sessions on the exercise equipment, but I hadn't used it yet. I hadn't yet decided if they were being helpful or insulting. They'd moved to Denver about the time I came back to Paradise, so they weren't around to see that I'd let the gift languish. Now that I was here, I was a little surprised at the people who came to the center after working all day, and it occurred to me that maybe I should consider using that gift after all.

Marshall Ames had apparently ducked out of the restaurant for a while. I saw him mopping his face with a towel as he headed into the locker room. Quentin Ingersol, a real estate agent whose office was just around the block from Divinity, came out of the locker room wearing the same cheesy smile all of Paradise had been seeing in the new advertisements he'd plastered all over town. Nicolette Wilkes wiggled past, and only the fact that she's a good friend kept me from hating her for looking good in spandex.

After I tired of people watching, I counted rows of bleachers and lights in the ceiling. And when I was finished with that, I had nothing else to do but think.

I wondered if Hendrix objected to me personally, or if he would have objected to anyone in my position. I had a pretty good idea that he was one of those people who liked thinking of himself as king of the universe, which made it easier not to take his obnoxious attitude personally.

Seeing Nicolette and a few other women in the hallway also made me wonder if this team I was helping to coach was all-male because the city had never gotten around to making the league coed, or because Coach Hendrix had cut any female players before they could make it this far. Maybe the current female population of the under thirteen set just wasn't interested in basketball.

I don't know how long I'd been daydreaming when Hendrix blew his whistle and shouted at the boys. The tone he used grated on my nerves, but the boys didn't seem to think anything of it. While Hendrix chewed out his star forward, I chewed my thumbnail (much easier than filing) and argued with myself about just how much to butt heads with Butthead my first day on the job.

My personal threshold for ignorance is low, but all I had to do was look at Brody as he raced from one end of the court to the other, and I remembered that I wasn't there for myself. I was there for the boys. So unless Butthead stepped over the line, I'd do what he asked and try not to embarrass my nephews.

I even managed to keep that promise for about ten minutes. That's when the Butthead in question blew another shrill whistle and shouted at the boys to stop what they were doing. All ten stopped running abruptly and turned to face him, faces red, chests heaving from exertion, eyes bright with expectation, as if they thought he held the keys to fame and fortune in the NBA.

"All right," Hendrix shouted. "Line up at the free throw line—the A team on the north end, B team on the south." He strode onto the court in the midst of them, his back rigid, his expression haughty. Brody immediately moved toward the north basket, but Caleb hesitated.

He stood in the middle of the court, his spindly legs sticking out the bottom of his red and white uniform shorts and disappearing again inside shoes that looked twice as big as he was. His pale hair lay plastered against his head, and his nostrils flared as he struggled to catch his breath. Something strong and maternal flared inside me, and I had an almost uncontrollable impulse to sweep him off the court and fill him full of electrolytes.

But I was their aunt, not their mother. If Caleb and Brody had wanted someone maternal around, Elizabeth would be sitting in my place. That convinced me all over again to keep my mouth shut. And I would have, if Coach Hendrix hadn't suddenly focused on Caleb. "What are you doing, Shaw?"

Caleb sucked in a breath and tried to speak. "I—I'm—"

I gripped a towel in both hands, hoping that would keep my backside firmly glued to the bench.

"You're *supposed* to be under your team's basket. What are you doing standing there?"

"I—I can't—"

"He can't breathe, you moron." I tossed the towel onto the bench and walked onto the court. "Can't you see that these boys all need a five-minute break, or don't you care?"

Blood rushed to Coach Hendrix's face, and he peered at

me as if I'd crawled out from under a rock. "You're out of place, Shaw."

"I don't think so." I moved to Caleb and put my arm around his shoulders. Half a heartbeat later, I realized that might embarrass him, and I pulled it away again. "I'm just asking you to give them five minutes, not forever."

"And I'll give them five minutes when they need it." His beady eyes bored into Caleb, who already looked less red. "You okay, kid?"

Caleb nodded eagerly. "Yeah. I'm fine."

"Are you sure?"

He nodded again without looking at me. "I'm fine. *Sheesh*. I'm not a baby."

Well, terrific. I'd been on the job barely more than an hour, and already I'd stuck my foot in it. Caleb hadn't wanted or needed rescuing, and I'd embarrassed him thoroughly in front of his friends. "No. Of course you're not," I said. "I know that. I wasn't only worried about you."

Caleb lifted one shoulder and took his place beside his teammates. "Whatever. I'm okay. You can sit down again."

Right.

Under the weight of Coach Hendrix's disapproving glare, Caleb's resentful one, and Brody's blank-eyed stare that probably meant he was pretending he didn't know me, I returned to the bench and asked myself again what I was doing there.

Coach Hendrix blew his whistle, and the boys began another drill. I counted bottles of sports drink, straightened the stack of towels, and made a list of people I wanted to thank for this experience, starting with Karen.

After what felt like hours, practice was finally over, and Coach Butthead traded places with me. While I returned balls to the wheeled carts and gathered stacks of sweaty used towels, Hendrix sat on the bench and leafed idly through a magazine.

By the time Brody and Caleb emerged from the locker room, I'd convinced myself that I'd made a huge mistake. There was no way I could sit on that bench day after day eating whatever Hendrix dished out for me. No way I could bite my tongue when I thought he'd pushed the boys too far. No way I could suffer the indignity I instinctively knew would be present whenever Kerry Hendrix and I were in the same room.

A mens' pickup team had reserved the court for the time slot directly after ours, and an odd assortment of players were taking warm-up shots as the boys and I walked through the gym to the doors leading to the back parking lot. Practice had lasted so long, the sun had already dropped behind the western mountains by the time we stepped outside.

All the way across the shadowy parking lot, I tried to figure out the best way to break the news of my quitting to my nephews. I unlocked the car doors and slid behind the wheel. Brody claimed shotgun, which left Caleb in the backseat by himself. I put the key into the ignition but waited for both boys to buckle themselves in before I started the car.

They were both depressingly silent. Caleb wouldn't even look at me, and Brody kept sliding glances in my direction whenever he thought I wasn't looking. Look on the bright side, I told myself. After what had just happened, maybe they'd be glad to find out I was bailing out.

"Listen, you guys," I said as I started the car and put it into gear, "I've been thinking."

Caleb's little head shot up, and his worried eyes met mine in the rearview mirror. "You're not gonna quit, are you?"

"No, you dork, she's not gonna quit." Brody's eyes locked on mine. "*Are* you?"

What could I say to that? I knew I should say yes, but I couldn't form the word. I shifted in my seat so I could see Caleb better. "I thought I embarrassed you in there. Why do you want me to stick around?"

He shrugged, just the almost imperceptible lift of one little shoulder, and his gaze drifted to his knees. "You did, kinda, but only because Coach thinks I'm a sissy."

My heart shattered at the look on his face. "He what?"

"He thinks Caleb's a sissy," Brody said slowly, as if he was talking to an old woman.

I shifted my gaze to him. "How do you know that's what he thinks?"

"Because he says so. He says it all the time."

"He says Caleb's a sissy? In front of the other boys?"

Brody nodded, but he seemed unconcerned. "Yeah. Why?"

"Because Coach Hendrix shouldn't say things like that, especially not in front of the other kids." I struggled to keep my voice from cracking with anger. "It's not right."

"How else is he going to get Caleb to toughen up? Coach says he's the worst player on the whole team."

"Caleb's almost three years younger than you and some of the other boys. He can't be expected to play at the same level."

Brody shrugged and glanced into the backseat at his brother. "I was better than him when I was his age. He's gotta focus, you know?"

I couldn't remember when I'd been so angry, but I reminded myself that Brody was just a kid. He was only parroting things he'd heard. If I was going to get angry with anyone, it would be the jerk whose truck was parked three rows over, and I wasn't going to get angry with him tonight. The boys had already suffered enough because of adults who couldn't shut up around them.

Pasting on a smile that I hoped would encourage poor Caleb, I said, "Look, kiddo, you're doing just fine. And you're not a sissy. You're a nine-year-old boy." I had a few other things to say, too, but just then I saw movement near Coach Hendrix's truck, and for the third time in the space of as many hours, I completely changed my mind.

Maybe I *should* say something to him, I told myself. Just a word or two. Nothing that would upset the boys, though. Just a quiet word of warning . . .

I split a glance between my nephews and shut off the car. "Stay here," I said. "I'll be right back." Outside, I bent to make eye contact once more. "I mean it. Stay here."

Brody nodded, Caleb offered up a soft promise, and I was off across the parking lot as quickly as I could walk. "Coach Hendrix? Can I talk to you for a second?"

A head appeared above the truck bed, but it wasn't high enough off the ground to be Kerry Hendrix's. Maybe one of the boys had carried the equipment out after practice. "Sorry. I thought you were the coach. Do you know where he is? I need to talk to him for a minute."

Something heavy clattered to the ground beside the truck, and the shadowy figure began to run.

"Hey!" I shouted, taking off after him. "Wait a second!"

About twenty feet from the truck, the figure veered sharply to the right, and I saw him clearly for the first time. He ran awkwardly, dragging one leg behind him, and the shock of recognition brought me to an abrupt halt. I shook off my surprise and started running again, but my hesitation had given the man a large lead.

Maybe I should have gone back for the car, but Brody and Caleb were in there, and I didn't want to put them in danger. Kicking myself into high gear, I ran flat out. After only a few yards, my lungs burned, and my legs felt like rubber. While I was still at least forty yards away, the limping man jumped into a dark-colored SUV that had been idling at the curb, and the car shot away from the curb. I tried to get a look at the license plate, but I wasn't close enough. By the time I reached the street, the only thing left to see were their taillights.

Chapter 9

"Aunt Abby!" Brody's voice cut through the wind and pulled my gaze away from the tail end of the car. Still fighting to catch my breath, I whipped around to see why Brody sounded so close. In spite of my warnings to stay where he was, he'd left the Jetta and Caleb. He stood about thirty feet behind me, looking like a kid who'd just seen Santa Claus.

A gust of cold November wind swept around me, and I shivered. The shock of seeing Brody standing there in the dark brought me back to earth in a rush. Brody and Caleb were my responsibility at the moment, and I'd just been hideously *ir*responsible by leaving them in the car alone. Sure, we were in Paradise, where the crime rate still hasn't risen to match the rest of the country, but still . . . bad things happened to good people every day.

Trying to look stern, I started across the pavement. "What are you doing out of the car? I thought I told you to stay put."

Brody wore only a light T-shirt and a pair of jeans. Even from a distance, I could see his bottom lip quivering from the cold, and his breath formed wispy clouds above his head. "That was the guy, wasn't it?"

His question startled the stern right out of me. "What guy?"

He craned to see around me. "The *guy*. The one with the limp. That was him, right?"

Praying that he wouldn't catch cold and earn me a black mark in his mother's book, I put my hand on his shoulder and turned him toward the car. "What do you know about the guy with the limp?"

"I heard you telling Mom and Dad about him." He twisted away from me so he could see the road. "That's the guy who got shot, right?"

"Nobody got shot," I said firmly. By now, that was obvious even to me.

"Uh-huh. Remember? Last night when you came back to get my dad."

Brody was obviously too excited to listen. I caught him by the shoulders and made him look at me. "Nobody got shot," I said again.

"But you said he did."

"You shouldn't have been listening to our conversation," I said, sounding so much like my mother, I winced. "Did Caleb hear what we said last night?"

Brody nodded, and his chin quivered in the cold. "Yeah, but don't worry, he's okay. And I *wasn't* eavesdropping. You were in the kitchen, and that's right under our bedroom. We can hear anything anybody says through the heat vent."

My skin tingled, but I couldn't tell whether it was from irritation with myself or from the weather. I knew how those old farmhouses were built. I should have known the kids would hear us.

Still trying to look like someone Brody should pay attention to, I pointed toward the car and snarled, "Back. Right now. If you're not inside that car with your seat belt done up by the count of three, I'm quitting the team."

Brody stared up at me for half a second, judging my sincerity, then spun away and raced back to the car. I joined him there, checked to make sure Caleb really was all right, and started the car again.

I turned up the heat and shifted in my seat so I could look at both of them. "Do your mom and dad know that you heard us talking?"

Brody shook his head quickly. "Are you kidding? Dad would be all right, but Mom would have a fit."

"Well, then listen to me," I said, "and listen good. Nobody got shot last night. Whoever it was, they were just pretending."

Caleb leaned forward as far as his seat belt would allow. "Pretending to get shot?"

"That's right. Pretending to get shot."

"He's getting away," Brody pointed out with a worried frown. "We should go after him before he can hide."

I looked him square in the eye, hoping to make some kind of contact with his excited little-boy brain. "We're *not* going after him."

"But he's getting away!"

"He's already gone," I said. "And even if he weren't, I'm not putting you two in danger just to chase some creep with a limp who was trying to steal my car."

"He wanted to steal your car?" Caleb asked.

Brody shot an exasperated look into the backseat. "They do it all the time, Caleb. Don't you ever watch TV?"

"I watch it all the time," Caleb protested. "But why would they want *this* car? It's old."

Brody sighed heavily and shook his head. "You just don't get it, do you? For the *parts*."

He seemed so sure of himself, I didn't have the heart to tell him Caleb was probably right. The Jetta wouldn't be worth much, even stripped. Whatever the man with the limp wanted, it hadn't been my car.

"Was he trying to steal Coach's truck tonight?" Caleb asked.

I put the Jetta in gear and shook my head. "I have no idea what he was doing." But that didn't mean I couldn't take a look.

Detouring on my way across the parking lot, I pulled up next to Butthead's truck a few seconds later. He'd parked beneath a light, so it was easy to see the scratches in the paint as soon as we got close enough. I couldn't be absolutely certain the man with the limp had put them there, but it seemed like a pretty good bet that he had.

The only question was, why? It didn't make any sense.

"Ooooh, look at that," Caleb breathed from the backseat.

Brody's face puckered into a frown that made him look like his father. "Coach is gonna be piss—" he caught himself, shot a guilty look at me, "—really ticked off when he sees that."

Trying to keep her sons from using language like my brother is just one of the lost causes my sister-in-law has undertaken. My mother tried for years to keep Wyatt from talking like Daddy, and she'd failed miserably. Knowing how the boys looked up to their dad, I thought Elizabeth would have better luck beating her head against the wall.

"Speaking of Coach," I said with a glance toward the recreation center's doors, "I wonder what he's doing inside for so long."

"He always stays late," Brody said. "I think he works out in the weight room or something."

That made me think about the clang of metal as the limping man ran away, so I backed the Jetta up a foot or two and scoured the pavement for something he might have dropped. After a few minutes I saw a long piece of metal with an odd hook at the end lying a few feet from the truck.

With a stern glance at the boys, I slipped out of the car and picked it up by the ends, being careful not to smudge any fingerprints that might be on it.

I propped one end against my leg and pushed the button on the dash to open the hatch. When it popped up, I carried the metal piece to the back of the car and found a safe place for it. I slid behind the steering wheel and finally managed to get the Jetta all the way out of the parking lot—just as the door to the recreation center opened and Kerry Hendrix came outside.

For about two and a half seconds, I toyed with the idea of going back to tell him about the guy with the limp. But why bother? He probably wouldn't believe me, and I didn't want to subject the boys to another disagreement between us. Besides, Elizabeth would be expecting us, and I wanted to get the boys home on time.

I kept driving, never dreaming that such a small choice would turn out to have such large consequences.

Chapter 10

The next morning dawned gray and cold, a harbinger of the coming winter. The previous night's wind had stripped away the last remaining leaves from the trees, leaving the mountainsides looking stark and uninviting.

Before leading Max outside for his morning ritual, I threw on a pair of sweats and a jacket. The frigid air bit through both in short order. Teeth chattering, I tried to hurry Max along. Unfortunately, he enjoyed the brisk morning air, so the two of us were at cross purposes. As usual, he won. One of these days, I swear I'm going to convince him that I'm the boss.

When I finally got home again, I climbed into a steaming hot shower and stood under the spray until I felt some of the chill leave my bones. As I warmed up, I started to wonder why the man with the limp had turned up at the recreation center. Had he been trying to steal Kerry's truck? If so, he must not be very good at what he did. A competent thief would have had that truck open, hot-wired, and gone before I'd even noticed him messing around with it.

Hard on the heels of that thought came a flash of irritation with Elizabeth for her reaction when I delivered the boys safe and sound to her doorstep last night. Sure, we'd been fifteen minutes late, but it was only fifteen minutes, and we had a good reason. Wyatt had been concerned but cool. Elizabeth had started fretting about letting the boys go anywhere until somebody figured out what was going on in Paradise.

Unfortunately, the police wouldn't do anything until something really bad happened; meanwhile, the good people of Paradise could suffer a whole rash of irritating incidents.

One or two more, and I knew Elizabeth *would* keep the kids home—which seemed blatantly unfair. On the other hand, if I could figure out what was going on, maybe we could put a stop to all this nonsense before the whole thing got out of hand.

After attacking my hair with a blow dryer, I dressed in an oversized green sweater, a soft pair of jeans, and tennis shoes, then hurried downstairs to Divinity a few minutes before we opened at ten.

It was Sunday morning, so I wasn't expecting much foot traffic. I'd just finished making a pot of coffee and digging out the lone remaining piece of leftover coffee cake when the front door opened, and Jawarski stepped through.

I smiled when I saw him—right up until I realized he had his cop face on. Letting my smile evaporate, I poured two cups of coffee and shoved one across the counter at him. "You look down in the mouth. What's going on?"

Jawarski leaned on the counter, grabbed the mug with one hand, and wiped the other across his face. He has a nice face. A solid, steady, reliable kind of face that also happens to be sexy as hell. In the time I've known him, I've never seen him without his regulation cop mustache, and I'm not sure I want to. It suits him.

When he finally looked at me, I saw that his eyes were the color of storm clouds, and I knew I wasn't going to like whatever he'd come to say. Two seconds later, he proved me right. "Tell me what you were doing at the recreation center last night," he said.

"I was there for basketball practice. I'm assistant coach of the Miners this year."

One of Jawarski's eyebrows rose. "I heard about that, but I wasn't sure it was true. Since when?"

"Since yesterday. At least, yesterday was my first practice. I actually joined the team earlier in the week."

"Why *you* coaching basketball?"

I ignored the implied insult in that question and spooned sugar into my cup. "Why shouldn't I coach basketball?"

"No reason," Jawarski said quickly. "I'm just surprised, that's all. It doesn't seem like something you'd enjoy."

I slipped out from behind the counter and carried my cup and cake to one of the wrought-iron tables in the seating area. I settled in comfortably and helped myself to a chocolaty bite. "That shows how much you know. For your information, I wasn't always this sedentary. When I was a kid, I did a lot of things I don't do now."

Jawarski dipped his head, conceding the point, and joined me at the table. "So you just had a desire to turn back the clock, is that it?"

"No, Brody and Caleb asked me to take the job. They needed another adult on the coaching staff, or the team was going to fold. Now tell me why you want to know."

He propped his feet on an empty chair and scrunched down on his tailbone. The day had barely started, and already he looked beat. "I want to know because Kerry Hendrix thinks you vandalized his truck last night."

"What?" The coffee cup was halfway to my mouth when he said that, and the shock made me spill about half of it into my lap. I let out a yowl and stood, brushing ineffectually at the hem of my sweater and the front of my jeans. "Kerry Hendrix thinks *I*—? What a jerk! He thinks that *I*—?"

Jawarski listened to me sputter for a few minutes, then offered another bit of information. "He says he saw you in the parking lot when he came outside last night. Everyone else had been gone for half an hour or so, and you had no reason to stick around."

"What an idiot."

"He also says that you were upset with him for—" He consulted his notebook and read, "—'for putting you in your place in front of the boys.' " Jawarski gave me a long, slow look. "You want to tell me about that?"

"No, but I will if you insist. I thought he was pushing the boys too hard. He didn't agree with me, and he didn't like me challenging him in front of the kids. The boys insisted they were all right, and Hendrix sent me back to the bench to count towels."

"And why were you there so late?"

A couple of people slowed to look into the shop's windows. I waited until they'd walked on again to answer. It was the first time in a long time that I'd actively willed customers away from the store, and that made me even angrier.

"I was there," I snarled, "because I saw someone messing around with his truck. At first I thought it was Hendrix, but when I got closer, I realized the guy was too short, and it couldn't have been him. I shouted at him, and he ran away. That's when I realized that it was the same man I almost hit the other night—the man with the limp."

Both of Jawarski's eyebrows shot up at that. "You're sure it was the same man?"

I nodded, torn between feeling contrite and being pissed as hell. "I probably should have called and told you—and if I'd had any idea I'd need to prove my innocence, I would have—but how was I supposed to know that jerk would accuse me of vandalizing his truck?"

"Let me get this straight. You saw the guy with the limp at the rec center last night. The one you thought you hit. The one you *thought* had been shot."

"Unless there are suddenly two men with the same limp skulking around Paradise in the middle of the night."

"And you're saying *he's* the one who vandalized the truck?"

"I don't know for sure," I admitted, "but he was doing something, and when he ran away he dropped a long piece of metal."

"How do you know that?"

"Because I heard it hit the pavement. I don't know what it was, but he could have been using it on Kerry's truck."

Scowling, Jawarski pulled out the notebook he always kept in his shirt pocket. "Hendrix doesn't say anything about seeing a man with a limp."

"That's because he was long gone before Kerry ever came outside."

"So nobody saw him but you?"

I smiled and shook my head. "Brody and Caleb were with me. They not only saw the man with the limp, they also saw me pick up the metal piece he dropped."

Jawarski looked surprised at that. "You have it?"

"Of course I have it. After I saw what Kerry's truck looked like, I thought it might be some kind of evidence. It's in the back of the Jetta."

He gave me an atta-girl smile that pleased me a whole lot more than I wanted it to. "Did you happen to see where the guy ran off to?"

"I saw him get into a dark-colored SUV, but I couldn't get close enough to get the license number. I have no idea who was driving, and I didn't see where they went."

"Did the boys see the car, too?"

"Brody did. I'm not sure about Caleb."

Jawarski nodded, made a note, and slipped the notebook into his pocket again.

"You're not going to talk to them, are you?" I asked.

"Why not? If they corroborate what you've told me, Hendrix will have to back off."

"Yeah, and Elizabeth will pull the boys off the team. You know how protective she is. She's already talking about keeping them home, but the boys will be devastated if she does. Please don't drag them into this."

Jawarski looked at me for a moment, then shook his head. "If you say so, but I doubt Hendrix is going to believe that you're innocent just because *you* say so."

"I'll take my chances."

"Fine," he said with an exasperated shake of his head. "You want to show me that metal strip?"

He didn't agree with my decision, but I didn't care. With Brody working his way toward the starting lineup and Caleb trying to prove he wasn't a sissy, getting yanked off the team by a concerned mother was the last thing either of them needed.

The door opened, admitting two women into the shop, and I seized the opportunity to cut our conversation short. "Love to," I said, "but it looks like I'm going to have to work." I ducked into the kitchen, grabbed my keys, and tossed them to Jawarski. "I didn't have anything to pick it up with, but I tried to only touch it on the edges in case somebody left finger-prints."

The corners of his mouth lifted again, and before I knew what he was thinking, he leaned across the counter and kissed me soundly. "Well, at least there's one good thing that came from all of this," he said with a wink, "if you saw the guy with the limp, at least we know he's okay."

Chapter 11

Jawarski made off with the piece of metal, and Karen came through the door two minutes later. She seemed to be in an unusually good mood, and for some reason that grated up against the irritation I'd been feeling since Jawarski told me about Kerry's accusation. I didn't get a chance to ask why she was so happy until much later—after we'd waited on the customers who'd come in while I was talking to Jawarski and then ridden herd on a group of teenagers who stampeded into the shop a few minutes later.

When the last of the kids finally straggled out of the store, I pulled out the toffee bin so I could replenish the sample tray and checked to make sure Karen was still grinning.

She was.

"You're in an awfully good mood," I observed casually. "What's up? You and Sergio have time for a quick roll in the hay this morning?"

Karen laughed and shook her head. "Are you kidding? It's Sunday. He was still asleep when I left."

Conjuring up an image of Hendrix's face, I broke a slab of brittle into small pieces. It felt so good, I smashed another, and then rewarded myself by popping a piece into my mouth.

The buttery toffee filled my senses and made the world seem a little brighter.

"Well, something's got you grinning like the Cheshire Cat. What's going on?"

Karen bent to pick up a couple of napkins the kids had dropped on the floor and with a shrug, tossed the napkins into the trash. "I've found our new clerk. She'll be starting tomorrow morning."

I frowned slightly. "You found someone already? It's not one of the cousins, is it?"

Karen shook her head and started toward the small room on the other side of the shop. "No, it's not one of the cousins." She fluttered a dismissive hand over one shoulder as she walked, and stopped in the archway to look back at me. "It's actually someone who used to live here. She's come back, and she needs a job. She called yesterday after you left, so I had her come in for an interview."

"Do I know her?"

"I don't know. Her name's Liberty Parker."

The name didn't ring any bells, but with a name like Liberty, it seemed likely that she'd been born in the mid-seventies, which would make her . . . a few years younger than me. She'd probably been way below my teenage radar screen. "What do you know about her?"

"Not much," Karen admitted. "Just, like I said, that she's back in town, and she needs work."

"Did she have references?"

Karen's smile faded a bit. "I thought you were leaving the choice up to me."

"I did," I said with a patient smile. "Now I'm just asking for a few details. What made you decide to hire her? Does she have experience in retail?"

Karen hesitated ever so slightly before admitting, "I don't know."

"You didn't ask her?"

"I didn't think it was necessary," she said, lifting her chin defiantly. "She'll be fine. Trust me."

"I do trust you," I said, my patience slipping a bit, "but Divinity's a small shop. Whoever we hire is going to have a key to the shop and access to all our money. Please tell me you asked at least a few questions when you interviewed her."

Karen's chin jacked up another notch or two. "I asked plenty of questions." Her voice snapped like taut wire. "Nobody comes with a guarantee, Abby. I've talked to Liberty, and I think she'll work out just great. If my judgment isn't enough for you, maybe you should just do everything yourself."

I pride myself on being relatively smart—at least smart enough not to alienate the only person standing between me and failure in the candy business. It wasn't easy, but I slicked on a smile and poured bits of pummeled toffee into the sample tray. "I'm sure Liberty will be fine," I said, hoping I sounded as if I meant it. "I can't wait to meet her."

I thought Jawarski might call that evening to tell me what he'd found out about the metal strip, but I thought wrong. Max and I ended up sharing a bowl of candied popcorn while we watched a broadcast version of *My Big, Fat Greek Wedding* on TV, then going to bed depressingly early.

Next morning, I woke with the sun to find that a cold front had settled into the valley overnight. I pulled on a thick sweater and even thicker socks, then set off with Max for our morning walk. I had a lot to do that morning, and I wanted to get an early start.

A few minutes after eight, I let myself into the shop and got started making three dozen candy cornucopia centerpieces Richie Bellieu and Dylan Wagstaff had ordered for a dinner party the following week. Richie and Dylan were good customers, but they were also friends. Jawarski and I had both been invited to their dinner party, and I wanted the centerpieces to be special.

I dug out the grapevine cornucopia baskets I'd ordered from an online supplier and packed one with fruit drops in autumn-colored wrappers, dark and milk chocolate autumn leaves in colorful foil, and red, yellow, orange, green, and purple jelly candies wrapped in clear cellophane to let their colors shine through. I added molded milk chocolate balls filled with caramel and carefully positioned several small packets of Autumn Mix Jelly Beans.

Satisfied with the mix of color and texture, I wedged one of the large orange, yellow, and white swirled lollipops I'd made the previous week, positioned a few silk leaves, and voilà! instant horn of plenty. If you called an hour and a half "instant."

Twice in the space of an hour, the phone had rung with people calling in response to the want ad. Resisting the urge to take down their names and keep them as backup, I told both callers that the position had been filled.

Figuring I still had half an hour until the shop opened, I reached into the cupboard for ribbon. When I heard a knock on the front door, I dropped the roll on the floor and watched the satin make an autumn-colored trail across the floor.

Had I lost track of time? I checked the clock on the wall, but it was only a few minutes past nine thirty. Whoever it was could wait.

I started gathering ribbon, but the knock came again, longer and louder this time. Again, I ignored it. The store wasn't scheduled to open for another twenty-seven minutes, and I was in no mood to bend the rules for anyone.

When I had the ribbon under control, I began to roll the satin strip back onto the spool, but again the knock sounded, this time followed by a faint voice calling, "Hello-o-o-o. Is anybody in there?"

Barely keeping my irritation in check, I put the ribbon down and strode toward the front door. A young blonde woman of about thirty stood on the other side. She wore a sweatshirt and jeans, and her hair had a streak of black down the root line. When I was younger, that would have been a sign that she needed a visit to a hairdresser, but I had the sneaking suspicion that with her, the color was intentional.

She leaned against the glass and cupped her hands around her eyes so she could peer inside. "Hello?"

I moved in front of the door so she could see me and gestured toward the sign right in front of her. "We don't open until ten. You'll have to come back then."

"Oh, but I'm not a customer," she said, taking her hands off the glass and beaming at me. "I'm your new clerk. Karen hired me on Saturday."

I stared at her for a full minute, then unlocked the door and ushered her inside. "I'm sorry. Karen mentioned that she'd hired someone, but I wasn't expecting you until later." She was eager, I'd grant her that. Doing best to shake off my earlier irritation, I held out a hand and said, "I'm Abby."

"I'm Liberty." She pulled her sweatshirt off, sending black

and blonde hair flying in all directions. "Liberty Parker. Pleased to meetcha."

"Likewise." I think I sounded genuine, but I'm not sure. I was too busy wondering what I was going to do with her until Karen arrived. Locking the front door again, I motioned for Liberty to follow me into the kitchen. "Did Karen happen to tell you what time she'd be in today?"

"I don't think so. She told me I didn't need to come in until eleven, but I came in early. I wanted to make a good impression."

She'd made an impression, all right. "Why don't you have a seat right over there?" I said, nodding toward the table near the window. "I'm just finishing some centerpieces."

"Ooh, that sounds great. Can I help?"

Grudgingly, I gave her one more point for enthusiasm. "Another day, maybe."

Looking disappointed, Liberty sat at the table and watched while I began to crimp the ribbon between my fingers to make a bow. I'd just made the second loop when she let out a heavy sigh and said, "I feel kind of useless just sitting here and watching you."

"You're fine," I assured her. "Why don't you tell me a little about yourself while we wait for Karen to get here? Karen said you've lived in Paradise before."

"I lived here when I was younger, but I just came back a few weeks ago."

"Really? What brings you back?"

"My boyfriend. Rutger. He's going to be trying out for the OfficeCentral cycling team in the spring, and he wanted to come here to train. I wasn't sure I was ready to come back, but . . ." She let her voice trail away and finished her explanation with a shrug.

If that's what Rutger had come to Paradise for, he'd picked an odd time to make the move. "He's going to train in the winter?"

Liberty picked restlessly at a pile of grapevine pieces that had fallen from the baskets. "He loves to ski. That's the other reason he wanted to come here. He figures he can go other places to ride when the weather's bad, but there are only a few places in the country where the skiing is this good. And he's right, you know. It really is the best." Pausing only long enough to take a breath, she asked, "Is this garbage? I could clean up for you if that's okay."

Just being in the same room with her was making me tired. The woman exuded a level of energy I hadn't felt in years. I wasn't sure if I envied or resented it. "That's fine," I said. "I'm sorry I don't have anything else for you to do. I wasn't expecting you until later, or I would have been better prepared."

Liberty's smile faded. "I made a mistake, didn't I? I should have waited until eleven."

Had I hurt her feelings? If she was *that* tenderhearted, this was never going to work. I formed another loop for the bow, checked to make sure it was the same size as the others, and ignored the cramp forming in the base of my thumb. At least now I understood why Karen had swept her up so quickly. My cousin had a maternal streak a mile wide. Nothing made her feel better than playing mother hen.

"It's fine," I said. "When I'm finished with this, I'll call and let Karen know that you're here."

"Oh." A glimmer of hope returned to the girl's face, followed immediately by a contrite frown. "I don't want her to be upset with me, too."

"I'm not upset with you," I said again. "What kind of experience do you have? Have you worked in retail before?"

"Oh yes. Lots." Liberty's smile returned, and it appeared that all was well again. "I sold shoes at JC Penney when we lived in Denver, and I worked at a gift shop in Albuquerque. I've waited tables, too, but I'm not really very good at that." Her eyes flew wide, and the smile was gone again. "But I probably shouldn't tell you that, should I? You'll wonder if I can do this job."

"Don't worry about that," I said. "This job isn't anything like waiting tables. If it were, both Karen and I would both be dismal failures. What about candy? Do you have any experience with what we do around here?"

"No. Not exactly. But I can learn. Karen said she thought that would be okay."

I couldn't very well insist that she have experience when I had so little. "Of course it will," I said. "As long as you pay attention and learn fast. Did Karen tell you that you'll need a food handler's permit?"

"Yes, and I'm going to get one on my lunch break."

"Did she give you any paperwork to fill out?"

"No, she said she'd go over all of that with me today."

I heard the door rattle, realized that this time I *had* forgotten to open on time, and hurried into the shop to rectify my mistake. To my relief, my first customer of the day was Rachel Summers, a friend who owns a candle shop just down the block. "I was beginning to think you weren't here," she said as she burst into the shop on a blast of cold air. "Can you believe how cold it is? I *so* didn't want to get out of bed this morning."

And with that, the day had begun. It would be hours before I had a chance to catch my breath again.

Chapter 12

Karen showed up by ten fifteen and spent a couple of minutes clucking over Liberty before sweeping her off for training. Rachel had ordered her morning Coke and hurried off to Candlewyck, and I had the kitchen to myself again.

I turned my attention back to the centerpieces, but in spite of my determination to focus on the work in front of me, my thoughts flitted around ceaselessly. I wondered what Jawarski had found out about the vandalism charge against me. I thought long and hard about my promises to Brody and Caleb. And I couldn't stop thinking about Coach Hendrix and his ridiculous accusation that *I'd* carved up his truck.

I had no idea how the two of us were going to get through an entire season of Youth League basketball without killing each other, but I was more determined than ever not to let him run me off. I might quit on my own, but I would *never* run. I had a firm rule about that.

Still, if I was going to stick around, I'd have to convince Hendrix to take me seriously. Racing through the parking lot the night before had forced me to acknowledge how seriously out of shape I was. No wonder the coach didn't think I was capable of anything more taxing than counting towels.

By the time I moved the centerpieces I'd finished to a counter near the window, I'd decided that it was time to dust off that gift certificate from my parents. I didn't know when I'd find the time, but I'd figure that out somehow. First, though, I needed to buy clothes comfortable enough to exercise in.

After cleaning up the things I hadn't used that afternoon, I told Karen I was taking an early dinner break and left the shop. The temperature had dipped at least another ten degrees while I'd been working, and I was tempted to fire up the Jetta, but nobody in Paradise drove if they were only going a short distance, and who was I to buck tradition?

Max had been waiting patiently for a little attention all afternoon, so I hooked him to his leash and set off up the street. Walking warmed me up a little, and I was soon glad I'd decided to walk.

The whole town was filled with a restless kind of energy brought on by the dip in temperature. Thick, gray clouds shrouded the mountains on every side of the valley, and there was an edge to the cold that smelled of moisture. Snow was coming. We could all feel it.

In the past few weeks, we'd received almost enough snow in the mountains to open the ski resorts. One more good snowfall ought to do it, and we were holding our collective breath, waiting.

Max and I strolled to the end of the block, then across the square to Alpine Sports. Gavin Trotter had come to Paradise a few years earlier, and he'd spent megabucks turning an ordinary retail space into a faux Swiss chalet filled with all the exercise clothes and sporting equipment anyone could possibly need. I hoped he'd have something that would motivate me to get into shape.

Alpine Sports is only about three blocks from Divinity, but my nose and fingertips were numb by the time I got there. I tied Max to a wooden bench sporting a huge ad featuring Quentin Ingersol's face and copy urging Paradise to come to him with all our real estate needs. I couldn't imagine wanting to see my face all over town, but to each his own, I guess.

Max settled into a makeshift shelter created by the bench and a nearby garbage can. Satisfied that he'd be warm and safe, I hurried inside out of the cold. Gavin, a tall, thin man with salt-and-pepper hair, glanced up from behind the counter as I came in. "Abby? This is a surprise. What can I do for you?"

I stood on tiptoe, trying to see what I wanted on the round displays and wooden tables squeezed into the space. Gavin had come to town at exactly the right time to open his shop, while the real estate was still affordable. The way taxes had soared in the past few years, I doubted either of us would've been able to open a shop in the middle of town now.

"I'm looking for some exercise clothes," I told him. "Something I can wear to the gym or outside if I ever get brave enough to exercise in public."

Gavin squeezed between two round hanging displays and motioned for me to follow. "Taking up jogging?"

"Maybe." I knocked a shirt to the floor and bent to pick it up. "I've started coaching one of the Youth League basketball teams, and it seems like a good time to get in shape."

Gavin shot a look over his shoulder. "You're coaching? Which team?"

"Technically, I'm the assistant coach," I said. "My nephews are on the Miners."

That made Gavin stop dead in his tracks. "You're coaching with Kerry Hendrix?"

"Yeah. Don't ask."

He laughed without humor and started walking again. "Okay, I won't. But Kerry's not exactly an easy man to get along with. You probably ought to know that if you don't already."

"Thanks. I wish I'd talked to you last week. How well do you know him?"

Gavin reached a rack near the back of the store and stopped walking. "Well enough to know that he can be an asshole. Just don't let him push you around, okay?"

I smiled ruefully. "Thanks. It's hard to know how much to argue with him. I don't want to embarrass the boys."

Gavin smiled. "Yeah. Touchy. Kids that age have a tough time. So what kind of exercise are you thinking of doing?"

I shrugged. "My parents gave me a gift certificate for the recreation center last year. I thought maybe I'd check out their exercise equipment."

"So you're thinking treadmill? Stair-stepper? Maybe the elliptical?"

Just hearing him list the choices made me tired, but I nodded. "Something like that."

"Then you're going to want the stuff in this corner. You want me to help you find sizes?"

Was he kidding? I liked Gavin, but there was some information *nobody* had about me. "If I told you what size I wear," I said with a roll of my eyes, "I'd have to kill you. I can manage, thanks. Do you have any recommendations?"

He pointed out a couple of good brands, showed me where to find the dressing room when I was ready, and left me to look through the depressingly small, tight clothes by myself. The idea of stuffing myself into any of the things on the first rack almost made me choke, but I didn't let myself give up. There was no law that said I *had* to wear one of those spandex/sports bra combinations when I exercised.

Freeing myself from the constraints of selecting an outfit, I browsed for twenty frustrating minutes before I found two pairs of workout pants I thought might fit me, and two actual T-shirts, both of which looked like they belonged on someone Caleb's age. Inside the dressing room, I struggled into the first outfit, saw what I looked like in that T-shirt, and decided then and there that "stylish" and "workout" were not words destined to meet in my vocabulary. I'd leave style to Nicolette.

By the time I returned the T-shirts and carried the pants to the register, night was beginning to fall. Gavin rang up the sale, ran my debit card through, and folded the pants and receipt into a bag. "Enjoy," he said as he handed it over to me. "And forget what I said about Kerry Hendrix. He's not the nicest guy in the world, but he's okay."

"Don't worry," I assured him, "you didn't tell me anything new. He accused me of vandalizing his truck the other night, so I already know just how friendly he is."

Gavin's smile faded. "He accused you of what?"

Briefly, I explained about the truck and seeing the man limping away from it. "Of course Kerry doesn't believe that I'm innocent," I said as I finished the story, "because he didn't see the guy or the SUV that picked him up. I think Brody, Caleb, and I are the only people who *have* seen him."

"The guy with the limp?" Gavin asked. "Short guy? Hasn't shaved in a few days?"

My head shot up with a snap. "Yes, have you seen him?"

"Yeah, a couple of times. As a matter of fact, I saw him walk by the store while you were in the dressing room."

"Just *now*?"

"Yeah. Why?"

"Did you see where he went?"

Gavin shook his head. "He was walking past the store going west. That's all I know."

"How long ago?"

"I don't know. Five, ten minutes."

Maybe it wasn't the smartest thing to do, but I snatched the bag from him and bolted for the door. "Do me a favor," I called back as I ran. "Call the police and ask for Detective Jawarski. Tell him what you told me."

"Wait a second. *Abby!*"

He shouted something else, but I was already gone. The limping man had slipped through my fingers twice already. I wasn't going to let him do it again.

Chapter 13

Max was waiting for me right where I'd left him. He leaped to his feet when he saw me come through the door, alert and ready for anything. Too bad he couldn't tell me where the man with the limp had gone.

I glanced in both directions as I untied Max's leash from the bench leg. To the east lay the town square, mostly empty this time of night. To the west, Prospector Circle, City Hall and a bunch of other deserted city offices including the police station. Across the street a couple of customers milled about inside Curl Up and Dye. Beside it, the credit union's windows were dark.

Gavin had said that the limping man passed his store heading west, but it seemed doubtful that he'd make a run for the police station, which meant that he'd probably turned onto Twelve Peaks Road at the next corner. Where he'd gone from there was anybody's guess.

Chasing him might have been foolhardy, but I was still angry about the stunt he and his friend had pulled at Hammond Junction, and I wasn't interested in taking the rap for the damage he'd done to Hendrix's truck.

Holding on to the slim hope that I'd be able to find him, I ran to the corner and checked the street in both directions. Max followed eagerly, interested, if slightly confused, by this fun new activity.

"Where'd he go, boy? Did you see him? The man with the limp?"

Max planted his butt on the sidewalk and panted. I appreciated his enthusiasm, but I wished he could be a little more help.

The sound of hurried footsteps reached me half a second before a woman barreled around the corner. I was too distracted to recognize Paisley Pringle, owner of the Curl Up and Dye, until she was almost past me. "Abby?" She stopped so fast I almost expected to smell burning rubber. "Hey! How are you doing?"

Paisley's a friendly woman, if a bit ditzy. She's always trying to convince me to let her "fix" my hair. I don't mean to sound fussy, but if Paisley's hair was any indication of what I could expect, I'd pass.

Paisley fluffed her short reddish hair with the fingers of one hand. Last time I saw her, she had long, bluish black hair that fell to the middle of her back. Today, her hair was about two inches long. That's not unusual for Paisley. Her hair color and style are different almost every time I see her, thanks to the magic of dye and extensions. Even so, I've yet to see her wearing a combination I'd consider letting her re-create on my head.

That didn't mean I wanted to alienate her, though. Paradise is still a small town, and people here have long memories.

I tried to look friendly back. "I'm fine, thanks. Busy." I didn't want to open the door for a lengthy conversation, but my mother would have killed me if she saw me behaving that rudely. "How about you?"

"The same. Gearing up for the holidays. You know how that is. You're away from the shop early. Taking a little time off?"

"Actually, no." I said. "I'm running some errands, having an early dinner."

Paisley smiled and glanced at her watch, a chunky silver thing that looked as if it weighed about ten pounds. "Are you through for the day? I just had a cancellation. I have time to give you a quick cut and blow-dry if you're interested."

I had no idea how many times I'd have to say no before Paisley realized I meant it, but apparently it was at least one more time than I'd said it already. "No thanks. I'm right in the middle of something."

Paisley bent to scratch Max and ran a glance over the bag I was carrying. "I see you've been to Gavin's."

Paisley has a talent for getting people to spill their guts without asking a single question. I'm not sure how she does it, but I actually felt a twinge of guilt for not telling her what was in the bag. "Yeah," I said. "Listen, I need to get back. Karen's running the store on her own." Technically true. I considered Liberty too new to be of much help.

"Oh. Sure. Of course. I saw your ad in the *Post*. You're looking for help?"

I nodded, chafing at the delay and trying not to show it. "We decided it's time."

"Any luck so far?"

Since I'd just claimed that Karen was alone, I was hesitant to admit the truth. But Paradise is too small to tell a lie, especially one that could be discredited faster than a kid can eat a handful of gummy bears. "Actually, Karen found someone already, so I guess we're all set. That's . . . uh . . . that's why I have to get back. She's running the store *and* training the new clerk."

"Well that's great! Who did you hire?"

"You probably wouldn't know her," I said, relieved that she didn't seem suspicious about my conflicting stories. I glanced around again in case the limping man had come back, but I still couldn't see him. In the process, my gaze skimmed across Paisley's eager face, and another twinge of guilt plucked at me. Determined to prove that my mother had instilled a few manners in me, I tried to give Paisley my full attention. "Her name's Liberty Parker."

"Liberty? Of course I know her. She grew up here, you know."

"That's what she said."

"She'll be great. I remember her as being a very friendly girl. Popular. She'll be a good draw for you. If you're hiring, that must mean you're doing well."

"We're doing fine, I think. At least for now."

She smiled, and we shared a moment. Two small business women who understood that life as a shop owner was never stable. Every day brought a new challenge, and nothing was ever guaranteed. "I heard you talking as I came around the corner," she said just as I was about to make an excuse and leave. "You said something about a man with a limp?"

Had I? I dimly remembered talking to Max, but I couldn't remember what I'd said. "I thought I saw someone I know. I must have been wrong."

"The guy with a limp? You know who he is?"

She sounded more than idly curious, which piqued my own curiosity. "Why? Have you seen him?"

She nodded. "He's been hanging around for a couple of days. He never says anything, and he never tries to come inside, but he makes me kind of nervous anyway. But if he's a friend of yours—"

"He's not a friend," I said quickly, "just someone I ran into a few days ago. Do you have any idea where I can find him now?"

Paisley shook her head thoughtfully. "I saw him about ten minutes ago, but I have no idea where he went."

I was disappointed but not surprised. "Is he usually here at this time of day?"

She shook her head again. "No. He doesn't really keep a schedule that I've noticed. He's just . . . there sometimes."

That didn't surprise me either. It would have been nice to know when I could find him again, but I was thrilled to find two other people who'd seen him around town. I'd been standing still so long my fingers were beginning to hurt from the cold. I made a two-handed fist and breathed on it to warm my fingers. "Have you ever seen him with anyone? Getting into or out of a car?"

Paisley tilted her head to one side and thought a bit harder. "I don't remember seeing him with anyone else. I could ask Mom. She's seen him, too. Maybe she's noticed something I haven't."

"Could you ask and let me know? It's really important that I find him. But if you see him, please don't tell him I'm looking for him."

"Ooh," Paisley said with a grin. "That sounds mysterious."

I didn't want to spark a wholesale panic by telling her the truth, but neither did I want to leave her thinking that I was playing some kind of game. "It's not really," I said. "I need to talk to him about something that happened the other night. I think he's trying to avoid me, that's all."

Paisley's smile slipped, and the spark faded from her eye. "Oh. Okay. Well, then, I should let you get back to work, and I'd better do the same."

She trotted across the street, and I went back to trying to figure out where the limping man had gone. I couldn't see anything in either direction likely to interest him, but with dozens of alleyways, parking lots, and miniature parks dotting the city, he could be anywhere by now.

Swallowing disappointment, I decided to take the long way back to Divinity and turned south on Twelve Peaks. I still had fifteen minutes left of my break, and a brisk walk to clear my head seemed like a good idea.

Max fell in beside me, and we walked around three legs of a block. We'd just crossed the street and started the long pull up the steep incline that was Grandview Drive when Max's ears shot straight up, and he let out a high-pitched whine.

This wasn't the first time since he'd become my dog that he'd done that, and a warning bell sounded in my head right away. If Max followed his usual pattern, the next step in this dance was taking off at a dead run. I tightened my grip on his leash, but I was a split second too late. His claws scrambled for purchase on the pavement, caught, and he was off.

He darted through the sparse traffic and into the parking lot of Walgreens, while I panted after him. I could see him dodging cars in the parking lot, turning, and weaving through the line at the drive-up prescription window.

"Max!" I shouted as I headed toward the drive-through window. I knew it wouldn't do any good. When Max is in this mood, he doesn't pay attention to anything. "Come back. Max!"

Struggling to follow him, I prayed that, since we were just half a block from Divinity, he'd turn up at home if I couldn't catch him. With my lungs burning from exertion, I rounded the back of the building and saw Max straight ahead of me.

Miraculously, he'd stopped running, and his attention was riveted on the hedge growing between the drugstore and the stairs leading down the hill I'd just climbed.

Even from a distance, I could see something mounded there, and another warning bell went off in the back of my head. I told myself not to jump to conclusions, but I had the sick feeling that either Max had discovered a hundred-pound bag of kibble, or there was something in that hedge I didn't want to see.

My breath was coming easier now, so I tried calling him again. "Max? Come here, boy." I kept my voice light, hoping I could lure him away, but he didn't even lift his head.

"Max! Come."

He burrowed a little deeper into the hedge, still not interested in anything I had to say.

"Max!"

"Abby?" A man's voice came out of the darkness behind me.

My heart shot into my throat, and I whipped around on the balls of my feet, prepared to kick the living shit out of whoever it was. Marshall Ames materialized out of the shadows, and I breathed a sigh of relief.

I'd known Marshall since we were kids in school. We hadn't been friends as kids—he'd been part of one group; I'd been part of another—but we'd become a little better acquainted since I'd returned to Paradise, and he was a familiar, friendly face when I needed one most.

He strode toward me, lamplight gleaming off his blond hair and reflecting off the lenses of his glasses. "Is everything okay?"

I shook my head uncertainly. "I'm not sure."

"Looks like Max has found something to interest him. Want me to get him for you?" He started forward without waiting for an answer.

I let him take a couple of steps, then reached out and snagged his arm. "No, wait. Don't—"

"Hey, it's okay. Max likes me, don't you boy?"

"It's not that," I said, suddenly aware that a couple of people had paused in the act of getting into their cars to watch us.

I dropped my voice and moved closer so they couldn't over-hear. "I think there may be something wrong."

"What do you mean, wrong?"

"I mean—" I cut myself off. I had nothing but gut instinct to go on, and not even much of that. And what if my gut instinct was wrong? I'd look like a fool. I shook my head and backed a step away. "I mean he looks pretty intense. Maybe you should let me go up there."

Marshall grinned and shook his head. "What are you talk-ing about? He's fine, Abby. Look, he's even wagging his tail. Just stay there, and I'll bring him back to you, okay?"

I nodded and bit back the rest of my protests. Even if my instincts were right, there was no law that said *I* had to find the body. Marshall was a big boy. He'd survive the shock.

He crossed what remained of the parking lot and reached for Max's collar. Max looked up at him, his little dog face beaming with pride. Even as Marshall hunkered down beside him, I told myself that I was wrong. Marshall prodded the mound gently, and I told myself that my imagination was working overtime.

But in the next instant Marshall jerked backward, one hand over his mouth. He shot to his feet and tugged Max in-sistently away from the pile of rags in the hedge. I had to ad-mire his composure. He didn't say a word until he'd closed the distance between us. Then, in a very low voice only I could hear, he said exactly what I'd been expecting.

"We need to call the police, Abby. There's a dead body over there."

Chapter 14

It took the police a couple of hours to clear the scene and transport the body to the closest hospital. I phoned Karen to let her know that I wouldn't be back for a while, and why. She asked a million questions, none of which I had answers to. When she finally gave up asking, I hung out with Marshall and waited for the police to take our statements.

A small crowd of curious onlookers gathered along the sidewalk, and several inquisitive drivers pulled into the parking lot, hoping to figure out what the police were doing there. Red and blue lights bounced off the brick walls of the drugstore, casting eerie shadows all around us. Paramedics and police officers swarmed the scene, talking in solemn tones that didn't carry to where Marshall and I leaned against the trunk of a police car.

I'd had to identify the dead man as the same man I'd seen at Hammond Junction, and images of the times I'd seen him alive raced through my head while we waited. Over and over again, I saw his eyes meet mine through the Jetta's windshield and saw the horror reflected there. What—or who—had he been afraid of? Had someone actually tried to kill him that night?

All things considered, Marshall took the shock of finding his first dead body pretty well. At least, I think it was his first. I guess there's no way to really know something like that.

Once the ambulance carrying the body left the scene, most of those who'd gathered to watch lost interest and wandered away. I'd tried to keep an eye out for anyone who looked more interested in the body than he ought to be, but if the other person who'd been at Hammond Junction was also in the drugstore parking lot, he—or she—hid their interest well.

Once, I thought I saw Karen and Liberty hovering near the edge of the crowd, but the police didn't let anyone get close to the scene or to their witnesses. The next time I looked, they were gone.

Two hours after we found the body, Marshall and I were finally allowed to leave. He walked with me as far as Divinity, but we didn't have much to say. I guess we were both tired of talking about the murder and answering questions, so we walked in silence. Still, I was surprised to discover that I appreciated not having to make the walk alone.

Karen had already locked up the store, so after Marshall and I said good night at the bottom of the steps, I climbed to the third floor apartment and locked myself inside. Questions continued to race through my head while I changed into a pair of soft, warm sweats and the faded Sacramento Kings sweatshirt I'd brought with me from California.

Who was the dead man? What was he doing in Paradise? Why had he been at Hammond Junction on Tuesday night and at the recreation center on Saturday?

Eventually, the events of the day caught up with me, and I realized that I hadn't eaten since eight that morning. I dug through my refrigerator, which turned out to be an exercise in futility. I didn't want to open the box of leftover Chinese that had been in the fridge longer than I could account for, and I couldn't think of anything to make with mayonnaise and Mom's strawberry jam.

I wondered if Marshall had gone back to his restaurant. It was late, but Gigi didn't stop serving until nine or ten, and I'm sure he probably had paperwork to do. I decided he was probably back there now, indulging in something rich and hot and French while I tried to decide how old the lone can of soup in my cupboard was.

Yawning, I tried to decide whether I was hungry enough

to have something delivered or too tired to wait for food to arrive. In the middle of my contemplations, a knock sounded on the front door. I opened it and found Jawarski leaning against my doorframe, a six-pack of Sam Adams in one hand, a Gut Buster Special from Black Jack Pizza in the other.

He gave me that lopsided smile of his. "Hey, slugger."

My insides did the fluttery thing they always did when he smiled that way. "Hey yourself. You and Sam there at loose ends tonight?"

"Unfortunately. Know anybody who might be willing to let us hang out for a while?"

I wasn't sure which of the three looked best to me. I stepped away from the door so they could all come in. "You must have read my mind. I was just thinking about ordering something."

"I heard you were tied up at the drugstore for a while." Jawarski put the pizza box and beer on my battered old coffee table while I went after paper plates. "How'd you happen to be there when they found the body?"

I found the plates and tore off a few sheets of paper towel so we could pretend to be civilized. "I was taking a walk on my dinner break, and Max got away from me."

"And that's where he went?"

"Not immediately," I hedged. "But yeah. Eventually."

Jawarski slid a look at me from the corner of his eye. "So how did Marshall Ames end up finding the body instead of you?"

I felt myself tensing. "Is this a social visit or a thinly disguised interrogation?"

He had the good sense to look sheepish. "Sorry. Purely social."

"Good." I relaxed again and realized that Marshall had never actually said why he was at the drugstore during the dinner shift. "Marshall was there at the drugstore," I said, caving in spite of my protest and answering Jawarski's question. "He heard me trying to get Max away from the body. Of course, I didn't know it was a body at the time, but I wasn't having any luck, and Marshall offered to get him for me."

The look in Jawarski's eye changed slightly. "And you let him? That doesn't sound like you."

"I'd just run up Grandview. I was tired and out of breath. Now open up that pizza before I eat right through the box." Jawarski laughed and did what I asked, and we settled like an old married couple on the atrocious plaid sofa I'd inherited along with the apartment. I helped myself to a garlic bread stick first. "So what do you know about the dead guy? Any idea how he died?"

Jawarski put his feet up on the coffee table next to mine and pulled two bottles from the six-pack. "Multiple stab wounds. Nice and quiet. No pesky gunshots to draw a crowd."

I shuddered and uncapped my beer. "Do you know who he is?"

Jawarski took a long pull from his beer, then wiped his mouth with the back of his hand. "Not yet. He had no ID on him, his fingerprints aren't on file, and we haven't found any record of him at the local hotels. Yet."

"No fingerprints on file means no criminal record, I guess. Did you find any prints on that metal bar I gave you?"

"On the slim-jim? Yeah, a couple of partials. It's not wide enough to pick up a complete print."

At least now I knew what I'd found, but why use a lockout tool to vandalize a truck? Why not use it to open the door and steal it? I was too tired to figure out the answers, so I filed the questions away for another time and asked, "And do the prints from the slim-jim match the dead man's?"

Jawarski picked up a piece of pizza, cradling it just so to keep the toppings from sliding off. "They do, but that doesn't really tell us anything. The investigation's just getting started, though. We'll know more by tomorrow."

"In the meantime, you still don't know what he was doing in town."

"Not yet."

"But at least you know he exists," I said with a tired smile.

"That's a plus. I was getting tired of you thinking I was nuts."

"Nobody ever said you were nuts," Jawarski protested. "But I couldn't very well run around searching for a mysterious limping man when there was no proof he even existed."

"Nothing except my word." I leaned back against the couch and let out a sigh. "A couple of other people have seen him, too. He's been hanging around by the Curl. Paisley and her mom have both seen him, and Gavin has, too."

Jawarski's chewing slowed. "You've been asking around about him?"

"Does that surprise you? I couldn't let you talk to the boys, but I figured someone else must have noticed him. If I could find someone else who saw him, you'd have to admit that he existed."

"Hey, I believed you," Jawarski protested again, "but you know how things work. I take orders. I don't decide what I'm going to work on. If my lieutenant doesn't believe there's a mysterious limping man running around out there, it doesn't matter what I think."

I picked a piece of sausage from my pizza and popped it into my mouth. "Then you're forgiven."

Jawarski leaned across what little distance there was separating us and kissed me gently. "Thanks."

I might have returned the favor, but my stomach rumbled insistently. I bit the point off my pizza and closed my eyes as I savored the mix of flavors. Jawarski's a truly masterful kisser, but the Gut Buster Special is truly a pizza masterpiece, so you understand my dilemma.

I could feel Jawarski watching me, so I opened my eyes again and rejoined the regular world. "So what are you going to do now?" I asked.

"About—?"

"Finding out who the dead man was."

Jawarski polished off one piece and reached for another. "We'll keep looking. Keep trying. We've got a couple of guys checking missing persons reports, and that may turn up something."

"There's always a chance that he was staying with someone who lives around here," I pointed out. "Somebody was waiting for him at the recreation center, you know."

"Somebody in a dark-colored SUV? Come on, Abby, you know how many SUVs there are around here. If you'd seen even a partial plate, I'd have something to go on. As it is now . . ." He broke off with an expressive shrug and put his beer bottle on the coffee table. Slipping an arm around my shoulders, he pulled me close. "What do you say we stop talking about the murder for a while and do something more interesting."

I admired his ability to switch gears at will, but I couldn't make the jump so easily. He and I hadn't slept together yet, but we'd been drawing relentlessly closer to turning that corner. On the one hand, I wanted nothing more than to see if he was everything I'd built him up to be in my imagination. On the other, once we crossed that line, we could no longer pretend that we weren't involved. Besides, finding dead bodies isn't so commonplace for me that I can just tune out the images. The idea of making out with Jawarski while the dead guy limped unrelentingly through my head didn't exactly turn me on.

"Have you talked to local restaurants, the grocery stores, and gas stations? Somebody must have seen this guy around."

Jawarski tensed. "I know how to do my job, slick."

"I never said you didn't. It just seems to me that you're giving up without much of a fight."

Frowning, he pulled his arm away. "Who said I was giving up? I just don't want to talk about it anymore tonight, is that okay with you?"

I shrugged and pretended not to care. "Sure, that's fine."

"But?"

"But what? I said it was fine, and it is."

Jawarski shook his head and put some distance between us. "Right. Except that you're still thinking about the dead guy. Call me crazy, but I'd rather have you thinking about us."

"Then humor me. Answer a few more questions so I can."

Jawarski tossed a wadded paper towel onto the coffee table and stood. "Okay. Hit me. What do you want to know?"

Half a dozen questions had been building themselves into a list, but the look on his face made them all evaporate. "If you really want me to think about us, maybe you should try being a little less hostile."

He put his hands on his hips and paced a few steps away. "I'm not hostile, Abby, I'm frustrated. I thought we'd turned a corner in our relationship, but now I'm not so sure."

There it was, the *R* word we'd been avoiding like the plague for months. It fell into the space between us and rolled around for a while in the silence. "I think we have turned a corner," I said, still unable to say that word aloud. "But shouldn't there be some give and take? I know you don't want to talk about the murder. You've been at it for hours, nonstop. But I'm the one who ran into the guy on Tuesday night, I'm the one who saw him vandalizing a car I was later accused of damaging, and I was there when his body was found. I'm still wound up, and I can't just shut that off because you want to get friendly."

Jawarski hung his head and shook it slowly. "I *can't* talk about the case with you, Abby. You're not a member of the force. I can't give you classified information, and I'm not going to let you know what the investigators on the case are thinking. That's not how it works."

"I'm not asking you for classified information."

"How do you know?"

I had my mouth open, ready to argue some more, but his question stopped me in my tracks. "Well, I don't, but—"

"Then don't take offense where none is intended. I'm not shutting you down, Abby. I'm not that kind of guy. I'd think you would know that by now."

That shot a hole in my self-righteous sails. Feeling about two inches tall, I stood to face him anyway. "I know you're not. I'm sorry."

I have to hand it to Jawarski. He knows how difficult those two words are for me to say, and he accepts them in the spirit they're intended. Without another word, he closed the distance between us and pulled me into his arms. A heartbeat later, his mouth covered mine, and I knew that we were okay again. At least for now.

It took some effort, but I even managed to shut out the images I didn't want to see so I could concentrate on the man in front of me, and that made us both happy.

Chapter 15

"I can't believe you found a dead body," Liberty gushed as she stocked the display case with blueberry fudge the next morning. "And right down the street, too."

She'd been gazing at me for more than an hour while I worked on a candy mosaic background in autumn tones for the shop's display window. Somehow, finding John Doe dead in the bushes had transported me to rock star status in her eyes. She seemed barely able to focus on the work she was supposed to be doing.

I couldn't explain why, but her attitude made me faintly uneasy. I glanced around for Karen, thinking she might save me from this conversation, but she'd disappeared into the office to take care of some paperwork. "It happens," I said with a nonchalance I didn't feel. "Even in Paradise."

Liberty straightened from her task, her upper lip curled slightly. "Believe me, I don't have any delusions about Paradise. This town is no different than anywhere else."

We might all say it, but Liberty was probably the only other person inside city limits who actually believed it. With its granite mountain peaks, dense forests of aspen and pine, and clear mountain streams nearby, Paradise looks as if it belongs on a postcard. Those of us lucky enough to live here understand just how fortunate we are. I couldn't say that out loud, though, so I followed the unwritten script my relatives had been using for years. "People are people no matter where you go. There are good and bad everywhere."

Liberty stopped just short of rolling her eyes. "Right. So who do you think killed him?"

A little surprised, I paused with a shard of candy in one

hand, a brush loaded with edible glue in the other. "I don't even know who *he* is."

"I know. That's weird, isn't it? Around here, I mean." She seemed to remember that she was supposed to be working and scooped up two squares of fudge with a spatula. "It's hard to imagine that *nobody* knows the guy."

"I'm sure someone does." I pressed the candy shard into place and eyed the effect critically. I was becoming bolder when it came to designing the display windows at Divinity, and this one was the most daring yet. "I'm also sure the police will find the answers to everyone's questions soon."

Liberty looked up in surprise. "What? You don't want to talk about it?"

Again, an uncomfortable feeling slithered up my spine. "A man's dead," I said, my voice flat. "I don't get off on speculating about what happened."

From somewhere behind me came the sound of Karen snorting in disbelief. "Don't let her fool you, Liberty. She's not as immune to gossip as she tries to pretend."

I glared at the open doorway. Karen should know what I *meant*. I might have talked about murder with family and a few close friends in the past, but I barely knew Liberty. Karen should be able to understand the difference.

Liberty grinned and carried the empty fudge pan into the kitchen. She'd done something to her hair that morning that made her whole head look as if a skunk had nested on top of it. "It makes you wonder, doesn't it? I mean, I know what made Rutger want to come here, and you and I just came home again. But what brings somebody like this guy to Paradise?"

Terrific. Apparently, Karen had been gabbing about me with our new employee. "I suppose we'd have to know something about him to know the answer."

Liberty leaned against the counter and studied the mosaic closely. "Maybe finding out what he was doing here would help tell us who he was. Have you thought of it that way?"

"I haven't really thought about it at all," I said. And that was mostly true. Okay . . . partially true. I'd been *trying* not to think about it. That had to count for something.

Karen appeared in the office doorway, a scowl on her narrow face. "She has a point. You could have passed the murderer somewhere along the road. Did you see anyone you recognized?"

I shook my head slowly. "I've thought about it a hundred times, but I don't remember anyone in particular, other than Marshall. I was too busy chasing Max." And trying to breathe, but I saw no reason to mention that.

"The killer must have known where to find him, don't you think?" Liberty said abruptly. "Unless it was just a random act of violence."

"I don't think it was random," I said. "It's too much of a coincidence that he'd pretend to be killed one day and actually turn up dead a few days later."

"Then it had to be planned," Liberty pointed out.

"Maybe not," I said. "Maybe someone just saw an opportunity and took it."

Liberty cocked an eyebrow. "Someone who just happened to carry a knife with him in case he came across someone he wanted to get rid of?"

"Obviously the dead guy had some kind of connection to Coach Hendrix," Karen said, changing tactics. "Maybe he can identify the dead guy."

I covered another sheet of candy with paper towel and shattered it using a rubber mallet. "I hope you're not suggesting that I should ask him."

Liberty picked up a stray sliver of candy and slid it into her mouth. "Are you talking about Kerry Hendrix?"

Intrigued, Karen came further into the room. "Yeah. Why? Do you know him?"

"I used to. We went to high school together, but I haven't seen him in years."

My stomach dropped. "You and Kerry were friends?"

Liberty laughed. "I wouldn't say that. He was in the popular crowd. I spent most of my time in the parking lot or behind the bleachers."

I hoped she was telling me the truth; otherwise, I was going to have a really tough time letting her stick around.

"Popular crowd? No wonder he's so cocky," Karen muttered. She came all the way into the kitchen and sat at the table. "So why did this guy want to destroy Kerry's truck?"

"Unless Kerry's changed, it could have been anything," Liberty said as she joined Karen at the table. "When I knew him, he always got his own way. He pissed a lot of people off."

"He hasn't changed a bit," Karen said with a rueful grin. "People like him never do."

Liberty *seemed* genuine, at least. I wondered who Kerry's friends were now that he was older, and if any of them might know what connection he had with the murdered man. Not that I had any intention of asking. The more distance I kept between Kerry Hendrix and myself, the better I'd feel.

Coach Hendrix and I didn't exchange more than a dozen words at Wednesday afternoon's practice. Apparently, he was still convinced that I'd vandalized his truck. I was still offended that he'd think so and more than a little uncomfortable around him.

With the two of us taking such pains not to interact any more than we had to, practice dragged on until I thought pulling the hair out of my arms with tweezers would have been less painful.

Finally, eight o'clock came around, and I led Brody and Caleb to the Jetta. While we'd been at practice, snow had started to fall, and the parking lot and cars were already blanketed with a thin layer of sparkling white.

Brody and Caleb reacted like boys always do, sliding on the ice that had formed under the surface and trying to pack the dry powder into snowballs. Like generations of adults before me, I walked with my head down, trying to keep my shoes dry and my hair from frizzing.

Brody and Caleb reached the car a few steps ahead of me. Caleb opened the car door and climbed into the backseat, but Brody came to a wobbling stop at the end of an ice slide and pointed toward the other side of the parking lot. "Hey. Lookit that. Isn't that the car that guy got into the other night?"

I followed his finger and saw a dark-colored SUV idling next to Coach Hendrix's truck. I could see Coach's shadow behind the wheel of the truck, and someone else's behind the wheel of the SUV. "I don't know. It might be, but I didn't see it well enough the other night to be certain."

"It *is* the same car," Caleb said, practically tumbling out of the Jetta in his excitement. "You wanna know how I know?"

Brody and I turned to look at him at the same time. "How?" I asked.

"Look at the lights in front. The one on this side is broken."

Sure enough, where the headlights wrapped to the side of the SUV, one of the lights was missing its yellow plastic covering. My heart thumped hard against my rib cage, and my hands grew clammy. "Are you *sure* that's the same car?"

Caleb's chin jutted out stubbornly. "I'm not a baby, Aunt Abby."

"I know you're not," I assured him. "I just want to be very sure it's the same car. Next time I see it, I'll give the license number to the police. Now get in the car and let's get out of here."

Brody reached for the door handle, but he stopped there. "Do you want me to sneak over there and write down the number?"

"Absolutely not. We're leaving."

Caleb didn't seem to mind, but I could tell Brody thought I was being a sissy. "How are you going to get the license plate number if we leave?" he asked.

It was a good question, but I couldn't take chances with the boys. We weren't just dealing with a suspected carjacker anymore. A man had been murdered. Whatever these people were doing in Paradise, they meant business.

I herded the boys into the Jetta, swept away a layer of snow so I could see to drive, and got the car running. Leaving the headlights off so we wouldn't attract attention, I drove around the building so I could leave the lot by the front entrance. We might have been perfectly safe driving past the SUV, bold as brass, but it was a risk I didn't want to take.

This was the second time that SUV had been here, and it made me wonder what connection it had to Coach Hendrix. Did he know something about John Doe's death, or was he in danger himself? I pulled my cell phone from my pocket, flipped it open, punched in Jawarski's number, and hit Send. Nothing happened. I glanced at the screen and realized that once again the weather had blocked the signal. Service was patchy in Paradise in the best of times. In bad weather, it disappeared almost entirely.

Now what?

My tires hit a patch of black ice and we slid a few feet. Tossing the phone into the center console, I fought to steer us out of the skid. After a few seconds the tires found purchase, and I regained control of the car. It hadn't been a dangerous skid, but it was enough to convince me that it was time to get the boys home.

"Aunt Abby?"

"Yes, Caleb?"

"I think they're following us."

I tore my glance away from the road and checked the rearview mirror. I didn't know if someone was actually following us, but there were headlights behind us. "I see them, kiddo, but I'm sure there's nothing to worry about."

Brody strained against his seat belt to see the car behind us. "Turn around, please," I said. If someone *was* following us, I didn't want the boys to make it obvious that we knew.

"But they're still coming," Brody protested.

The headlights followed us around a curve in the road, and I saw the SUV's outline in the glow of a streetlamp. Nervous perspiration dampened my hands. "I can see that," I said, trying to stay calm. "Now please turn around and look straight ahead."

"Maybe I can see the license number."

"Brody! I said turn around, and I meant it."

"Sheesh. You act like we're babies or something."

The snow began falling more heavily, and flakes stuck to the windshield. I turned on the wipers and hit the defrost onto high. "I don't think you're babies, Brody, but this isn't a game. When you're with me, it's my responsibility to make sure you're safe."

He flopped back in his seat, looking sullen. "Fine."

"Fine. Now let me concentrate, okay? It's hard enough

driving in the snow without having an argument at the same time."

Brody folded he arms and scowled.

I ignored him and drove carefully down Pikes Peak to Cliffhanger Drive, and slowly, steadily, the SUV stayed behind us.

Chapter 16

The storm grew worse by the minute. As fast as the windshield wipers slapped away the snow, another layer covered the windshield. The defrost labored to keep a patch clear enough for me to see through, but all three of us were breathing so heavily, the fan couldn't blow fast enough.

"Brody, I want you to find my cell phone. Can you do that?"

"Am I allowed to move?"

"Don't pout. You're old enough to understand danger. I need you to find my cell phone and see if I have any service."

He dug around in the center console for a while. "Got it," he said after a few minutes. "You have one bar."

"Hopefully that will be enough." I turned onto Larkspur and waited to see if the SUV would make the same turn. We were halfway to the next corner when the SUV slowly turned behind us, and my heart shot into my throat. "Scroll through my contacts and find Jawarski's number," I directed, trying not to think about what lay in store along the highway between here and Wyatt's house.

Caleb looked out the back window, but I didn't snap at him about it. By this time, the SUV's driver had to know that we were aware of him.

It seemed to take forever before Brody piped up again. "I've got it. Now what?" The poutiness had left his voice, and a solemn note had replaced it.

"Try to get him on the phone. Tell him where we are and what's going on."

Nobody spoke while Brody punched numbers, but I could

hear Caleb breathing, and he sounded frightened. "There's no answer," Brody announced. "I've got his voice mail."

"Leave a message," I said.

Brody did, but whether or not Jawarski would be able to make sense of it was anybody's guess. When Brody hung up, the phone beeped to indicate that I had a message, and I talked Brody through the steps to retrieve it.

"It's from Mom," he said after a few seconds of silence. "She says it's snowing too hard for us to come home. She wants us to stay here in town with you."

Knowing I didn't have to make that long drive sent a huge wave of relief through me, but we weren't safe yet. I didn't want to lead the SUV driver to my apartment or to Divinity. I needed to find a public place and people. Not that being in the middle of town had saved John Doe, but at least it might give us a fighting chance.

We came full circle to Silver River Road, and this time I turned east, toward King Soopers, the grocery store. Piles of snow left by a snowplow lined the road, and slush had started forming on the road's surface.

"Where are we going now?" Caleb asked, his voice small and frightened.

"To King Soopers. There should be people there." I tossed what I hoped was a reassuring smile over my shoulder. "Try to relax, okay? I'm not going to let you get hurt." I just hoped I wasn't making a promise I couldn't keep.

One at a time, I took my hands from the wheel and wiped my sweaty palms on my pant legs. I couldn't remember when I'd been so nervous, or when I'd had so much at stake, and I hated the SUV driver with a passion I hadn't known I could feel.

We crept past the Silver River Inn, a bed-and-breakfast owned by my friends, Richie and Dylan. They'd have helped us, but the front door was two full flights of stairs from street level. Even if we could find a place to pull off the road, we'd never make it up the stairs before the SUV caught up with us.

A few feet farther along, I spotted the new antique store, the Ivy Attic. Its door was at street level, and for one brief moment, I let myself hope that it was still open, but all the windows were dark, the closed sign hanging slightly off-kilter in the front door.

We crept along two more blocks before a tiny voice broke the silence again. "Aunt Abby?"

"Yes Caleb?"

"I think they're gone. I can't see the lights anymore."

My eyes shot to the rearview mirror. I couldn't see the headlights either, but that didn't mean we were in the clear. "Did you see the SUV turn off somewhere?"

"Nope. He was there one minute and gone the next."

"What about you, Brody?"

"I didn't see anything either."

Had the SUV really stopped following us? Or had the driver done something more sinister, like turning off the headlights to keep us from knowing what was coming? "Keep watching," I ordered. "If you see anything back there—anything at all—tell me immediately."

But for the next three blocks neither of the boys said a word. I pulled off the road into the King Sooper's parking lot. It wasn't crowded, but there were enough cars there to make me feel safer than I'd felt in an hour. I found a spot that gave us a good view of the road, but it was close enough to the door to let us escape inside if we had to.

We sat there for almost thirty minutes before I let myself believe that the SUV had given up on us. As the realization that we were safe finally hit, the adrenaline pumping through my veins drained away, and bone-deep exhaustion hit like a sledgehammer.

Back home, I circled the block to make sure nobody was lying in wait for us, then dragged myself up the stairs behind my two silent little nephews. It was the first time I'd ever seen them so subdued, and I hoped it would be the last.

I woke the next morning to a thick blanket of snow covering everything in sight. The storm had moved out, leaving clear blue skies and brilliant sunshine behind. The boys were still sleeping when I took Max out for his walk, so we didn't go far. Seeing that no other tracks marred the snow made me relax even further.

Last night, I'd placed calls to both Elizabeth and Jawarski once we got home. I'd told Jawarski about the SUV, but the driver hadn't actually done anything or made any overt threats, so there wasn't much the police could do. I had to be satisfied with Jawarski's promise to act immediately if the driver ever crossed the line. We'd talked briefly about the murder investigation, but there wasn't much Jawarski could tell me. The police still hadn't identified the victim, and they were up to their eyeballs in interviews with people who'd been near the drug store the night of the murder—none of whom seemed to know anything helpful.

I'd been honest with Jawarski, but I'd played down last night's danger when I talked to Elizabeth. I'd have to tell her the truth this morning, but I'd seen no reason to upset her in the middle of the night with a snowstorm raging. I knew Elizabeth. She'd have risked her life to drive into town after the kids.

I made chocolate chip pancakes for breakfast, then loaded the boys into the car. This time, I let Max come along. In fact, it would probably be a long time before I'd go anywhere without him again.

After dropping the boys at school, I drove to my brother's house to have the conversation I'd been dreading all night. Elizabeth saw me pull into the yard and stepped onto the porch while I gathered the boys' uniforms and equipment from the backseat.

It was barely eight thirty, but I could tell that she'd been hard at work already. She'd pulled her hair into a ponytail, which she never did unless she was baking, and she wore a flour-dusted apron that told the rest of the tale. "You didn't have to drive all the way out here to bring that stuff," she called. "We could have picked it up."

"No problem." I slid on an icy patch of snow and almost lost my footing. "I need to talk to you about last night."

Elizabeth took Caleb's bag as I climbed the steps to the porch and ushered me into her big, warm kitchen. It smelled of coffee and yeast, which probably meant that she was making bread.

Motioning me toward the table, she cleared a spot for me

to sit. "Actually, I'm glad you came," she said. "I'm still not clear about what happened."

"That's probably because I wasn't very clear." I left my seat and poured a cup of coffee, then carried it back to the table. "It was a bit more involved than I told you on the phone."

"Oh?"

"Yeah. Somebody followed us, Liz. We came out of practice—later than the rest of the team because I had to put away equipment—and the SUV I told you about seeing the other night was in the parking lot."

Elizabeth took a slab of bread dough from a bowl, dusted the table with flour, and began kneading. "Are you sure it was the same SUV?"

"I'm positive. Caleb recognized the broken light on the side. Anyway, I was a little nervous, so I got the boys into the car and took off out the front entrance of the parking lot. The next thing we knew, the SUV was coming after us."

Elizabeth's hands stilled in the ball of dough. "Why didn't you call?"

"I tried calling Jawarski, but I didn't have any service because of the storm."

Apparently forgetting about the bread, she sat across from me. "Why would they follow you? My kids were in the car."

"Believe me, I know." Briefly, I told her the rest and watched confusion and fear battle it out in her eyes. "I don't know what they wanted, Liz. The boys are fine, but I wanted you to know."

She nodded slowly. Just as slowly, the fear and confusion were replaced by anger. "Why would they follow you?" she asked again. "Have you been 'investigating' again?"

Her venom surprised me. "No. Not this time."

"Then why? Why you? Why my boys?"

"I don't know."

"Oh come on, Abby. They didn't just pick you out of the air." She gestured wildly, almost knocking the bowl off the table. "There must be *some* reason they targeted you."

I gaped at her. "You think I'm lying?"

She stared at me for a long moment, then shook her head.

"I don't know. No. Yes." She stood and turned away, rubbing her forehead with one hand. "I mean, look at what's happened in the past. Can you blame me? What would you think in my place?"

"I'd like to think that I'd believe you. I didn't have to tell you what happened, you know. I could have kept quiet."

Elizabeth came back to the table and directed her frustrations into the bread. "Okay. I believe you. You wouldn't lie to me. I know you wouldn't."

"Thank you."

"But that still doesn't explain why somebody followed you."

"I can only guess, but maybe it's because we saw the SUV near Coach Hendrix's truck. Maybe the driver recognized us from the other night."

Her eyes shot to mine. "You think Coach Hendrix is mixed up in all of this?"

"I don't know. He could be, or he could be in some kind of danger."

"And he's coaching my kids? Putting every single one of the boys on the team in danger?" She dropped the dough on the table and reached for the cordless phone on the counter behind her.

I caught her arm and pried the phone from her fingers. "Don't do anything hasty," I said. "We don't have any way of knowing what's going on. There might not be any connection between them at all, and even if there is, Kerry may not know about it. I doubt he'd purposely put the kids at risk."

Elizabeth hesitated, so I pressed my advantage. "Let's not jump to conclusions," I said, "or we could make things worse. Let me talk to Jawarski and see what he says. You know he won't suggest anything that will put the boys in harm's way."

"And in the meantime, I just let the boys go to practice and games as if nothing's happening?"

"Unless Jawarski thinks there's a reason not to. But just in case someone *is* watching me, I think either you or Wyatt should take the boys to their practices—just until we find out what's going on." It just about killed me to make that suggestion. I loved the time I spent with the boys, but it was the right thing to do. "If it makes you feel better, stay for the practices. Kerry doesn't like parents to hang around, but he can't kick you out."

Elizabeth gave the dough a final punch and put it in a loaf pan. "I'll think about it, but I can't make any promises until I've talked to Wyatt."

"Understood." I checked the time, realized I had less than an hour until Divinity opened, and stood. "Are we okay?"

Elizabeth nodded. "Of course. I'm sorry I went off on you that way, but you have to understand where I'm coming from."

"It's no problem," I assured her. "I'd feel the same way if I were you." We hugged briefly, and I followed my footsteps through the snow back to the Jetta. I was exhausted already, and the day hadn't even started.

Chapter 17

I was almost back to Divinity when I spotted Coach Hendrix's truck idling outside the Stop-N-Go, a large cloud of smoke pouring from its exhaust into the chilly morning air. In spite of my caution around Elizabeth, I thought it was time somebody asked the man a few questions.

Without giving myself time to think twice, I jerked the wheel and pulled into the parking lot. I parked next to his truck and got out of the car to wait. He came out a few minutes later carrying a large coffee and an apple fritter.

His step faltered when he saw me. The hesitation was so slight I would have missed it if I hadn't been watching for it, but nobody could have missed the sour expression on his face. "What the hell do you want, Shaw?"

I wondered if he was this obnoxious with everyone, or if I was just special. "I need to ask you a couple of questions," I told him.

"Yeah? Well it's going to have to wait. I'm late for work."

His dismissal infuriated me even more. I took two steps and planted myself in front of the truck door. He could move me if he wanted to, but he'd have to manhandle me to do it. "This is important, Kerry. It'll only take a minute."

He looked as if he might explode, but it only took him a few seconds to reach the same conclusion I had and to realize that, at least for now, I had the upper hand. He'd never dare get physical in front of witnesses.

"All right," he said, spreading his hands in a gesture of surrender. "What's on your mind?"

It occurred to me that I ought to be nervous, but I must

have been too angry. My nephews had been terrified last night. *I'd* been terrified. And here he stood, cool as a cucumber and not even slightly concerned. "There was a dark-colored SUV near your truck outside the recreation center last night. The driver of that SUV followed me when I left," I told him, hoping he'd show some sign of decency. "Brody and Caleb were with me."

"Followed you?" Hendrix laughed through his nose. "Why would anybody want to do that?"

"That's what I'm asking you."

"How would *I* know?"

"Because you were talking to the driver just before he came after me."

He laughed again and shook his head in disbelief. "You're some piece of work, Shaw. I'm telling you, I don't know what you're talking about. Now get out of my way."

"Who was the guy with the limp?"

"What guy?"

His calm infuriated me. "The one who vandalized your truck. The one we saw get into an SUV just before you came outside. And the same one who was murdered just a few days later."

"You're the only one I saw anywhere near my truck that night."

"I didn't touch your truck, and you know it." A man walking across the parking lot turned at the sound of my voice, and I realized that I was almost shouting. I lowered my voice before I spoke again. "I don't know what's going on with you, but if you're involved in something dangerous, you'd better not bring it anywhere near the boys on the team."

Hendrix laughed under his breath. "What's this? A threat?"

"Consider it a friendly warning," I snarled. "Do whatever you want on your own time, but keep it away from those kids."

Without waiting for a response, I got back into the Jetta and drove off. It wasn't until I'd put a couple of blocks behind me that I realized I was shaking like a leaf.

I couldn't help but wonder if Hendrix had sent the driver after us to frighten me. I was almost convinced he had, and the possibility made my blood boil. But as Jawarski had pointed out, I couldn't prove a damn thing. All I had were my suspicions.

Still shaking, I pulled into the parking lot next to Divinity a few minutes after ten. I could have crawled into bed right then and there and slept the whole day away, but I had too much to do. Thanksgiving was less than two weeks away, and I needed to make several batches of Aunt Grace's gourmet lollipops. They weren't difficult to make, but I still occasionally had trouble getting the air bubbles out of my poured sugar confections, so they took concentration—a quality in short supply lately.

Most of the fear I'd felt last night had dissipated with the rising sun, but a tight knot remained lodged just beneath my heart. I'd have been happy to keep Max by my side all day, but the health department frowned on dog hair in the kitchen, and there was still too much snow on the back porch to chain him up back there. I left him upstairs in the apartment with strict instructions not to chew anything and made myself go to work. If the temperature warmed up as the day wore on, I could always bring him down later.

I put on coffee, then checked the mosaic for the display window to make sure the edible glue was dry. It had been an ambitious project, and I felt ridiculously pleased with the results. Deciding that I'd ask Karen to help me set it up in the window when she got to work, I moved on to the next task: gourmet lollipops for the upcoming holiday.

After making sure I had the recipe I wanted, I started gathering the ingredients I'd need that morning. I pulled a bag of candy corn from the cupboard and checked a piece with my thumbnail to make sure it was fresh. In spite of the fact that the company that makes it sells 35 million pounds of candy corn a year, I've always considered it an unappreciated and overlooked candy. I'm not sure why, either.

Candy corn, has a long, proud history more than a hundred years old, and I think anything that has stood the test of time for that long should be given its due. I'm sure George Renninger, the inventor of candy corn back in the 1880s, would agree with me. It seems commonplace to us now, but George's tricolor design was actually considered revolutionary when the candy first hit the market, and the public went nuts for it.

After determining that the candy was fresh, I opened a new supply of lollipop sticks, found sugar, corn syrup, and the flavor oils I wanted. It took me a few minutes to find the plastic bags I'd need to wrap the pops in the supply cupboard, and I made a mental note to reorganize the supplies when I had a free hour or two.

Karen and Liberty came in as I was pulling the molds I wanted from a bottom cupboard. They were both flushed with the cold and laughing about something. Something vaguely uncomfortable darted through me, followed immediately by the thought that I might be jealous of Karen's easy friendship with Liberty. But that was ridiculous. Why would I begrudge Karen a friend? It's not as if she and I hung out together away from the shop, and I certainly didn't want to get buddy-buddy with Liberty.

Whether or not it made sense, I realized that in the last few days I'd started feeling like a third wheel in my own shop. Maybe I should make more of an effort with Liberty. And maybe trying to worm my way into their friendship would make me feel worse.

They chattered between themselves while Karen stomped snow from her boots and peeled the scarf from around her neck and Liberty rubbed her arms for warmth. After a while, Liberty seemed to realize I was in the room. "Good morning," she said as she headed for the coffee. "Want me to pour you a cup?"

I shook my head and lifted the mug already in front of me. "I'm fine. You two both seem to be in good moods. Any special reason?"

"Are you kidding?" Liberty gaped at me as if I'd asked something unspeakably stupid. "Have you been outside this morning?"

"I was out earlier," I said. "Caleb and Brody spent the night with me, so I drove them to school."

Liberty filled two more mugs and handed one to Karen. "How was practice?"

I hesitated for a moment over my answer. Her question was innocent enough, but the answer was complicated. I still felt reluctant to confide in someone I barely knew, especially someone who'd already admitted she knew Kerry Hendrix. But I had no reason to believe they were friends, and she was doing well at her job. Karen liked her, so it looked as if she might be around for a while. Uncomfortable as I was discussing all the strange goings-on with a stranger, I was even more uncomfortable with the idea of censoring every conversation.

"Practice was fine," I said. "Kerry and I avoided each other like the plague."

Karen laughed. "Well, that's probably for the best. At least the team didn't have to deal with all the tension between the two of you."

"Yeah." I picked up the molds I'd selected and started lining them on the counter so I could fill them later. "It's what happened after practice that put a damper on the evening."

Liberty's gaze jumped to my face over the rim of her mug. "Why? What happened?"

I told them briefly about the night before. Karen's expression grew more worried as I spoke. Liberty's grew more animated.

"Are you sure it was the same vehicle?" Karen asked when I'd finished talking.

"I wasn't," I admitted, "but Caleb was absolutely certain of it. He pointed out a broken light and swears the SUV that picked up our John Doe the other night had the same light missing."

"No kidding?" Liberty carried her mug to the table and settled in. "Maybe they weren't actually following you. Maybe they were just on the way home and happened to be going the same way."

I shook my head. "Not the route I took. I'm convinced the driver was following us. I just don't know why."

"Maybe you should ask Kerry," she said. "If he was talking to the driver, he probably knows him."

"He claims he doesn't know what I'm talking about, but I know that's not true. I *saw* him sitting in his truck."

Liberty shrugged. "Well, he's always been kind of a jerk. I have to admit that."

I turned back to look at her. "I thought you said you didn't know him."

"I didn't, but I knew who he was. Everybody did." She sipped her coffee cautiously to test the temperature. "The girls were crazy about him, and the guys all looked up to him. You know the type."

Yeah, I did. I didn't like the guy, that was for sure. But being a jerk didn't automatically mean that he was involved in anything illegal. He'd been the victim of vandalism, I reminded myself, and that was his only connection to the dead man. Even a horse's ass like Kerry wouldn't murder somebody for scratching his truck. At least, I hoped not.

Chapter 18

I was about to turn back to the candy when I saw Marshall Ames coming into the store. He held a cardboard drink tray with two cups of coffee in one hand, a white pastry bag in the other, and he was grinning like a kid who'd just brought home a treasure. He spotted me at once, and his grin broadened. "I was in the neighborhood and thought I'd stop by. Do you have time for a quick break?"

Questions about Kerry and the SUV were swirling through my head, but Liberty and Karen had gone back to work, and curiosity about the reasons for Marshall's visit got the best of me. "Sure," I told him. "Come on back."

Marshall followed me into the small room that we used for an office and waited while I swept a stack of filing from the heavy wooden chair I keep in there for the occasional visitor. Most of the time it also does duty as a filing cabinet.

As soon as we were settled in our seats, Marshall laid out his miniature picnic and gestured grandly. "*Et voilà, madame*. I hope you like the huckleberry muffins from Parsons Bakery. I would have brought dessert from Gigi, but stopping by was a spur-of-the-moment decision."

I smiled, slightly uneasy now that I was alone with him. I've known Marshall since we were kids, but we'd never really been friends. I was too much of a tomboy, and he was too much of a nerd for us to find common ground back in school. We'd met up again about a year ago, and I'd been surprised by the changes in him. He didn't seem like such a nerd now, and that's what bothered me. When I looked at him, I didn't see nerdy little Marshall. I saw Marshall with the broad shoulders and narrow waist. Marshall who'd turned out kind of hot.

"So what's all this?" I asked.

He shrugged and nudged his glasses up on his nose. "I just wanted to make sure you were doing okay after the other night. Finding a dead man isn't an everyday occurrence."

"I've been fine," I assured him. "Unfortunately, this isn't the first dead body I've seen."

"That's true. It's not." Marshall reached for a muffin and gave me an odd look. "I'd almost forgotten that you're almost an old hand at this. Maybe you should have brought *me* muffins."

I laughed and felt myself relax. "I'm sorry I didn't think of it. I guess I've had too many things on my mind."

"You sound busy." Marshall peeled back the wrapper and took a large, appreciative bite. "Anything you need to talk about? I'm a good listener."

I started to respond with a simple "No," but I thought of all the times Karen had lectured me about opening up to people and decided to fight my instincts. "It's nothing major," I said, "just a lot of little things all at once. There's the murder, of course, and we're training a new clerk."

"I noticed. She looks familiar. Is she from around here?"

"She used to be. Her name's Liberty Parker, and she just moved back a few weeks ago."

He tilted his head to one side, then shook it slowly. "I'm sure I've seen her before, but the name doesn't ring a bell. Is she working out okay?"

"I think she'll be fine. It just takes time."

Marshall nodded understanding. He knew about the trials of dealing with employees and planning work shifts and paying taxes, and it felt good to talk with someone who understood how trying each of those things could be. "How long has she been working here?"

"Just a couple of days," I said, pulling back the wrapper from my muffin and breaking the muffin in half.

"She'll probably be reliable enough," Marshall said. "Once you get her trained, you'll be glad you have her."

"I'm sure I will. I'm just edgy, I think. Things have been kind of weird around here for the past week."

"Why? What's been going on?"

I realized that I'd never told him about the incident at Hammond Junction, so I filled him in quickly and said, "It's been driving me crazy, trying to figure out what really happened that night. And nobody wants to admit they knew the dead man, but I'm *sure* he had business with someone here in Paradise." I broke off with a rueful grin. "I'm positive someone tried to kill him that night. I just can't figure out how they missed and why they let him get away."

Marshall had listened to my story with an ever-deepening scowl. "You're sure that what you heard were gunshots?"

I nodded. "I'm positive. I watched him crumple to the ground like a sack of potatoes. I could have *sworn* he'd been shot but, like I said, there was no sign of him or of any blood when we got back there."

"And all this happened when?"

"Last Tuesday. The sixth."

"So that means that he was in town then."

"Yeah. I think he's been in town for a while. Have you heard anything?"

"Me?" Marshall seemed surprised by the question, but the surprise didn't seem entirely genuine. He laughed and shook his head. "Sorry. Nobody tells me anything, and I'm okay with that. The less involved I am in the guy's murder, the happier I'll be."

I probably should have felt the same way, but I didn't. "I saw him one other time before the murder," I told Marshall. "Outside the recreation center after practice."

Marshall cocked an eyebrow. "Practice?"

"I've been roped into being the assistant coach for the Miners, one of the Youth League teams. I don't know how long that will last, though. Coach Hendrix hasn't exactly become a fan of mine."

"You're working with Kerry?"

Kerry? I eyed Marshall warily. "You know him?"

"He's been in the restaurant a few times," Marshall said. "He's got quite a temper."

"Terrific," I said with a grimace. "That's good to know, since he's not exactly thrilled to have me hanging around. I saw the dead guy messing around with Hendrix's truck one night and tried to stop him, but Hendrix is convinced *I'm* the vandal."

Marshall looked outraged. "He *said* that?"

"He not only said it, he filed a complaint with the police."

"I knew I didn't like that guy." Marshall frowned so hard his forehead rutted. "What was the dead guy doing with the jerk's truck?"

"I don't know, but I'm convinced there's some kind of connection between the two of them. There's also a third person involved—someone who drives an SUV."

Marshall laughed without humor. He tossed his muffin wrapper into the trash and leaned forward, resting his arms on his thighs. "That could be almost anybody in this town."

"Yeah, but this is a dark-colored SUV with a broken running light on the side. I've seen that SUV twice now: once when the vandal got into it after messing with Hendrix's truck, and again Monday night."

Marshall sat up slowly, his eyes locked on mine. "You probably don't want my advice, but if I were you, I'd steer clear of this whole thing. It sounds dangerous. Hell, it *is* dangerous. One person is already dead."

"Yeah, but why? What do all of these people have in common? That's what's driving me crazy."

"Who knows? But really, Abby, think about what you're doing. You're messing around with murder. Just because you've done it before and come out okay, that's no guarantee you'll be safe this time."

Marshall's vehemence surprised me. "I'm not *that* far involved," I assured him. "I'm just trying to find the answers to a couple of questions, and when I do, I'll go straight to the police. Besides, if Coach Hendrix is involved or being targeted, I can't just turn my back and let him be alone with all those boys, can I? Don't I have a duty to make sure they're safe?"

Marshall noticed a trail of crumbs on my desk and swept them into his hand. He stood and brushed the crumbs into the trash can, then came around the desk to stand over me. "Let the police save the world, Abby. It's their job, not yours." And before I knew what he intended, he leaned in close and touched his lips to mine. The kiss didn't last long, but it left me speechless and totally unable to form a coherent thought long after he walked away.

I was still trying to process what had happened when a soft knock on the office door brought me back to the present. Karen stood in the open doorway, a deep scowl on her face as she watched me. She'd clearly witnessed Marshall's kiss. "What was all that about?"

"All what?"

"You and Marshall."

Still confused, I could only shake my head. "I have no idea. He came by to make sure I was okay after finding the body the other night—at least that's what he said."

Karen came into the office and sat in the chair Marshall had vacated. "Well, it's pretty obvious that's not all he wanted."

"Maybe." I gave up a thin smile and tossed the uneaten half of my muffin into the trash. "He's a nice enough guy, but that wasn't what I was expecting."

"Judging by the look on his face, you'd better expect it next time you see him. He's got the hots for you. So, are you going to tell Jawarski?"

"About that?" I laughed lightly. "Why? Nothing happened."

"Marshall kissed you," Karen reminded me, which wasn't exactly necessary. "I don't think Jawarski will consider that 'nothing.' "

"Jawarski doesn't own me," I said sharper than I'd intended. "We're not an item, and we're not exclusive—unless he's made some decisions without consulting me. We're friends who occasionally go out."

"Yeah," Karen said, giving me a *look*. "But only because you don't want to take things further. Jawarski's crazy about you. You're the only person in town who doesn't know it."

Uncomfortable with the conversation, I stood. "You don't know that. He's no more ready to make things official between us than I am." I wasn't in the mood to dissect my personal life right then, so I walked into the kitchen.

Karen followed and planted herself in front of me. *The look* had intensified in the time I'd had my back to her. "Don't try to avoid the subject, Abby. If Jawarski finds out about you and Marshall from someone else, you could lose the best thing that's ever happened to you."

"Who else is he going to find out from? The only people who know about it are you, me, and Marshall. I'm certainly not going to tell anybody, and you'd better not tell anybody . . ."

"Which leaves Marshall. I saw the look on his face. If something happened to break you and Jawarski up, he would *not* be unhappy."

I laughed and pulled a couple of Cokes from the old refrigerator we keep around for personal use. "You make it sound like we're living in a soap opera or something," I said, handing a can to Karen. "It was a simple kiss on the spur of the moment. It didn't *mean* anything, and it's certainly not something I'm going to tie myself in knots over."

Karen rolled her eyes as if she had never met anyone so naive, but she didn't argue. One of the things I like best about her is that she knows when to back off. "Fine. Have it your way. But if you screw up your relationship with Jawarski, just remember I warned you."

As if I could forget.

Chapter 19

I worked the rest of the morning situating candy corn and lollipop sticks in the molds, then pouring the hot syrup and slowly, carefully, tapping the bubbles out of the candy.

I *was* right, and Karen *was* wrong. But no matter how many times I told myself that I had nothing to worry about with Jawarski, Karen's warning needled at me all day. Which was ridiculous because I wasn't even interested in Marshall. *I* hadn't initiated that kiss. I had nothing to worry about.

When I finally had three dozen lollipops cooling, I spent an hour filling orders we'd received over the phone. By the time I had the orders ready to ship, the sun had melted most of the snow that had fallen overnight, so I packed the boxes into a canvas bag, climbed the stairs to let Max out of exile, and walked with him through town to the post office.

My route took me past Walgreens which, of course, started me thinking about the dead man again and the lack of information about his identity. Somebody had to know who he was. Somebody had to know who owned that SUV and why it had followed me last night. And I'd have bet everything I owned that someone living in Paradise had the answers I wanted. But where to begin? That was the million-dollar question.

Thankfully, the lines at the post office were blessedly short, so I was in and out in record time. Knowing that Karen had Liberty to help her at the store gave me a new feeling of freedom I hadn't had since I took over the store. I decided to take a leisurely stroll back to work. Maybe even do a little window shopping.

I saw Vonetta Cummings driving past in her Buick and waved hello, then turned my face to the weak sun high overhead. Max sniffed at everything we passed with enthusiasm, lunging after a piece of wood one minute, stopping to check out something only he could smell the next. At the rate we were walking, it took a few minutes to reach the Curl Up and Dye, and I calculated that it would take a good fifteen minutes to get back to Divinity, but I didn't push Max to go any faster. After last night and the morning I'd had, it felt good to clear my head.

I waved to Gavin Trotter, who stood in the window of Alpine Sports, and thought about crossing the street to say hello. But when I realized that Annalisa Kelso's teal Jeep Cherokee was in the Curl's parking lot, I changed my mind.

According to Paisley, her mother had seen the man with the limp on more than one occasion. Maybe Annalisa would know something that could help the police identify him. I found a warm, dry spot for Max and pushed open the door. Immediately, a wash of chemical scents rushed over me, and I wondered how Paisley and Annalisa could breathe that air all day long. The scents are just as overpowering inside Divinity, but chemicals can't compete with chocolate, butter, and sugar.

Inside the Curl, it's easy to forget that Paradise has become a cross between old and new. The walls are a pale, buttery yellow, the hair dryers a ghastly shade of pink, and white eyelet curtains hang at the windows. It's pure Mayberry.

Annalisa Kelso stood over a customer at the shampoo station near the back of the salon. Closer to the front, Paisley frowned in concentration as she worked a hair dryer over a customer's new hairdo. Paisley didn't seem to notice me, but Annalisa, a sturdy woman with dark hair and a warm smile, looked up as I entered.

"I'll be right with you, Abby. Have a seat while I finish up here."

I settled in with a magazine on the rock that masquerades as a sofa and waited while Annalisa rinsed and repeated. Finally, she wrapped a towel around her customer's head and steered her toward a haircutting station.

"Sorry about that wait," she called out, tottering on swollen feet toward the register. "What can I do for you? Haircut? Maybe a shampoo, cut, and style? We're running a special."

I did my best not to look horrified by the suggestion. "No thanks. Actually, I just came by to ask you a couple of questions. Is there any chance you could take a quick break?"

Annalisa looked over her shoulder at the woman with the dripping hair. *"Now?"*

"I know you're busy, but it will only take a minute."

"That may be so," Annalisa said with a tight smile, "but it's really not a good time—unless you want to talk while I cut Joyce's hair."

I'd have preferred to talk with her alone, but I'd take what I could get. "That's fine if you and Joyce don't mind."

"Not a bit. We can kill two birds with one stone. Come on back."

I followed her and sat in the empty chair beside her workstation.

"Now," she said as she picked up a comb, "what do you want to know?"

"I ran into Paisley the other night, and she mentioned that you might have seen a man with a limp hanging around this area in the past few days. Is that true?"

Her customer turned her head so she could look at me. "Are you talking about the guy who was killed over by Walgreens?"

Annalisa put her fingers on the woman's chin and turned her back so she was facing the mirror. "I need you to hold still, Joyce, or you're going to be very unhappy with your hair when you leave here."

Joyce giggled and muttered a soft, "Sorry."

Annalisa dug around in a drawer and pulled out a handful of pastel hair clips. "Yes, I did see the man you're talking about. He was out here in our parking lot a couple of times and standing around on the corner once or twice. Why?"

"The police haven't been able to make a positive ID," I said. "I'm trying to help them figure out where to look next."

Which was true. In a roundabout way. Anything I learned, I'd eventually share with Jawarski.

Paisley glanced over her shoulder and said, "I heard he had a thousand dollars in his pocket when they found him. Is that true?"

I shook my head. "I don't know. If he did, I haven't been told about it."

"I have no idea who that poor man was," Annalisa said, continuing our conversation as if Paisley hadn't spoken. "But I know who might be able to tell you. I saw the man get into a car one day."

"Is it true that he was a drug dealer?" Joyce asked, turning her head again and causing Annalisa to lose her grip on another strand of hair. "I heard that he was."

Rumors and gossip always spread fast in a town like Paradise, and obviously this time was no exception to that rule. I was itching to hear what Annalisa had to say, but I felt an obligation to nip rumors in the bud. "Where did you hear that?"

"I don't remember," Joyce admitted. "I think somebody at the school told me. Or maybe it was the clerk at King Soopers."

"I wouldn't believe anything you hear unless it comes in a statement from the police. Now, Annalisa, the car he got into . . . was it a dark-colored SUV?"

"An SUV?" Annalisa shook her head firmly. "No. I saw him getting into a light-colored sedan. I don't know anything about an SUV."

"How did he die?" Joyce asked. "Is it true that he was stabbed to death?" She met Annalisa's eyes in the mirror and confided, "Thomas says that he was stabbed, but you know how *he* is." She smiled at me and dropped her voice to a confidential whisper. "My husband's a bit of a know-it-all."

I knew the answer, but I hadn't seen an official statement about cause of death from the police, so I shook my head. "I'm afraid I can't say for sure," I told her, and turned to Annalisa once more. "Are you sure it was a sedan?"

"Of course I'm sure," Annalisa said with a laugh. "I know the difference between a sedan and an SUV."

I sat back in the chair and tried to take in what she'd just told me. I'd been so focused on the SUV and Coach Hendrix, it had never occurred to me that John Doe might have had contact with other people in Paradise. "Do you have any idea whose car it was?"

Joyce sat up straight in her chair. "Ooh, do you, Annalisa?"

Pleased by the attention, Annalisa pinned up another section of hair and shrugged casually. "Sure. I saw the man driving it clear enough." She gestured toward the street and said, "They met right out here on the corner."

That made me sit up a little straighter, too. "Who was it?"

Annalisa looked at me over her shoulder. "It was Quentin Ingersol."

"Quentin Ingersol?" I said, making no effort to hide my surprise. "Are you talking about the real estate agent? The one whose picture is on the billboards and benches all over town?"

Paisley led her customer to the register and punched a couple of buttons. "One and the same."

"What was the dead guy doing with him?"

"I'm sure I don't know," Annalisa chided gently. "I only saw the dead man getting into Quentin's car. I didn't hear what they said."

"Of course not." I smiled an apology. "I'm just a little surprised, that's all."

Annalisa picked up a pair of shears and steadied Joyce's head again. "If some new guy came to town and wanted to buy property, this Quentin guy is probably the first one he'd go see. He's got his name everywhere."

The man I'd seen out at Hammond Junction hadn't looked like your typical property owner, but what did I know? So Kerry Hendrix wasn't the only person in town with a connection to John Doe. It would be interesting to find out just what Quentin Ingersol knew about the dead man.

Chapter 20

I would have liked to track Quentin Ingersol down right then and there, but a quick check of my watch told me that I'd already been away from Divinity for nearly an hour. Max and I hurried back, but I had trouble concentrating for the rest of the day.

Between customers, I spent the afternoon making more centerpieces for Richie and Dylan's dinner party and listening to Karen training Liberty. I had to admit that Liberty seemed bright and eager. She picked up everything Karen threw at her easily, and the questions she asked convinced me that she had processed the information.

The never-ending stream of chatter about everything from Rutger's favorite restaurant to Rutger's favorite television show to Rutger's lucky socks grated on my nerves after a while, but Karen didn't seem to mind, so I did my best to tune it out.

At seven, I tucked the bank bag under my arm and crossed the street to make the day's deposit, leaving Karen and Liberty to lock up behind me. The bank had long since closed its doors, but its after-hours window was still open when I got there, and two other people were already in line. I moved behind them and settled in to wait.

At the head of the line, a bulky man wearing a too-tight T-shirt and jeans that sagged from his hips argued mildly with a young teller named Chloe about a problem cashing the check he'd given her. I didn't intend to eavesdrop, but we were stuck in a ten-by-ten foyer together. There really wasn't any way to avoid listening.

"I'm sorry," Chloe said for the third time since I came through the door, "there's nothing I can do."

"Sure there is," the man argued. "Cash the check. I guarantee it's good."

Chloe shook her head firmly. "I can't cash a check of this size. Not from an out-of-state bank. You can deposit it into your account if you want, but I have to put a five-day hold on it because of the amount. It's the best I can do."

"That's bullshit. I've been a customer of this bank for most of my life. Just cash the damn thing, and let me be on my way." Torn between natural curiosity and a reluctance to gawp at someone else's misfortune, I took another look at the man at the window, and this time I felt a shock of recognition.

Dwayne Escott. He just kept growing more charming every time I saw him.

Chloe's cheeks flushed pink, but she held her ground. "I can't cash the check, sir, I'm sorry."

"Then get your manager."

The woman in front of me shifted uncomfortably at Dwayne's tone, and an uneasy feeling traced my spine. What was it with this guy? When had he become such a jerk?

"You're more than welcome to talk to the bank manager," Chloe said, "but you'll have to come back tomorrow. He's gone home for the day."

"Well isn't *that* terrific. Okay, there must be *someone* around here who knows what they're doing," Dwayne insisted. "Find them. I'll wait."

Irritation began as a low tickle at the base of my stomach and slowly worked outward. I tried to ignore it. I had enough trouble on my plate, I didn't need to ask for more. But I couldn't ignore the look on Chloe's face or the tone of Dwayne's voice as he chewed her out.

"I know what I'm doing," Chloe said, but by this time her face had grown beet red. "I can't cash the check for you, sir. I'm sorry." She lowered her voice, but it still carried through the small bank lobby. "I'm afraid your account is overdrawn and has been for several weeks. This isn't the first time, either. I can't give you cash, but if you'd like to make a deposit—"

"Hell no, I don't want to make a deposit," Dwayne thundered. "How many times do I have to tell you that? I want the damn cash. I *need* the cash."

That niggling feeling of irritation spread through my arms and down my legs. I've always hated bullies, ever since I was a kid—especially when they badgered others over problems they'd created themselves. Back then, I didn't always have the courage to stand up to them, but I wasn't a kid anymore, and my conscience wouldn't let me stand by and let Dwayne badger the poor girl any longer.

Swearing softly under my breath, I reached past the woman in front of me and tapped Dwayne on the shoulder. "She's explained why she can't cash the check," I said. "Why don't you give her a break?"

Dwayne whipped around to face me, and for a minute I thought he might hit me. When he saw who I was, he choked back whatever he'd been about to say and growled instead, "I don't see what business it is of yours."

"You're making it my business," I said, still trying to sound moderately pleasant. "I've been waiting here fifteen minutes while you try to bully that poor woman into breaking the rules of her job. If she can't do it, she can't do it. Just come back tomorrow and talk to someone who can."

Dwayne's eyes narrowed a little further with every word I spoke. I'd been carrying a mental image of him as a geeky kid, but as we stood there staring at each other, it occurred to me how much larger—and no doubt stronger—he was than me.

To my surprise, he snatched the check from the counter and turned away from the teller window. He rammed into the woman behind him with his shoulder, knocking her off balance, but he didn't seem to notice.

He only had eyes for me. "You know what your problem is, Abby?"

I refused to let him intimidate me. "No, and I'm not in the mood for you to enlighten me."

"Your problem is you don't know how to mind your own business. One of these days, you're going to get yourself into big trouble."

In light of the past few days, his threat sent a shiver up my spine. This was the second time Dwayne had said something vaguely threatening, and I wondered if I should be worried. I decided to get angry instead. "Why don't you can the tough-guy attitude, Dwayne? Nobody's impressed. Just go home, get a good night's sleep, and come back in the morning."

He leaned in close and lowered his voice. "Yeah, I'm going. But you might want to be more careful driving around out by Hammond Junction. Next time you're out there in the middle of the night, you might not be so lucky."

Dwayne's warning echoed through my head even after he slammed out of the bank's lobby, and so did about a hundred questions. Had he just been trying to act tough, or had he threatened me? I wondered if his attitude meant that he was connected in some way to the strange things happening around Paradise, or if he just had issues.

He lived near Hammond Junction where the dead man had first vaulted into my life. He could easily have chased the limping man into the junction and then vanished. But was Dwayne capable of murder?

When it was my turn at the teller window, Chloe smiled as if she'd just found her new best friend. "Thanks for the help with that guy," she said. "I just hope he doesn't decide to take it out on you later. He looked pretty upset."

I glanced over my shoulder at the sidewalk and turned back with a shake of my head. "Don't worry about him. He's just a big blowhard. I don't think he'd ever *do* anything."

Chloe unzipped the bag and removed the day's receipts. "I hope you're right," she said as she began to run the numbers on her calculator. "I don't mind admitting I've been nervous ever since they found that dead guy over at Walgreens. I hate working this shift."

"Are you the only one working tonight?"

Chloe shook her head, and her mouth curved in a sly smile. "No, the night manager is in the back. I just didn't want to tell that creep."

I grinned at her, surprised by her spunk. "Well, I wouldn't worry too much about the murder," I said, hoping to reassure her. "I don't think it was a random killing."

Her dark eyes shot up from my deposit. "Really? Do you know something about it?"

"Not as much as I'd like to."

Her smile disappeared. "So you're just saying that to make me feel better?"

"Not at all. I'm pretty sure that whoever killed that guy was somebody he knew."

Chloe let out a squeaky laugh. "Well, that doesn't help much. Not in a place like Paradise, where everybody knows everybody else."

I grinned and shook my head. "You think it's bad now, you should have seen it twenty years ago. Besides, I think the victim was just in town visiting someone."

"Really?" Chloe gave that some thought before going back to the calculator. "You might be right, except when he came in here, it sure seemed like he was planning on staying."

The hair on the back of my neck stood up. "He came in here? The man with the limp?"

Chloe nodded. "Yeah. A couple of times at least. Opened two accounts and everything." She shot a guilty glance at the door behind her and dropped her voice. "I can't believe I said that. I'm not supposed to talk about our customers' business, so pretend you didn't hear me, okay?"

I nodded, ready to promise anything. "Sure. But does that mean you know his name?"

She nodded again, but she didn't look at me, and her fingers moved faster on the keys. "I do, but I can't tell you what it is. I've already said too much."

I couldn't very well yell at Dwayne for badgering her and then do the same thing myself, so I swallowed all the arguments that occurred to me. "You can tell the police, can't you?"

"Probably, but I think they already know." She finished calculating and tapped the checks into a neat pile. "They were in here talking to Frank Ogden for a couple of hours this afternoon."

The police had talked with the bank president? I wondered what they'd found out and whether Jawarski would tell me. It wasn't just idle curiosity that made me wonder. After everything these creeps had put me through in the past week, I thought I deserved a few answers.

Chloe returned my empty bag and receipt in the tray. "I wish I could be of more help," she said with an apologetic smile, "but I can't afford to lose this job."

"That's okay," I assured her. "I understand. Just one more thing. Did the guy ever come in here with someone else?"

"You mean a friend?"

"A friend, a business associate." *A realtor.*

Chloe shook her head slowly. "I don't think so. Mostly he just came in for a few minutes at a time, to make deposits into his account."

Interesting. "Do you know where the money came from? Do you remember the names on any of the checks?"

"Oh, he didn't deposit checks," Chloe said. "He always brought in cash."

"Nothing but cash?"

"Not that I ever saw. Of course, I didn't help him *every* time, so I can't say he never, ever brought in a check. But *I* never saw one." She tilted her head to one side, and a frantic look flashed across her face. "I can't talk about this anymore. My manager is going to hear me, and I'll lose my job."

I was eager to hear more, but I didn't want to be responsible for her being fired. Reluctantly, I picked up my bag and receipt and turned away.

Chapter 21

Outside the bank I stood for a minute in the gathering dusk, watching streetlights blink on and the tiny white lights in the trees along Prospector Street turn the old mining community into a fairyland—as long as I didn't look too closely. There were a handful of reasons why I should have just walked across the street and gone home, but Chloe had touched a match to my already smoldering curiosity. I was dying to know what Quentin Ingersol would have to say about his association with the dead man, and I was almost positive that I'd never find out unless I asked for myself.

I checked my watch and realized with disappointment that the real estate office would be closed by now. I had no idea if Quentin would even agree to talk to me, but I probably stood a better chance of getting to him if I showed up during regular business hours.

Forcing myself to do the right thing, I spent the rest of the evening balancing Divinity's checkbook while Max chewed on a hunk of rawhide bone. I climbed into bed before the nightly news was even over, but I kept reliving my conversation with Elizabeth, remembering John Doe's eyes as he looked at me through the windshield, and wondering who had been out at Hammond Junction with him that night. Dwayne seemed easily capable of murder, but his only link was proximity to the Junction. Kerry seemed connected, but I had no clue what his motive would be. And Quentin Ingersol . . . I tried telling myself that John Doe was probably just a client, but if that was the case, why hadn't he come forward to identify him?

I have no idea what time I finally fell asleep, but I woke

the next morning to clear blue skies, springlike weather, and a town full of long faces brought on by the realization that the ski resorts probably wouldn't open for Thanksgiving.

The morning flew by in a flurry of phone calls and paperwork. I even finished the centerpieces for Richie and Dylan. At a few minutes after eleven, I left Divinity for lunch and set off down the stairs that would take me down the hill to Ski Jump Way. Five minutes later, I opened the door to the small first-floor office of Big Horn Real Estate.

A young woman who looked familiar sat behind the reception desk just inside the building. Her dark hair and wide, almond-shaped eyes blended with her deep olive complexion to hint at an exotic ancestry. The nameplate on her desk said Elena Whitehorse, but that didn't help me place her.

She smiled as I came inside. "Good afternoon. Can I help you?"

"I hope so. I'm looking for Quentin Ingersol. Is he in?"

She nodded and lifted the receiver from her phone, then waited with one finger poised over the keypad. "Who should I tell him is here?"

I couldn't believe my luck. Maybe things were finally looking up. "My name is Abby Shaw."

"Are you a client?"

"No, but this won't take long. I just need to ask him a couple of questions."

She punched in a series of numbers. "I'll see if he has time to see you. Why don't you have a seat over there?" She nodded me toward a row of chairs near the window. She spoke for a few minutes in hushed tones, then replaced the receiver and smiled as if we were friends again. "Quentin can give you five minutes," she said. "His office is down this hall, the last door on your right."

I thanked her and wandered down the hall until I found Quentin's office, where he was waiting for me. I guessed his age at late twenties to early thirties, a husky guy with blond hair and a tuft of hair just below his bottom lip. He wore jeans and a striped blue shirt under a sports jacket, and he strode toward me wearing a broad smile and holding out a hand for me to shake. "Ms. Shaw, what can I do for you?"

I shook his hand and followed him into the sunny office, the walls of which were covered with framed certificates and licenses. Just in case I had any doubts about his qualifications, I guess. I settled into a nicely stuffed chair across the desk from him and waited until he sat to tell him why I was there. I figured it would be harder for him to throw me out if I'd already laid claim to something solid. "I know this sounds odd, Mr. Ingersoll—"

"Call me Quentin. Please. 'Mr. Ingersoll' makes me feel like an old man."

I smiled and started over again. "I know this sounds odd, but I'm wondering if you can give me some information about a man I believe was a client of yours."

Quentin looked surprised by the question, but he leaned back in his seat and rocked slightly. "That is an odd request. What do you want to know?"

"I'd like to find out who he is, and if you know why he was here in Paradise."

"Was?"

"He's the man who was murdered outside the drugstore the other night. Someone told me that they saw you picking him up a couple of times."

His eyes shuttered, and the expression on his face gave nothing away. "Whoever told you that must have been mistaken. I never met the guy."

"How can you be so sure? Did you see the dead man?"

"Of course not. The police came by the businesses on the block with a photograph. I couldn't help them, and I can't help you. Even if I had known him, I wouldn't be able to tell you anything about him. We take our clients' privacy very seriously."

Between the blank-eyed stare and the stony expression, I had a hard time believing that he was being truthful with me. "And I'm sure your clients appreciate it. But these are kind of unusual circumstances, so I'm hoping you'll make an exception."

"And what's so unusual—besides the fact that someone killed the poor guy?"

"I nearly ran into him out at Hammond Junction one night.

I thought he'd been killed that night. Obviously he wasn't, but I guess that near accident made me feel responsible for him somehow. I'm curious to know who he was."

The edges of Quentin's lips curved slightly. "That's understandable, I'm sure. But as I said, I didn't know the guy."

"Are you sure? I've talked to a couple of people who are sure he got into your car on more than one occasion. If he wasn't a client, maybe he was a friend."

Slowly, Quentin folded his hands in the center of the desktop. "I don't know where you heard that rumor, but I can assure you it's not true. I've never met the man who was murdered the other night."

What was with these people? First Kerry Hendrix, now Quentin Ingersol, both denying things I *knew* must be true. "If you did, it's only a matter of time until the police figure it out."

Quentin's lips tightened into a thin line. He tugged on his cuffs to adjust his sleeves, and I had the impression he was trying to buy time. "I have to admit, I find this all very troubling. Why don't you satisfy my curiosity and tell me who's spreading these nasty rumors?"

Did I look that gullible? I shook my head and matched his smile. "That's not important."

His gaze grew as stony as his face, but I wasn't ready to give up. "The dead man was out at the recreation center last week. I saw him myself. He got into a dark-colored SUV with a broken light on the side. Do you know who owns that SUV?"

Quentin's eyes locked on mine. "How would I know that? There must be hundreds of SUVs in this part of the world. The man is dead, Ms. Shaw. Why don't you just let him rest in peace, whoever he was?"

"I wonder if someone who has been murdered can rest in peace."

Quentin didn't even bother with a reply. He stood, making it clear he considered our conversation over. "I'm sorry I can't help you, Ms. Shaw, but I'm afraid you're wasting your time. Now, if you'll excuse me, your five minutes are up, and I have a busy schedule."

I couldn't think of an argument that might change his mind, so I stood and handed him one of Divinity's business cards. "If you change your mind, give me a call."

"Of course." He tossed the card into a desk drawer where it would probably stay until he emptied the drawer into the trash. I could feel him watching me as I walked down the hall, and I saw him step back into his office as I left the building.

That, I told myself as I walked away, had been a monumental waste of time. Other than validating my suspicions about Ingersol, I'd only succeeded in frustrating myself more than I already was. So far, what I knew about the dead man and his reasons for being in Paradise could fit on the head of a pin and leave room for a blog entry or two.

I thought about stopping at the bank to see if Frank Ogden would talk to me, but I know a dead end when I see one. Frank Ogden would rather eat rocks than tell me about an account holder, dead or alive. Besides, I didn't want to get Chloe in trouble for telling me about the dead man's accounts in the first place.

I'd climbed the first couple of steps leading back to Prospector Street when I heard someone call my name. I turned back and saw Elena Whitehorse hurrying toward me, her pretty face pinched with worry. She checked over her shoulder as she walked, and I had the distinct impression she was trying to make sure she wasn't being followed.

Intrigued, I turned around and descended the stairs again. Without saying a word, she snagged my sleeve and tugged me toward an alcove nestled beneath the stairs. A quiet little voice inside my head whispered caution, but her behavior was so odd I ignored the warning and went with her.

Chapter 22

A cool breeze circled through the alcove as Elena and I hid beneath the stairs. Darting concerned glances at people passing by on the sidewalk, Elena spoke in a soft voice. "Quentin will kill me if he finds out that I'm talking to you. He thinks I'm getting coffee."

My heart beat a little faster. "Why wouldn't he want you talking to me?"

"I overheard your conversation," she almost whispered. "He's not telling you the truth."

That wasn't exactly a news flash, but she'd piqued my curiosity. "How do you know that?"

"Because the guy who was killed over at the drugstore came into our office more than once. I know. I saw him there."

"How do you know it was the dead man? Did you see the picture the police have?"

She nodded. "I stood as close to him as I'm standing to you right now."

My breath caught in my throat. "Have you told the police about this?"

"Not yet." Elena's gaze flickered away, then snapped back to my face. "I probably will. No, I'm *sure* I will. I just . . . well, it's complicated, and it has nothing to do with the murder."

"You're withholding information, Elena. That could mean serious trouble."

Her dark eyes clouded. "I'll tell them. I promise."

I wasn't sure I believed her, but I'd done what I could. "So who was the guy? Was he there to meet Quentin?"

Elena nodded and leaned forward a fraction of an inch so she could check the traffic on the sidewalk again. "Yeah. I made the appointments for him."

"Do you know who he was? You know his name?"

Elena shifted her gaze back to my face and nodded. "I can give you a couple of names, but I'm not sure either of them were real. At first, he told me his name was Arthur Hobbs, but I heard Quentin call him Lou a couple of times."

Neither name rang any bells with me. "Why was Hobbs meeting with Quentin? Was he a client?"

Elena shook her head. "I don't think so. If he'd been looking at property, Quentin would have said something about the listings he was showing, or he'd have taken keys with him when he left the office. He didn't do either. He just took off when they had an appointment, or sometimes they'd just go into Quentin's office and shut the door."

"How often did they meet?"

Elena shrugged. "Once a week."

"For how many weeks?"

"The last month or two, I think. I can't remember, but I could check my calendar if it's important."

The dead guy had been in town that long? That surprised me. "It might be important," I told her. "Did you ever hear what they talked about?"

She shook her head. "When they were here, Quentin always made sure I had something to do that kept me away from my desk."

She seemed sincere, but after getting stonewalled by Kerry, Quentin, and Dwayne Escott, her willingness to talk seemed a little suspicious. Was she being honest with me or setting me up? "Why are you telling me all of this?"

"Because I know Quentin's hiding something. He knew the man who got killed, and now he's claiming that he didn't. Why would he do that unless he has something to hide?"

"Maybe he just doesn't want to get involved in a murder investigation."

She shook her head firmly. "I don't think so. That's not like Quentin. He's hiding something, and I don't want any part of it."

She had a point. "Do you think he is involved in something illegal?"

"I think he might be," she said with a dark scowl. "I know the signs. I've seen them before. But my family doesn't need any more trouble. My mom's been through enough."

Finally, I remembered where I knew her from. I hadn't seen her since she was a girl when her stepbrother was accused of assaulting a girl a few years younger than me. Ben had been in and out of trouble for most of his teenage years, and last I'd heard, he'd been sentenced to prison for aggravated assault. Elena was right. Her family didn't need any more trouble.

Now that I remembered her, I shoved my suspicions aside. "If Hobbs wasn't a client, were he and Quentin friends?"

Elena shook her head. "I don't think so. In fact, I don't think Quentin liked Hobbs at all. He always seemed annoyed when Hobbs was around, and when I'd tell him that Hobbs had called or something, he'd swear or slam his desk drawer shut or bang the phone down. To tell you the truth, I think Hobbs made him nervous."

"Then they must have had business together. But why would Quentin do business with someone he felt that way about?"

"I wish I knew. Whatever it was, Quentin was doing it off the books." Elena darted another nervous glance at the sidewalk. "I've been gone too long. I should get back before Quentin gets upset."

I touched her arm gently. "Are you afraid of him, Elena?"

The question seemed to catch her offguard. "He has a temper," she said after a brief pause. "And *somebody* killed Hobbs on Sunday night."

"Do you think Quentin did it?"

"I don't know. He's not normally a violent person, but you never really know about another person, do you?"

Maybe she didn't *know* if Quentin was guilty, but she thought he might be. "Why would he want Hobbs dead? What's his motive?"

Elena bit her lip, and her eyes shuttered, as if she realized she'd said more than she'd intended to. "I don't know why I said that," she said, backpedaling. "Quentin's all right, really. And you're probably right. He's probably only denying that he knew Hobbs because he doesn't want to get dragged into the investigation."

She tried to leave, but I caught her hand. "You don't really believe that," I said, "or you wouldn't have come after me."

"Even if he *did* kill Hobbs, I don't know why he'd do it. I've only worked for him for six months. I don't know him that well."

"Wait! One more question. Does Quentin have any listings near Hammond Junction?"

Confusion clouded Elena's dark eyes. "Two. Why?"

"That's where I saw Hobbs for the first time. Which properties is Quentin handling?"

"The old Davenport house is on the market, and Colby Tilley is selling off about twenty acres near the creek."

I had no idea whether the information was important or not, but I filed it away just in case. "Do you know where Hobbs was staying?"

Elena dug a Post-it note from her pocket and slipped it into my hand. "I don't know where he was staying, but I called him twice at that number. Maybe that will help." And before I could stop her, she was gone.

I watched until she disappeared around the corner, then glanced at the note. The number had a local area code but not a prefix I recognized, which meant the number probably belonged to a cell phone. That would make it just about impossible to track—at least for me—and that made it just another dead end.

With the phone number Elena gave me burning a hole in my pocket, I picked up a sandwich and a Coke and carried them back up the hill. Karen and Liberty had worked out a lunch schedule so that one of them was always at the store, but I didn't want to take advantage of my newfound freedom.

The adrenaline rush that had carried me through my meeting with Quentin began to fade as I climbed the steps, and by the time I reached street level again, a sudden wave of exhaustion made my limbs heavy. I paused to catch my breath and saw Liberty come out the front door of Divinity across the street from where I stood. She shivered in the cold air and crossed her arms tightly over her chest, then turned away from me and started walking quickly downhill.

She looked small and alone, and a pang of guilt stirred uncomfortably. She was a good worker. Eager. Always on time. Karen seemed to like her. Really, I told myself sternly, I should be more friendly toward her.

I jogged across the street during a break in traffic and my thoughts had just started to drift back toward other things when I saw Liberty stop walking abruptly. She turned slightly in the direction of a man, just stepping out of a nearby shop. For a heartbeat, I thought he might be the mysterious Rutger. In the next breath, I recognized the lumpy body of Dwayne Escott.

They were too far away for me to see expressions or hear what they said, but Liberty seemed pleased to see him. I don't know what made me stop walking to watch them. There was no reason Liberty and Dwayne couldn't be friends. But watching them together made me uneasy.

For the first time, I wondered about Liberty's story. Did Rutger actually exist, or had she made him up to explain why she'd come back to town? If she wasn't here because of "Rutger" was the timing of her return a coincidence? She'd come back at roughly the same time Hobbs showed up, and I wondered if there was some connection between them.

Liberty must have felt me watching them because she glanced up the street quickly. Instinctively, I stepped into the recessed doorway of Picture Perfect so she wouldn't see me.

"Abby? What on earth are you doing?"

The woman's voice, so unexpected, almost made me drop my sandwich. I wheeled around to face my friend Rachel with an embarrassed laugh. My reaction had been purely instinctive, and I must have looked ridiculous, ducking into the doorway like that. "I don't know," I said, stepping onto the sidewalk and hoping to regain a little dignity. "Don't ask."

Rachel's a beautiful woman whose life's ambition is to be a plus-sized model. I've only seen her a handful of times without full makeup, her dark hair just so, and outfits topped off with carefully coordinated accessories. Most mornings, I'm doing well if I can remember to put on a watch.

While Rachel waits to be discovered, she makes and sells candles at a shop just down the street, and she's usually in and out of Divinity several times a day. Like me, she must have been planning to eat lunch while she worked because she carried a bag with noticeable grease spots and a large soda in a paper cup.

She glanced down the street in the direction I'd been looking. "What are you doing, spying on Liberty?"

I was embarrassed to admit the truth, so I hedged a bit. "Not exactly. I haven't seen you for a few days. You must be busy down at Candlewyck."

Rachel gave me a knowing look. My subtle attempt to change the subject hadn't fooled her in the least. "I am. It's that time of the year, you know. I sell more candles during ski season than I do the rest of the year. What about you? Are you getting orders for holiday candy already?"

"Some." We started walking slowly toward Divinity. "The pace should really start picking up as we get closer to Thanksgiving."

"How's Liberty working out?"

I lifted one shoulder in a casual shrug. "She seems fine. Karen's pleased with her."

"But you're not so sure."

"She's fine," I said firmly, but I wasn't sure which of us I was trying harder to convince. "She hasn't done anything to make me unhappy with her."

"But—?" Rachel nudged me gently with a shoulder. "Come on, spill it. I can hear the hesitation when you talk about her."

I stopped walking a few feet from Divinity's front door. Uncertainty about Liberty had been nagging at me for days, and the urge to confide in someone was almost overwhelming. But if we were going to have this conversation, I didn't want to have it in front of Karen. "It's nothing I can put my finger on. There's just something a little . . . off about her."

Rachel's dark eyes clouded. "What do you mean?"

"Have you ever met her boyfriend?"

"Rutger?"

I nodded. "I've never seen him. Have you?"

Rachel blinked in confusion. "You think she's making him up?"

"I don't know. That's the trouble. She came back to town about the same time the dead guy showed up. What if there's some connection?" I glanced down the street to see what Liberty and Dwayne were doing now, but they'd disappeared.

"I think you're a little paranoid," Rachel said. A sigh laced with exasperation escaped her lips. "Have you heard anything about the murder? Do the police have any suspects?"

Maybe she was right. For Karen's sake, I *hoped* she was. "No suspects that I know of."

"And the victim? Do they have any idea who he was yet?"

I filled her in on everything I'd learned since I saw her last, told her about the guy who'd been following us the other night, my visit to Quentin Ingersol's office, and my conversation with Elena. "That may not even be his real name," I said when I'd finished, "and none of it may help the police, but I'll call Jawarski and tell him what I found out as soon as I get back to the shop."

Rachel frowned thoughtfully. "No wonder you're paranoid. Do you have any idea who was following you?"

"None."

"I would have been totally freaked out," Rachel said.

"Believe me, I was. And the boys were terrified. The whole thing's starting to get to me, I guess."

"I should just put the whole thing out of my mind and focus on things I can actually do something about—like work."

"What you need is an evening without work and without the basketball team. A night all your own." Rachel fell silent for a moment, then turned to me with a grin. "I know the perfect thing. Come with me to that new antique shop after work. I've heard good things about it, and I'm dying to see what they have."

"I don't know—"

"Come on. It will be fun. We can get dinner somewhere when we're through."

"It sounds tempting," I admitted, "but this schedule I've

been keeping recently is kicking my butt. I think I'd be smart to stay in tonight and catch up on my sleep."

"Your *sleep*?" Rachel laughed and shook her head. "How boring is that?"

"I know. I know. I'd love to go to the antique store with you another time, though."

"Okay. Sure. I can wait a couple of days." She glanced at her watch, and her mood changed abruptly. "I've got to run. I'm alone in the shop today, and I locked up when I left. The note I left on the door said I'd be back ten minutes ago."

"That's all right. I need to get back, myself."

"And don't worry about Liberty," she said as she started away. "I really think she's okay."

Chapter 23

Divinity was empty of customers when I let myself inside so, wrapped in blessed quiet after Karen left on break, I called Jawarski and filled him in on my conversations with Quentin and Elena. He didn't return the favor, but that didn't surprise me.

After I finished talking to Jawarski, I stared at the phone for a full minute, trying to argue myself out of doing what I did next.

It didn't work. Curiosity was way too strong.

Holding my breath, I dialed *69 to keep my identity from showing up on caller ID and punched in the phone number Elena had given me. I chewed on my bottom lip while the phone rang. I desperately wanted to find out who the phone belonged to, but what if *69 didn't work this time, and I gave myself away?

The phone rang a handful of times, then transferred to voice mail. Even that didn't give any clue about the phone's owner because the recorded message was the generic one that had been programmed into the phone at the factory. Disappointed, I disconnected, stuffed the number into my pocket, and glanced around the store.

I'd been so preoccupied for the past few days, I felt as if I was seeing it for the first time after a long absence, and that added a layer of guilt to what I was already carrying after taking time away for the basketball team.

Time to get my priorities in order, I told myself. I'd let myself be distracted long enough. As customers came through the door, I put everything out of my mind and gave the shop my full attention.

My run-in with Dwayne Escott the night before had reminded me of my promise to deliver a box of caramels to Marion the next time I was in her neck of the woods. Between customers, I boxed up a selection of candies especially for Marion: caramel squares, walnut caramels, caramel peanut candy bars, pecan caramels, ginger cream caramels, butterscotch caramels, and, in honor of the season, pumpkin caramels.

I took my time, selecting carefully to make sure I included time-honored favorites and a couple of new selections Karen and I had recently added to Divinity's repertoire. Once I had the box packed to my satisfaction, I peeled off my gloves, closed the lid, and positioned one of Divinity's gold-edged labels over the seal.

It wasn't until Liberty burst through the door like a cyclone, upsetting the peaceful atmosphere I'd been enjoying, that I realized she'd been gone for lunch far longer than an hour.

She blew through the seating area, tossed her sweatshirt into a corner behind the counter, and beamed in my direction as two customers approached the register. "Go on," she said, shooing me away. "You've got plenty of things to do. I can take care of this."

She smiled brightly and chatted with the women about the weather, keeping them engaged in conversation as she rang up their sales. She seemed to have everything under control, so I went into the kitchen. The sticky molds I'd used for the lollipops were still on the counter, waiting for my attention. I filled the sink with warm, soapy water and gave them what they wanted.

A few minutes later, I heard the bell over the door, and silence descended until I heard a voice behind me. "Abby?"

I turned to find Liberty in the open doorway. "Yes?"

"Need any help?"

"Thanks, but I'm just washing up a few things. Didn't Karen leave you anything to do?"

Liberty nodded. "A few things."

"Go ahead and do that. I'll be finished here in just a few minutes."

"Okay." Liberty started to turn away but stopped herself. "Have I done something to offend you, Abby?"

I shook my head quickly. "Of course not. Why do you ask?"

"You always seem so . . . distant. It's almost as if you don't want me around. If that's the case, I'll go. Just say the word."

Standing in the kitchen and looking into her wide blue eyes, I felt about two inches tall. "You haven't done anything to offend me," I assured her. "I've just been busy. And distracted. A lot has happened in a very short time, and I'm not going to be around all the time. We hired you because I can't be here to help Karen the way I used to be."

"Oh. Okay."

I turned back to the sink, but she didn't move, and I realized we weren't finished talking. "Is there something else?" I asked over my shoulder.

"Can I ask you a question?"

"Okay."

"Karen told me that you came back to Paradise after living away for a long time."

"That's right."

"How did you get people to accept you being here again?"

The question touched a nerve. I shook the water from my hands and grabbed a towel. "Are you having trouble?"

Liberty let out a soft laugh. "You could say that. I guess part of the problem is that I don't really know that many people anymore. I didn't spend a lot of time in class when I was in school, and most of the kids I hung out with are long gone now." She leaned against the counter and crossed one foot over the other. "The ones who are still around are . . . I don't know . . . they're just not the kind of people I want to associate with now. I've changed, I guess."

"So what's the problem?"

"Well, I want friends. Rutger's always busy, and I hate being alone. But you and Karen are the only friends I have, and I'm not sure *you* even like me."

Heat crept into my cheeks. "I don't dislike you, Liberty. I just don't know you very well yet. It takes me a while to warm up to people, that's all. The rest of the town is a lot the same way," I assured her. "Folks around here have long memories, but they're loyal. Just give them time."

She didn't say so, but I could tell by the look in her eyes that she didn't believe me.

"Obviously, you know people around town," I said, trying to encourage her. "I saw you talking to Dwayne Escott earlier." Okay, so I had a *tiny* ulterior motive for bringing that up. Sue me.

Liberty's gaze shot to mine, but I couldn't tell if I'd surprised or frightened her. "Dwayne. Is that his name? I recognized the face, but I couldn't remember who he was."

My eyes roamed her face as I tried to decide if she was lying to me. "Don't worry. I'm sure he never suspected a thing. You looked like you were saying hello to an old friend."

"Really?" She let out a relieved sigh. "Well, that's good. I mean, it was obvious that he knew me, and I'm always so embarrassed when that happens."

My feelings about her did another about-turn. "Yeah," I said with a smile, "I hate that, too. So how do you know Dwayne?"

"We went to high school together. No, that's not really true. We were in the same class in high school, but we didn't really know each other. I wasn't in class often enough for any of those guys to know me. I was surprised he even recognized me."

"Those guys?"

"Yeah. He was one of the kids who ran around with Kerry Hendrix."

"Dwayne Escott was?"

"You didn't know that?"

I shook my head, trying to picture Kerry and Dwayne in the same room, much less the same teenage clique. I just couldn't get the image to form. "I had no idea. They were close friends?"

"Yeah, those two and a couple of others. I forget their names, though. I wouldn't have remembered Dwayne's if you hadn't told me." She slipped an apron over her head and grabbed the glass cleaner and a rag. "And then there were the girls. Always a dozen girls or more hanging all over them. To tell the truth, I had no use for them *or* the girls who thought they were so hot."

There was another image that just wouldn't pull together for me: Dwayne Escott being fawned over by teenage girls.

"Well, look," Liberty said, "I've kept you from the dishes long enough, and Karen wanted me to clean those candy jars before she got back from lunch, so I'd better get busy."

I nodded absently, still trying to piece together what she'd just told me. Lou Hobbs—or whatever his name was—had known Kerry Hendrix. Kerry Hendrix and Dwayne Escott were good friends, or at least they used to be. And Lou had been "shot" a few hundred yards from Dwayne's front door. If *that* was a coincidence, I'd run down Prospector Street in nothing but my underwear.

Chapter 24

I slept fitfully that evening, dodging dreams about Marshall and Jawarski all night. By the time I finally gave up trying to sleep and climbed out of bed the next morning, I was not only exhausted but irritated with Karen for planting the idea that Jawarski might be upset over that stupid kiss in the first place.

My irritation took an upswing when I stumbled across the bag still holding the exercise pants I'd bought at Alpine Sports. I hadn't even managed to remove the price tags yet, nor had I bothered to buy T-shirts to go with them. Tossing the bag aside, I went through my usual morning routine from walking the dog to opening the store.

When Karen arrived, I loaded the centerpieces I'd made for Richie Belieu and Dylan Wagstaff into the hatch of the Jetta, settled Max in the backseat with a couple of rawhide chews, and pointed the car toward the Silver River Inn.

Like all of the historic buildings in Paradise, the Silver River Inn has survived a number of different lives since it was originally built. Back in the 1840s it began as a one-room schoolhouse, then grew as new rooms and extra floors were added on, started over as a miner's hospital, then becoming a library and finally an office complex.

Almost five years ago, Richie Bellieu and his partner, Dylan Wagstaff, bought the place, gutted it, and spent the next two years bringing it to life again as a bed-and-breakfast.

I grabbed a box of centerpieces and led Max up the two flights of stairs from the street. Inside the hushed, elegant atmosphere of the B & B I resisted the urge to tiptoe and turned toward the lobby, the sound of Max's claws scrabbling on the polished hardwood floor making me wince as we walked.

Richie stood behind the registration desk, and Dylan was busy with something near the front windows. As always, they both seemed delighted to see Max . . . and pleased to see me.

They've been life partners for at least ten years, but unlike other couples, they don't seem to be turning into each other as the years go by. Richie, who'd become a blond since the last time I saw him, is flamboyant, filled with enthusiasm, and usually more feminine than I am. That morning, though, he wore jeans so faded they were almost white and a sweatshirt with a peace symbol fading across his chest over a thin white turtleneck. It was an unusual choice for Richie.

Dylan, who is typically more reserved than his partner, keeps his light hair neatly trimmed and his clothing conservative. He wore dove-gray slacks and a chic gray and black matching sweater that seemed more suited for Richie's closet than his own. Maybe they *were* turning into each other, after all.

Richie swept out from behind the desk and wrapped his arms around Max, planting noisy kisses in the air near the dog's head. "Max, you old devil, you. We weren't expecting you until tomorrow—were we, Dylan?"

Dylan agreed they weren't, and Max, who adores both men, wagged his little stump of a tail with delight. Dylan pulled himself away from the lovefest first and grinned up at me. "Are those the centerpieces?"

"They are. You want to take a look?"

"Are you kidding?" Richie ruffled the hair on Max's head and stood to face me. "I can't wait to see what you've done this time."

I love that Richie and Dylan are both fans of my work, but I'm also a little nervous whenever I work for them. So far, they've been wildly enthusiastic about everything I've created for the inn, but nobody bats a thousand all the time.

Dylan took the box from me and carried it to a table in the dining area of the great room. "It's not very heavy. Are they all in here?"

"I have another two boxes in the car. I thought I'd show

you what I've got first. If you want me to make changes, I'll take them back with me."

Richie clasped his hands together under his chin and swayed slightly from side to side. "Well, don't tease us. Show us!"

I opened the box, removed the protective wrapping, and placed a single cornucopia centerpiece on the table. Silk leaves and candy "fruit" filled the horn of plenty and spilled onto a piece of cardboard I'd cut into an eggplant shape and covered with dark green felt. Richie clapped his hands in delight.

As always, Dylan's response was more restrained. "They're going to look fantastic with the china," he said with an appreciative smile. "They're exactly right."

Richie grabbed one of my hands in his and tugged me toward a large leather sofa positioned in front of a blazing fireplace. "I don't know why you worry so much. You've never let us down."

Almost giddy with relief, I laughed. "Maybe one of these days I'll start to develop some confidence in myself, but I'm still worried about living up to Aunt Grace's reputation."

"Well, stop worrying. The centerpieces are perfect. Now, what about Monday? You *are* coming, are you not?"

I nodded. "I'll be here. Do you want me to come early and help with anything?"

"Don't be silly. You're a guest. What about Pine?"

"He'll be here, too—at least he said he would be last time I talked to him."

With a satisfied nod, Dylan headed for the sidebar where they kept fresh coffee and cookies round the clock. He held up a silver coffeepot that looked old and wickedly expensive. "Coffee?"

Leaving the sofa, I crossed the room to look at the piece. "Is this new?"

Richie trailed behind me, clearly delighted that I'd noticed. "Yes, it is. Gorgeous, isn't it?"

"It's beautiful." The coffeepot wasn't the only thing new on the sideboard. A four-piece coffee service sat on a matching silver tray, each piece elaborately decorated with curlicues and silver roses. I don't know a lot about antiques, but I recognize quality when I see it. "Where did you find this?"

Dylan laughed aloud and nodded toward the street. "There's a new antique shop across the street—the Ivy Attic—and it's *fabulous*. This set is nineteenth-century, German sterling silver."

I ran a finger across the rose on the sugar bowl's lid. "I've heard about the shop, but I never dreamed they'd be selling something like this. It's breathtaking."

"And it's just the beginning." Richie dragged me back to the sofa again. "You should *see* some of the pieces she has over there. There's a pair of nineteenth-century French wall mirrors in the back room that I'm head over heels for." He smiled at Dylan across the room. "Not that anything could take *your* place, love."

Dylan returned the smile and filled three cups. "As you can tell, we've found a new hobby. It's all I can do to keep Richie from going over there every day."

Richie wagged a hand in a dismissive gesture. "He thinks I'm going to bankrupt us, but I'm not *that* far gone. I just don't think a few well-placed pieces would hurt our reputation, that's all."

I didn't want to get drawn into an argument between them, so I accepted the cup Dylan offered me and said, "The coffee set certainly is beautiful. How long has the shop been there?"

"A month?" Richie shared a look with Dylan, and they spoke in shorthand the way couples who've been together for a while do. "One? Are you—?" . . . "Didn't she open the weekend—?" . . . "Oh, that's right. That's when—" . . . "Exactly. Shae and Donovan, and that *horrid* sweater." With the details decided, Richie looked at me again. "About two months, I guess. She opened around the first of September. You really should go check it out. You might even find a few things for Divinity."

I was suddenly, strangely envious of the closeness they shared. My ex-husband and I had had that once—at least I'd thought we had—and I missed it . . . or at any rate, I missed believing that I had it. Finding out about Roger's affair had left me wondering about everything I'd once believed in.

Watching Dylan and Richie exchanging glances, I thought about Marshall kissing me and about Karen's warnings that I should tell Jawarski or risk losing him. It was hard for me to believe that Jawarski would make a big deal out of a little kiss, especially when I hadn't even been a willing participant. But what if I was wrong?

I didn't want to be with someone who flipped out over little, inconsequential things, and I hated the idea of jealousy, but deep inside I knew that Jawarski wasn't the type to fly off the handle without reason.

The kiss wouldn't bother him . . . but the lie would.

Chapter 25

Maybe I *should* talk to Jawarski, but I couldn't see any reason to rush things. I needed a little while to think about how I was going to approach him, exactly how to tell him about Marshall without making it sound as if I'd stepped over the line or that I was imagining a line that didn't exist.

We'd spent so many months tiptoeing around each other, I didn't really know where we stood, and I didn't want him to think I was assuming more than he intended. In short, it was a conversation I knew I had to have but still didn't want to.

No matter how slowly I sipped, it didn't take anywhere near long enough to drink the coffee, and in spite of my protests that he didn't have to, Dylan insisted on carrying one of the two remaining boxes of centerpieces up the stairs, cutting another excuse for procrastination in half. For once, Richie's accounting package worked without a single glitch, and less than half an hour later I descended the stairs for the final time.

I was almost to street level when the ornate sign for the Ivy Attic, in the window of a Victorian-style house across the street, caught my eye and gave me the excuse I'd been looking for to put off talking to Jawarski. Not that we needed antiques at Divinity, but as Richie said, you never knew. Besides, as a member of the Downtown Merchants' Alliance, it was my civic duty to welcome a new business owner to the community.

Pleased with myself for my ingenuity, I led Max across the street and clipped him to a piece of fencing that surrounded a yard filled with old metal farm implements. When I let myself in through the front door, the musty smell of old buildings greeted me—unusual for our area of the world. Buildings, no matter how old, don't pick up that moldy smell when there's no humidity to cause it.

A large bureau stood flush with the door, and two tall windows flanked a Victorian secretary made of what looked like mahogany. A narrow opening between the bureau and the cash register revealed a long room filled with pieces, the sheer size and volume of which made me feel claustrophobic.

"See anything you like?" A woman's voice sounded close to my ear and caught me off guard.

I pivoted to face her and found myself eye to eye with a woman a few years younger than me. Her copper-red hair was so bright, I knew the color couldn't be natural, and her eyes were slightly puffy, as if she'd been crying recently or suffering from hay fever.

To my surprise, I recognized her. I just couldn't figure out why Marshall hadn't mentioned that his half sister had returned to Paradise. "Ginger?"

Her smile drooped a little, and she moved into the light so I could see a sprinkling of freckles trying to make themselves visible beneath layers of foundation and powder. "Yes. Do I know you?"

Paranoia returned full-force, and suddenly Marshall's visits, that kiss, and his presence at the murder scene seemed almost sinister.

But that was ridiculous. Marshall? No way he could have been involved in Hobbs's murder . . . could he? Shaking off my suspicions, I smiled at the woman standing in front of me.

"You did once. Abby Shaw. I went to school with Marshall."

"Oh my—" Her smile regained all of its brilliance, but it seemed almost unnaturally bright. "Well, of course it's you. I would have figured that out sooner or later. How are you?"

"I'm doing well, thanks."

"Last I heard, you'd fled the coop, too. Don't tell me we both came crawling back."

"I didn't exactly come *crawling*," I protested, even though I had. "I came back almost two years ago after my Aunt Grace died. I own her candy shop now."

"Really?" Ginger reached somewhere above my head and pulled down the largest cat I've ever seen. She held it close to her chest and scratched under its chin, and the thing let out a contented rumble. "I've just been back a couple of months, but I love this store. Do you like it?"

I nodded and glanced into the room behind me. "I've heard some wonderful things about it. In fact, I decided to stop in because several friends have mentioned your place, and my friends at the B & B across the street couldn't stop raving. The coffee set they bought from you is exquisite."

Ginger beamed. "Isn't it? I was really proud of that find." She shifted the cat and cast a pleased glance around her. "Are you looking for anything in particular? I'd be happy to point you in the right direction."

"Actually, I'm just here to take a look around. I'm killing time until another appointment."

"Well, feel free to look around all you want, and give me a shout if I can help you find anything." She deposited the cat on the top of the bureau, disturbing a layer of dust, and wiped the hair from her hands onto her pant legs.

I battled a sneeze and felt a strong urge to escape the cramped store and grab a lung full of fresh air. But I'd told Ginger I was there to browse, so I felt obligated to at least give it a quick look. I wandered idly through one room after another, slipping past mounds of crockery, headboards, dressers, silver teapots, and an occasional vanity, sidling past stacks of mismatched dinnerware, coat trees, mirrors, and picture frames.

On sheer volume alone, her inventory was impressive but a bit baffling. The freight charges for hauling all of this furniture up the mountain would have been astronomical, but I doubted there were this many antiques in the whole basin. It was hard to believe that she'd accumulated this much by going on a massive antique hunting binge once she got here.

I wondered how Richie and Dylan had found anything of value in all this clutter, and whether any of the pieces I was dismissing with barely a glance were actually valuable. Just when I was about to give up the whole visit as a waste of time, I came across a nearly hidden selection of teacups and saucers that caught my interest. I didn't think they were worth much, and the price tags stuck to the bottom of the saucers confirmed my suspicions, but they struck a chord with me, and I imagined the cup with the lavender roses filled with purple hard candies and bound up with cellophane and a bow made from antique-looking ribbon.

It was the first time since I took over Divinity that an artistic design had sprung into my mind, fully formed, and my heart beat a little faster in response. I spent the next several minutes looking through every cup and saucer and picking five of my favorites. Five should be enough to test the idea without spending a lot of money.

Carefully, I stacked the saucers together and picked up three of the cups by hooking my fingers through their handles. As I reached to pick up the other two with my free hand, I heard footsteps behind me. I turned to see Marshall come through the door of what I thought must once have been the kitchen.

He smiled when he saw me, and I was struck again by how good-looking he'd become since we were kids. "Ginger told me you were back here. I didn't know you liked antiques."

"I don't know much about them," I admitted, "but I'd heard good things about the store and thought I'd check it out. Why didn't you tell me Ginger was back in town?"

"I didn't realize you knew her; she's so much younger than we are."

I made a face at him. "We're not *that* old. I was an aide for her Girl Scout troop for a couple of years. I would have come by to see her weeks ago if I'd known she was back."

Marshall bowed slightly at the waist, a teasing light in his eyes. "My humble apologies. I won't make the same mistake again."

I laughed and picked up the last two cups. "It's no big deal. I was just surprised to see her when I came through the door. She has quite a store here."

"Doesn't she?" Marshall stepped in front of me and shifted a chair to make it easier for me to get past it. "And it's quite a success so far. People seem to love it."

"I'm happy for her," I said, and I honestly meant it. The

place might make *me* feel as if the walls were closing in, but I still wished her well. "You're both doing well, aren't you? Gigi seems to be getting more popular all the time.

He laughed softly and shifted another chair out of my way. "It's amazing, huh? Who would have thought the Ames kids would make good like this?"

I stopped walking and studied his face. "What do you mean by that?"

"Oh come on, Abby. I know what a geek I was in school, and Ginger wasn't exactly the homecoming queen. We both struggled. I'm just saying, I think it's kind of funny how the world changes." He started walking again slowly, and I moved with him. "I mean, look at somebody like Kerry Hendrix for example. He was king of the world while he was in high school. Captain of the football team. President of the senior class. Everybody loved him. Girls couldn't keep their hands off him. Now look at him. He's working at the bowling alley and coaching Youth League basketball. How the mighty have fallen."

"I don't remember Kerry Hendrix in school," I admitted.

"He was in Ginger's class," Marshall explained. "She had a killer crush on him, but he didn't really give her the time of day. You know. Typical high school crap. You were gone by the time they got to high school, but the whole town made a big deal out of him back in those days."

Suspicion zapped me again. Everything I'd been hearing about Kerry explained his arrogance, but Marshall seemed oddly emotional about Ginger's childhood. "Well, I'm sorry for Ginger, but she's obviously survived and thrived, so she doesn't appear to have suffered."

Marshall laughed, and the moment was gone. "You're right. Oh, man, listen to me. I haven't even thought about that stuff in years. It must have been talking about him at your place yesterday that brought it all back again."

"In that case," I said with a small grin, "I offer *my* most humble apologies." We reached the front of the store, and I put the cups and saucers on the counter. "So you're not friendly with Kerry these days?"

"If I were, would I have told you to watch out for him?"

I shook my head and laughed. "No, I guess not," I said. "What about Ginger?"

"Are you kidding?"

"Silly question, I guess." I stretched out my hand to ring the bell that would let Ginger know I was ready.

Marshall put his hand over mine and said, "Before you do that, I need to ask you a question."

With Karen's warning ringing in my ears, I drew my hand away slowly. "What?"

"Have dinner with me."

"Dinner?"

"Yeah. It's a meal, generally eaten in the evening. I thought it might be nice to eat one together."

Even with Karen's prediction, Marshall's invitation stunned me. Words jammed up in my throat, and it took me a minute to get any of them out of my mouth. "That's really nice of you, and I appreciate the invitation, but I can't. I'm . . . seeing someone."

Marshall's smile inched a little wider. "I know all about the guy you're seeing, Abby. I know he doesn't appreciate you, and I know he doesn't spend nearly enough time with you."

"I know it probably looks that way from the outside, but you really can't tell what's going on between two people from outward appearances. Jawarski and I are both content with our . . . with the way things are. Really, Marshall, I'm flattered, but I really don't think it's a good idea."

He studied my expression for a long time, then shrugged and worked up a smile. From a distance, the smile might have been convincing. Close up, it definitely lost the battle. Maybe because I could see the embarrassment in his eyes. There was something else in his expression, too. I just couldn't put my finger on it.

"Well, you can't blame a guy for trying, I guess." He glanced over his shoulder, ran a quick look over his watch, and backed a step or two away. "Listen, I've gotta—I need to get back to the restaurant."

"Oh. Sure," I said with a smile. "Business is always first, right?" I tried again to figure out what that emotion was in the back of his eyes, but again it eluded me. Probably nothing, I told myself firmly. I'd hate to see what would be in *my* eyes right after someone turned me down for a date. "Listen, Marshall, just because we can't go out, that doesn't mean we can't be friends."

"Right. Friends. That's good. It's cool." He stepped backwards again and the cat, which must have been hiding under a chair, let out a yowl of pain. A flush rushed into Marshall's face, and he turned away quickly. "I'll see you around, okay?"

"Absolutely." I kept smiling until he shut the door behind him, then let out a breath and closed my eyes. I told myself that he'd taken the rejection well, but I couldn't stop thinking about that look on his face and wondering just what it was I'd missed.

Chapter 26

My conversation with Marshall convinced me that I couldn't put off talking to Jawarski any longer. Not only did I want to find out if knowing Lou Hobbs's name had unearthed any new information, but I had a sudden, intense need to make sure he and I *were* as comfortable with our . . . whatever it was . . . as I'd told Marshall we were.

I put the box holding the cups and saucers in the hatch and stuffed an old sweater and my emergency kit around it to keep the box from sliding. Then, loading Max into the backseat, I turned the Jetta toward town again.

It was mid-afternoon by the time I got there, and the parking lot the police department shared with other city offices was packed. I drove up and down several rows before I found a spot closer to the library than the police station. The weather was mild, but I had no idea how long this conversation would take, and I didn't want to leave Max cooped up in the car. Hooking him to the chain again, I found a spot where he could lie in the shade or bask in the sun, depending on his mood, then pushed through the glass doors of the white brick building that housed Paradise's finest.

Since Jawarski and I had started spending more time together I'd become, if not a regular fixture around here, at least not an unexpected one. I waved at the women working dispatch, signed in with the officer working the front desk, and climbed the stairs to the second floor.

The detective division is all the way at the back of the building, down a long, brightly lit corridor that stretched from one end of the building to another. That's why I had no trouble seeing the blonde with the killer body standing just outside Jawarski's office. I didn't have any trouble seeing Jawarski either, for that matter. He lounged in the doorway wearing a broad, appreciative smile as he listened to what the blonde was saying.

I'm sure there were at least half a dozen explanations for what I was seeing, every one of them legitimate and non-threatening. I skipped over every one of them and went straight back in time to the night I walked into the bedroom I shared with my then-husband and discovered him on the floor with the reason my marriage had been falling apart.

I stopped halfway down the hall, wanting to turn around and get out of there before Jawarski noticed me, but unable to move. I was rooted to the spot, staring at the very thing I didn't want to see with the horrid fascination of someone who's just witnessed an accident.

After what seemed like a very long time, Jawarski looked away from the blonde and noticed me. He said something to her and waved me closer. "Hey there," he said as the woman turned and walked away. "What are you doing here?"

Angry with myself for my reaction, I moved into his cluttered office, but I couldn't get out the words I'd come to say. Instead of asking him to grab some dinner at my favorite Thai restaurant, I heard myself say, "I wondered if the information I gave you earlier was of any use."

His expression closed down, just as I'd known it would, but right then it was easier to deal with him as a cop than as the man I cared way too much about. "You came about the murder?" he asked, his voice stone cold.

I nodded once and sat in one of the chairs in front of his desk. "Did the name help you? Could you find anything on either Arthur or Lou Hobbs?"

Jawarski dropped heavily into his chair, but the glare I expected didn't appear. Instead, he smiled as if he'd just won the lottery. "Not yet, but we're still pursuing a few angles, trying to find out if he has any other aliases."

"Do you know where he was staying while he was here in town?"

"If I did, is there a reason I should tell you?"

The question stung, but I wasn't sure whether I resented it

because of the blonde, because of Marshall, or just because Jawarski was being an ass. "You should tell me," I snapped, "because I may have some information that I can share with you."

"Really? And what would that be?"

"I have a phone number that Elena Whitehorse from Big Horn Realty used to reach him when she set up appointments for him with Quentin Ingersol." I'd copied the number onto a piece of scratch paper, and I pulled that out of my pocket now and dropped it on Jawarski's desk. "If you don't already know where he was staying, maybe that will help."

He picked up the note and studied it for a long moment. "How'd you get this?"

"That doesn't really matter, does it? What matters is that Quentin Ingersol knew Hobbs, but he's lying about it for some reason."

His gaze shifted from the paper he held to my face. "And you know that how?"

"I told you I talked to him earlier. He denied knowing Hobbs at all."

Jawarski let out a sigh heavy with frustration. "Yeah. I've been meaning to talk to you about that."

"Don't bother giving me the lecture, because I already know it word for word, and you already know I'm not going to listen anyway."

He shook his head and ran a hand over the bristle on his head. "What did this Elena Whitehorse tell you?"

"Just that Hobbs was in Quentin's office more than once, and she called that number when she needed to make an appointment. And she said that she thinks Hobbs made Quentin nervous."

"Have you tried calling the number yourself?"

I thought about saying no, but he'd see right through me, so why bother? "Yes, and I'm pretty sure it's a cell. It went straight to voice mail with the factory recording. I don't have any idea whose phone it is."

I was trying hard not to be prickly with him, but the mix of emotions churning in my blood made my skin itch. Was I jealous? Feeling guilty? All of the above?

"Is that it?"

I stood and walked to the other side of the room, pretending a sudden interest in a stack of books he had on a table. I didn't want a guy who flipped out over inconsequential things, and here I was tying myself in knots over something far less threatening than a kiss. The worst part was that I had to finally admit that I felt more than friendship for Jawarski.

Doing my best to keep my voice casual, I asked, "Who was that woman I saw you talking to when I came in?"

"Stephanie?" I could hear the surprise in his voice, the effort he made to follow me onto this new track. "She's a detective with the narcotics division, why?"

"I've just never seen her before," I said, darting a thin smile over my shoulder. "I wondered if she was a friend or someone you work with."

"She's both, but not in the sense I think you mean." He stood and came toward me, but he stopped before he got too close. "What's this all about?"

I turned to face him and forced myself to be honest. "I wish I knew. When I saw you talking to her, I felt a whole bunch of things I didn't want to feel."

His blue eyes darkened slightly. "You didn't have to. She's a friend, and she's a fellow officer, but that's it."

I nodded slowly, trying to work up the words to tell him about Marshall and wondering how I'd explain something I didn't understand myself. "I know it's short notice, but I really came by to see if you're free for dinner. I was going to give you the phone number then."

"Tonight?"

"If you're not busy. I was thinking maybe we could grab some Thai at the Lotus Blossom . . . unless something else sounds better."

"I wish I could," he said with a frown, "but I've already made other plans. How about a rain check? I'm free tomorrow night."

Whatever I'd seen in Marshall's face earlier was probably reflected on mine just then. Logic told me that Jawarski wasn't brushing me off, but all those old insecurities made my stomach ache. "Yeah. Sure. Tomorrow's great." *Tell him,* the voice inside my head whispered, but I convinced myself this wasn't the right time or the right place. "I have practice until six, so do you want to just meet there at about eight?"

"Eight's fine." Jawarski took a look at my face and put a hand on my arm. "What I've got going tonight isn't really important. If you want me to cancel, I will."

I shook my head quickly, wishing I could appreciate the offer but just feeling a whole lot more guilty. "No, don't be ridiculous. We can go tomorrow."

"You're sure?"

"Of course I'm sure," I snapped. Immediately, I wanted to take the words back, but that's the thing about words: They last forever. I forced a smile and wished I could crawl into a hole and disappear. "I'm sorry. I didn't mean to get hostile or anything. I'm just a little confused right now, and I'm trying really hard to figure out what I'm feeling."

"Because of Stephanie?"

It would have been easy to say yes and let it go, but I knew that Jawarski and I wouldn't stand a chance if I did that. I shook my head and turned to look at him. "Partly, I guess. I've spent the past year convincing myself that you and I are friends—*good* friends, but still just friends. But friends don't get jealous the way I did when I walked down that hall."

Jawarski gave that smile that always makes my heart flutter a little. "I'd like to think we're more than friends, but I know you're nervous about moving ahead, and I'm not going to pressure you. You know that, don't you?"

I nodded and felt my courage fail me again. What was *wrong* with me? Why was I such a coward? "It's not just that," I said, pushing through my hesitation. "Marshall Ames came to see me yesterday. He said he was just checking to make sure that I was okay—you know, since we found the body together and everything."

Jawarski didn't say a word, he just waited patiently for me to spill my guts.

"Anyway, we talked for a while, and he did what you always do. He told me to stay out of the investigation, warned me about staying safe . . . you know, all that stuff."

"It's a lost cause. Should I warn him?"

The joke made me feel even worse. "The bottom line is, he kissed me," I blurted. "I didn't expect it to happen, and I didn't ask for it to happen, but he did, and I thought you should know."

Jawarski studied my face for an uncomfortably long moment. "Did you kiss him back?"

I shook my head. "I don't think so."

"Did you like it?"

"I don't think so."

"But you're not sure."

"No, of course I'm sure. I was shocked, that's all. I had no idea he felt that way about me."

"You didn't? It seemed pretty obvious to me when I saw the two of you together the other night."

I gaped at him. "The night of the murder?"

Jawarski nodded and perched on the corner of his desk. "The man likes you, Abby. The question is, how do you feel about him? Because I'm perfectly content to be patient and let you figure out how you feel about us, but I'm not going to wait around if there's another guy in the mix."

My stomach dropped. Or maybe it was my heart. *Something* slid to the ground by my feet and left an empty hole inside me. "There's not another guy in the mix," I said firmly. "I just told you, I had no idea what he was going to do."

He dipped his head once. "Fair enough."

I could feel myself doing what I always do when my back's to the wall. I got angry. "And don't sit there looking all morally superior, either. Stephanie would be all over you if you gave her half a chance, and don't pretend you don't know it."

"But the point is," he said with aggravating calm, "I don't give her half a chance."

"Meaning, by implication, that I did give Marshall a chance."

"I didn't say that."

"You didn't have to."

"Don't put words in my mouth, Abby."

"Don't imply something and then pretend you didn't. I'm not the only one who's confused around here, Jawarski. And

I'm not the only one dragging a bunch of baggage around with me. You're no more sure of what you want us to be than I am, so don't pretend you are."

"I know what I want," he said, his voice low. "But sometimes I wonder about you. Do you really have feelings for me, or are you just interested in what I can tell you about whatever case I'm working on?"

We were standing there, staring at each other and waiting for the other one to look away or say something, when an officer put his head into the room. "Hey, Jawarski, we've gotta roll. Got a call about a domestic disturbance down in Swede Alley."

Jawarski broke, nodded at him, and glanced back at me. "Sorry. We'll have to finish this later."

I didn't know whether to feel relieved or irritated. "Sure," I said, plunging my hands into my pockets and heading for the door.

"We still on for tomorrow at eight?"

I stopped in the doorway and looked back at him. "Only if you want to be."

"I'll be there."

And I knew I would be, too. I just wished I could get some idea of how the rest of the conversation was going to play out before I got there.

Chapter 27

At seven o'clock on the dot, I led Max onto the porch of Wyatt and Elizabeth's house, handed a cellophane-wrapped teacup filled with pastel candies to my sister-in-law and a bottle of wine to my brother. Wyatt grunted, but I couldn't tell if he appreciated the wine or wished I'd brought beer.

Since Jawarski and I weren't having dinner tonight, I'd called to see if Wyatt and Elizabeth were free. I didn't know how seriously to take Marshall's warning about Kerry Hendrix and his temper, but he wasn't the only person who'd expressed doubts about Kerry. With all these warnings ringing in my ears, it didn't seem right to keep my mouth shut while ten innocent boys spent time around someone who might be dangerous.

Elizabeth kissed my cheek and whispered a thank-you for the teacup, and set it on the counter. She bent to take something from the oven. "I'm so glad you agreed to come for dinner. We don't do this often enough."

Wyatt put the wine on ice and pulled a beer from the fridge. "You said you had something important to talk about?"

"I do, but I think it would be best to wait to talk about it until after dinner. I'm not sure I want the kids to know until you've decided what you want to do. Now, what can I do to help you, Elizabeth?"

She waved away the offer. "Dana and Danielle are going to set the table, and that's about all that's left. Just sit down and relax. You want some wine?"

The lack of sleep and the stress of the past week were all

starting to catch up with me. "Maybe a Coke," I said. "I still have to drive home."

Wyatt found a Coke in the fridge and handed it to me. "If you want to talk about the kids, now's probably a better time than later. Once they come down for supper, it'll be a madhouse around here until almost eleven."

Unexpected longing for a family of my own almost knocked me over. Most of the time I keep that old dream under control, but once in a while it breaks through and knocks me flat. Doing my best to ignore it, I glanced at the vent over Elizabeth's head and pictured the boys hovering over it on the second floor. "That might be a good idea. Do you mind if we go into the living room for a minute?"

"The living room?" Elizabeth looked aghast. "But dinner's almost finished."

Wyatt followed the direction of my gaze, and realization dawned. "Just turn everything down for a few minutes," he told Elizabeth. Then to me, "We won't be long, will we?"

"Not long at all," I promised.

Elizabeth scowled, but she did as we asked, and we migrated into the other room. Keeping my voice low just in case, I filled them in on everything I'd learned about Kerry and my concerns that he was either connected to Hobbs in some way or in danger himself. "I don't know what you want to do," I said when I finished. "I don't have any proof that Hendrix is involved in the murder, and I can't prove that he sent the driver of the SUV after the boys and me, but I didn't want to leave you in the dark."

Wyatt rubbed a hand across his face and shared a look with Elizabeth. "I don't want to say a man's gone bad just because he rubs a few people the wrong way. Hell, if people started thinking that way, I'd be on dozens of lists, myself."

"It's not just that he rubs people the wrong way," Elizabeth said, her face creased with concern. "If you ask me, there's too much going on here to ignore. It seems pretty obvious that Coach Hendrix knew Hobbs, but he's lying about it for some reason. I don't like it."

"That doesn't necessarily mean that he's guilty of murder," I pointed out.

Elizabeth sighed heavily. "I know that, but we don't know for sure, do we? What if he's involved somehow? What if he's in danger, himself? Can we afford to take that chance?"

Wyatt shook his head slowly. "Hell if I know."

"Well, I do," she said firmly. "I don't want the boys on the team anymore. Not if Kerry Hendrix is going to be coaching."

"What are you going to do?" Wyatt asked. "Tell Hendrix he has to quit?"

"If we have to. The boys shouldn't suffer because of his decisions."

Wyatt chuckled. "When you're in charge of the world, sweetheart, you can make sure everything works out fair. This isn't an easy problem to fix. Hendrix isn't the type to quit, even if we threaten him."

"Then let's go to the other parents and warn them," Elizabeth suggested. "If we all band together and demand that he step down, what choice would he have?"

"If he's innocent," I said, "he might sue you for slander. I'd be careful about going that route. Even if he couldn't prove his case, he could make your lives miserable for a long time, and he's just the type to enjoy doing that."

Elizabeth deflated a bit. "But what other choice do we have?"

"I don't think we have one," Wyatt said. "If we want to make sure the boys are safe, we're going to have to pull them from the team."

"I guess you're right," Elizabeth said with a frown. "They're going to be upset, but we can't just let them keep going to practice and games, with so many bad things happening and so much that's unexplained."

Out of nowhere, Caleb spun into the room like a Tasmanian devil, his little face red with fury. "You can't make us quit. That's not fair!"

Elizabeth looked stricken. Wyatt tried to catch his son and stop him from shaking. "It's just for a little while," Wyatt told him, his voice surprisingly gentle. "Just until we can figure out what's going on in town."

"I don't *care* what's going on in town. If you take me off the team, all the boys will say I'm a sissy!"

"Oh, honey, no they won't," Elizabeth said, trying to reassure him.

"Yes they will. They already think I'm a baby, and you're going to make it worse."

"It won't just be you, sport," Wyatt said gently. "Brody will have to sit out for a while, too."

"So?" Caleb shouted. "*He* doesn't have everybody calling him names."

The poor kid looked so miserable, I thought my heart would break. "Caleb, please try to understand—"

He turned on me the instant he heard my voice, and the anger on his young face made me catch my breath. "All the other boys are gonna hate me," he shouted, "and it's all your fault."

"Caleb!" Elizabeth shot to her feet. "You don't talk to your aunt that way. Apologize to her right this minute."

"No. I won't. It *is* her fault. It's *all* her fault." As quickly as he'd appeared, he was gone. I heard his little footsteps thundering up the stairs, and I was dimly aware of the blur that was Wyatt racing out of the room after him.

Chapter 28

"He's only a little boy. He didn't know what he was saying," Karen said when I told her about it the next morning. She stood in a patch of sunlight that streamed inside through the kitchen windows, which made the day look far warmer than it actually was. She shivered and nudged up the thermostat a couple of degrees. Like other old buildings, Divinity is notoriously drafty.

"He knows he hates me," I said as I measured three cups of raisins into a bowl. Caleb still hadn't forgiven me, and I was feeling horribly sorry for myself. Making rum raisin balls seemed like a reasonable way to lift my mood. If the scents of melting chocolate and the steps involved in making the candy didn't work, the rum might. "I wish I could figure out what connection Kerry Hendrix had with the dead guy. He's the one who should be leaving the team."

"Why?"

"Because I don't like him."

"That doesn't make him a murderer," Karen pointed out. "And even if it does, let the police prove it."

Deep down, I knew she was right. I had to have faith in the system. I had to believe that right would prevail. And I *did* . . . deep down. Closer to the surface, I felt like I'd failed my nephews, and I hated knowing that they agreed with me.

I covered the raisins with rum, set them aside to soak for the next three hours, and tried to shake off the foul mood that had been plaguing me all morning. "Is everything ready for the book club meeting?"

"Almost," Karen said. "Liberty's setting up the new meeting room even as we speak, and I've almost finished putting together the sample trays." The Paradise Pageturners had been holding their monthly meetings at Divinity for the past several years. In all the excitement of the impending holiday, the murder, and our new clerk I'd nearly forgotten that the Pageturners had rescheduled their meeting for today. Once again, Karen had covered my backside.

The ladies of the club left the selection of candies up to us every month, and we tried to give them a few old favorites along with a couple of new varieties each time.

Usually, I created the sample trays for the group, but Karen had been chomping at the bit for more responsibility for months. She'd worked part-time at Divinity for Aunt Grace while I was off living my other life, yet Aunt Grace had left the store to me. Feelings of guilt over my inheritance and gratitude toward Karen for helping me learn the ropes convinced me that it was only fair to let her exercise her creative side once in a while, so I'd turned the task over to her this time. This morning, with my nerves on fire and my mood in the toilet, I almost regretted the decision.

"Don't worry," Karen said. "Liberty and I can handle the book club meeting."

"I know you can," I said with a thin smile. "I'm just in a strange mood this morning. Ignore me."

The bell over the front door jangled, and Karen turned away with a grin. "You got it." She was almost out of the kitchen when she turned back. "If you need something to do, why don't you run over to Walgreens and pick up the stuff on that list?" she said with a nod toward a sheet of paper she'd tacked to the bulletin board. "It'll save us time later."

I knew she was just trying to get rid of me, but maybe she was right. My mood wasn't doing anyone any good. I pulled the list from the bulletin board and scanned it quickly. Apparently, we were out of almost everything from paper towels to ibuprofen. I grabbed my keys and the company checkbook from the office and drove the half block to the drugstore so I wouldn't have to haul the supplies back to Divinity on foot.

Inside the store, I managed to get the cart with the wobbly

wheel, and my mood dropped even lower. I could have traded it for another cart, but I was so consumed by self-pity at that point, I couldn't even make myself do that. Battling the cart's determined efforts to circle to the right, I loaded the basket with the items on Karen's list and added a few of my own. By the time I'd gone around the store a couple of times looking for everything, my head had begun to pound to the rhythmic *whap-whap-whap* of the wheel as it hit the metal casing surrounding it.

Finally, I turned toward the cash register, where a young blonde of about eighteen popped her gum and waited for something to do. Britnee, according to her name tag, barely acknowledged my presence, which was fine with me. I wasn't in the mood for idle chitchat anyway. Behind her, a young man worked a feather duster across a row of film with as much enthusiasm as Britnee showed over helping me.

When Britnee was almost finished ringing up my purchases, the young man turned his head and said, "Hey, Brit. Do you know if the schedule for next week is up yet?"

Britnee popped her gum and shook her head. "I don't think so, Chase. She said she might not even do it today."

The young man muttered something under his breath, and Britnee rolled her eyes in response. "I know. I know. But don't tell *me*. Talk to her." She hit the Total button and flashed a bored glance at me. "Comes to ninety-five ninety-eight."

I said a silent prayer of thanks for Liberty's enthusiastic attitude and pulled out the checkbook. As I began to fill out the check, the fog that had been hovering around my head all day lifted, and I realized I was standing in the middle of a potential gold mine of information.

Tossing off a friendly smile, I asked, "Do you mind if I ask the two of you a couple of questions?"

Britnee flicked another couldn't-care-less look in my direction. "About what?"

"About last Monday night. Were you working that night?"

A veil of thin blonde hair fell when Britnee moved her head. She hooked a finger through it and tucked it behind her ear in a movement so automatic, I'm sure she didn't even know she'd done it. "I can't talk to you. My boss has a fit if we stop working to talk to anybody."

Which might explain her stellar people skills. I glanced around quickly, saw no one standing in line behind me, and pulled handful of items from the nearby bargain bin. Still trying to look friendly, I dropped them onto her conveyer belt. "There, now you have to talk to me. Just ring them up slowly, and tell me if you were working last Monday night."

Chase looked up from his dusting. "The night they found the dead guy in the parking lot? We were both here."

Britnee scanned a rubber ball with colorful spikes sticking out all over it and shuddered at the memory. The lock of hair escaped from behind her ear and fell down in front of her face again. "Was that not the freakiest thing ever?" she asked, hooking and tucking without missing a beat.

For the sake of argument, I agreed that it was, indeed, the freakiest thing ever. "You know, I'm the one who found the body. At least, my dog did. Did either of you see it happen?"

"The murder?" Britnee looked almost impressed by my claim to fame as she scanned a closeout can of Pringles and slid it into a bag. "I didn't see a thing, thank God. Did you?" She glanced longingly at Chase, as if she could feel a protective aura emanating from his scrawny body.

Chase ran his feather duster across a rack of magazines and puffed up a bit, no doubt trying to look tough. "I didn't actually *see* it happen, but I came close. I took a bunch of boxes out to the Dumpster about five minutes before they found the guy's body."

Britnee scanned the last item on her belt, but I still had questions. I held up a finger in a signal for her to wait and went back to the bargain bin. I loaded up again, checking price tags quickly to make sure I wasn't going to empty the bank account for a chance to hear what these two had to say.

"Did you see anything unusual?" I asked as I unloaded two decks of cards, a canister of tennis balls with one missing, a couple of kitchen towels, and a bubble pack of flavored lip gloss.

I could tell that Chase wanted to say yes, but he shook his

head reluctantly. "No. I mean, there were cars coming and going, you know? And there were people outside. But I didn't see the dead guy at all."

"That's because he was in here," Britnee said, startling us both.

"He came inside?" I asked.

She nodded solemnly and went through the motions of tucking and looping that errant lock of hair behind her ear once more. "I ought to know. I'm the one who rang him up."

Chase gazed at her with new admiration, as if she'd survived a brush with death in the last twenty seconds, and he'd been there to witness the miracle. "What did he buy?"

"A pack of gum, I think. I don't think he actually wanted it. He was just trying to get away from the guy who was bugging him."

I was finding Britnee more fascinating by the moment. "What guy?"

"The guy he was trying to get away from." Her tone suggested that I needed to pay better attention.

"Right. This is the first I've heard of that," I said. "Do the police know?"

Britnee shrugged lazily. "I guess so."

"You don't know? Does that mean you haven't told them?"

She lifted her gaze to mine. "I didn't talk to them, Sissy did. I don't know what she told them."

"Who's Sissy?"

"The night manager," Chase explained. "If you ask me, she's gone a little nuts since she got her promotion."

I knew the type. There's one in nearly every workplace. "So you didn't actually talk to the police yourself?" I asked Britnee.

"No, Sissy said she had to do it because she's the manager. I told her that was stupid. I mean, *she* didn't see anything, but she didn't care. She wanted to look important."

I sincerely hoped Sissy was about twelve; otherwise, I'd be frightened by the stupidity of that decision. "Did you contact the police later and tell them what you knew?"

Britnee shook her head. "No. I don't want to lose my job."

"And Sissy *would* fire her," Chase said. "She's like that."

They were so young, it was almost painful. "She can't fire you for talking to the police," I assured them. "There are laws."

Chase laughed through his nose. "Yeah? Well, tell Sissy that. But don't expect it to do any good. She'll just do whatever she wants."

I could have enlightened them on a few facts about employment law, but we were losing focus. "Did you see the other man's face? What did he look like?"

Britnee swiped the three-pack of fruity lip gloss across the scanner and pulled a flyer from a stack at the end of the counter. She pushed the flyer toward me. I picked it up and found Quentin Ingersol beaming up at me from a grainy photograph. My head shot up, and my breath caught. "He looked like this guy?"

"No, he *was* that guy."

My heart thumped with excitement. "Are you sure?"

Britnee secured the wayward lock of hair behind her ear again and nodded. "Sure I'm sure. That guy's in the store at least twice a week. I know who he is."

"But you haven't told the police that he was talking to the dead guy right before the murder?"

"No." *Duh!* Britnee shook her head and frowned as if she was losing patience with me. "It's not like he killed the guy. I mean, he's one of our regulars. He's in here all the time." She glanced at the empty conveyer belt and glanced back at me. "Is that it?"

She wasn't the only one losing patience, but I tried to hang on to mine with both hands. I pulled two magazines and a container of breath mints from the rack. "Did you happen to hear anything they said?"

"Who?"

"This guy and the dead guy. You said they were arguing . . ."

Britnee scowled at me. "No I didn't. I said that the dead guy was trying to get away from the other guy."

"Do you know why?"

"This guy—" she tapped Quentin's face with her fingertip, "—kept telling the other guy to back off."

"What did the dead guy say?"

"He laughed. Like it was some kind of joke."

"Do you know what this guy wanted him to back off from?"

"No." Britnee stopped working again and cocked an eyebrow, waiting for me to toss a few more purchases onto the belt.

I decided I'd spent enough on worthless junk and held up both hands. "You didn't hear anything else?"

"I didn't hear anything except that," Britnee said. "The guy in the picture told the dead guy to back off, and the dead guy laughed." She hit the total button and rattled off a new amount, sliding a glance past me to something behind me. "You'd better go anyway," she said softly. "Sissy's back there watching."

Chase, in a self-protective measure, had already moved away. I wrote out the check and tossed it onto the conveyer belt along with two business cards. "Do me a favor, okay? If either of you think of anything else, will you let me know? You can find me at the candy shop on Prospector Street."

Chapter 29

I left Divinity earlier than usual that afternoon for
basketball practice. I hadn't seen Kerry since our run-in at the
convenience store, and now that Wyatt and Elizabeth had
taken Brody and Caleb off the team, I had no idea what his
mood would be. If he was going to cop an attitude with me, I
wanted him to do it before the boys arrived.

I'd called Elizabeth earlier to see how Brody and Caleb
were feeling about being sidelined. Neither of the boys
wanted to speak to me, but Elizabeth assured me they'd get
over their disappointment soon. Kids were resilient, she assured me. I hoped she was right.

The parking lot was nearly empty when I pulled in, so it
wasn't hard to make sure there were no dark-colored SUVs
lurking in the shadows. Even though lights spilled out of the
windows and illuminated the sidewalks, I didn't see another
soul until I let myself through the front door and into the reception area.

There, a young woman with curly dark hair sat at the front
desk, the phone wedged between ear and shoulder. She
smiled vaguely in my direction as I walked past her, but she
was so deep in conversation, I wasn't sure she actually saw
me. The windows of the administrative offices were already
dark, indicating that the office staff had already gone home,
but the faint sound of exercise equipment floated up the stairs
from the work-out room in the basement. At least one hearty
soul was in the center that evening.

I checked the gym to make sure Kerry wasn't already
there, then stepped into the ladies' room. I had a few minutes
to kill and nothing to do, so I spent a little while pretending to

make myself presentable: a quick sweep of a brush through my hair, a swipe at the lips with the remnants dug out of an old pot of Carmex I found in the bottom of my bag, a quick adjustment to the shoulders of my sweater, and a tug at the hem. I'm not sure I made any real difference to my appearance, but at least I'd tried.

After washing my hands, I reached for the door handle, but the sound of raised voices somewhere nearby made me stop with the door only partway open. Two men, from the sound of it. Two very *angry* men speaking in hushed, heated tones.

Deciding that discretion was the better part of . . . something, I let the door inch shut again. Almost. Curiosity trumps discretion any day. Maybe I was eavesdropping, but how else would I know when I could leave the bathroom without interrupting?

I couldn't make out what the men were saying at first, but it didn't take long before my ears adjusted to the ebb and flow of background noise and I began to pick up snippets of their argument.

". . . if anybody finds out, I'm through. You know that don't you?"

"Quit being so damn melodramatic. Who's going to . . . ?"

Intrigued, I leaned a bit closer to the narrow opening I'd left myself. The men couldn't be far from where I stood. I could make out shadows moving on the wall across from me as they talked.

". . . proof somewhere. You know she's got it."

"And she'll be taken care of. Don't worry about that."

That sent a chill through me, and suddenly eavesdropping on their argument stopped being only a mildly entertaining diversion. Who was "she"? And what did he mean by "taken care of"?

"That's good," the first man said, his voice suddenly crystal clear and so close I caught my breath, "because if you screw this up, I'll lose everything. I'm already damn close to losing it now. This is *not* what we agreed on."

"Relax, would you?" His companion must have moved

closer, too, and I suddenly recognized one of the speakers. "You know why she's come back," Quentin Ingersol said. "You know what we need from her. Once we have that, it'll be over."

My breath caught, and my heart thudded in my chest. Two women had recently returned to Paradise: Liberty and Ginger. Which one were they talking about?

"It had better be," the second man growled. "Because if it's not . . ." His voice sounded vaguely familiar, but I couldn't place it. It didn't sound like Kerry, but I was pretty sure that whoever it was, I'd talked to him recently.

The voices faded away, and the shadows on the wall moved toward the front of the building, too far for me to hear what the men were saying. I leaned my head against the cool tile wall and concentrated on breathing while I replayed the bits of conversation I'd heard in my mind. Who were they talking about? What did they need? And who was the second man?

I stood there shaking, running through the list of men I'd spoken with in the past week or so. Dwayne, Marshall. Kerry. Who else? Richie, Dylan. Gavin. I racked my brain, not daring to step out of the ladies' room until I knew I wasn't alone in the hallway with a couple of killers.

When I heard the first of the boys arrive for practice, I sucked it up and let myself out of my tile-walled sanctuary.

Kerry was already in the gym with the kids, and his posture stiffened noticeably when he saw me. "About time you joined us, Shaw. I need you to gather up the permission slips for the away game the boys took home last time. And the equipment's in my truck." He lobbed his keys across the court toward me. "Go get it."

It took a lot of nerve to treat a fellow volunteer with such scorn, and I was in no mood for Kerry's attitude. I caught the keys and lobbed them back at him. "I don't think so. Considering the accusations you've made against me, I think it would be better if I kept my distance from your truck."

Color rushed into his face, and his eyes grew cold. A muscle in his jaw twitched repeatedly. Very slowly, he dragged his gaze away from mine and tossed the keys to Jason Pacheco, one of the older boys on the team. "Take someone with you, Jason."

Jason bobbed his head once, jerked his head at Ryan Goddard, and jogged toward the rear doors. Coach and I stood for a long moment staring each other down until a bored voice sounded in the doorway behind me. "Coach Hendrix? Phone call for you on line one," and broke the tension. At least for the moment.

I had enough time after practice that evening to run home, change into clean black slacks and a sweater, and run a brush through my hair before meeting Jawarski for dinner. Brody and Caleb might not be on the team at the moment, but I'd made a promise to all the members of the team, and I felt an obligation to their parents to make sure they were safe.

On a whim, I replaced the old Carmex with a layer of the strawberry-kiwi lip gloss I'd picked up at Walgreens and brushed a hint of blush on my cheeks. A couple of minutes after eight, I pushed through the glass door to the restaurant and stepped into a crowd of people waiting to be seated. I knew Jawarski was already there, because I'd seen his truck in the parking lot when I cruised through.

Inside, soft Asian music played on a PA system, and the host, a young man of about twenty, spoke rapid Thai into the house phone. The door shut behind me, setting off the oddly discordant yet soothing sounds of bamboo wind chimes. I glanced into the dining room, peering between bamboo plants strategically placed to give the illusion of privacy.

Jawarski had already been seated, and he waved me over to our table. I was starving and more than ready for dinner, but seeing Jawarski sitting there in a crisp white shirt under his good black jacket wiped all thoughts of food out of my head for a full thirty seconds.

He stood as I approached the table, a gentleman of the old school, and his eyes lit with an appreciative gleam. I thought that was only fair, since I'm sure mine were pretty well lit also. He pulled out a chair for me, held it the way boys used to be taught in school, and then resumed his seat across from mine.

"You're looking terrific tonight," he said. "Basketball must agree with you."

I laughed, so relieved that we were going to start off on a pleasant note I probably sounded giddy. "I'm not so sure about that. It may just be the death of me."

Jawarski signaled the waiter, and a moment later a glass of Thai tea appeared on the table. I'm a pushover for touches like that, and he knows it. I took that as a sign that he'd calmed down enough to realize that I hadn't exactly tripped Marshall and then beat him to the floor to get that kiss.

"Trouble on the team?" he asked.

I shrugged and stirred my tea. "I'm not sure if there's trouble on the team or just with my portion of it. Wyatt and Elizabeth pulled the boys from the team, and the boys blame me."

I waited for one of those *Well, what did you expect?* faces, but that's not what I got. Jawarski's eyes softened, and he touched my hand gently. "Ah hell, slugger. I'm sorry. I know how much those kids mean to you."

I could have handled an I-told-you-so, but that just about did me in. His eyes were so kind, I had to look away, and only Karen's voice running through my head and warning me not to screw this up kept me from pulling my hand away from his. A solid block of something filled my throat, and my eyes burned. I hate crying more than almost anything, but still I forced myself to stay where I was. I just hoped Jawarski would appreciate my sacrifice.

Finally, I found the ability to move my head and managed a small nod. "It's fine."

"Yeah." Jawarski ran his thumb across the back of my hand, then slowly let it go. "I can see that." He leaned back in his chair and gazed around the restaurant, giving me a few seconds to pull myself together.

That's the problem with Jawarski. One minute I'm so frustrated by him I'm ready to turn around and walk away; the next he does something so thoughtful I wonder what my life would be like now if he disappeared from it. That thought terrified me. After the breakup of my marriage, I'd vowed never to let myself become dependent on a man again. I'd been so careful to draw clear lines between my life and Jawarski's. I'd kept him at arm's length longer than he wanted me to, and much longer than I wanted to, yet I still hadn't managed to achieve the measure of independence I wanted for myself.

"So," he said after a lengthy pause, "where were we, when we were so rudely interrupted the other day?"

"I think you were accusing me of encouraging Marshall Ames."

Jawarski gave that some thought and shook his head. "No, if I remember right, we'd already worked through that, and you'd just observed that I'm an emotional wreck of a man carting around so much baggage, you keep tripping over it." His face didn't betray any emotion, but his eyes danced with amusement, and I knew we'd both moved past the edge of the cliff we'd been standing on yesterday.

"I think you're right," I conceded. "I *was* in the process of pointing out how annoying all that baggage can be for someone as emotionally healthy as I am."

Jawarski grinned lazily. "Yeah?"

"Yeah."

He sobered again and said, "Listen, Abby. About what I said yesterday . . . It was a shitty thing to say."

I felt my own smile slide from my face. "Yeah," I said. "It was."

"I shouldn't have said it."

"No," I said. "You shouldn't."

He fell silent, and his eyes slowly roamed my face. After a long time, he shrugged. "That's all. I just wanted you to know that it was a shitty thing to say."

I like the fact that he's not sappy. I'm not either, so it seems to work. "You're a little late, Jawarski. I knew it was horrid the minute it came out of your mouth."

"Well, then, next time how about filling me in?"

"You got it." I waited for a second and tried to look annoyed. "That's it? You're not even going to apologize?"

He pretended to think about that for a few seconds, then shook his head. "Nope. I think that's it."

I reached across the table and punched his arm with more affection than irritation, and we spent the next few minutes poring over our menus and discussing the pros and cons of several choices. After we'd ordered, Jawarski rested both arms on the table and smiled slowly. "Thought you might be interested to know that we got a lead on Hobbs today."

Jawarski offering me information about a case was so unexpected, I choked on my tea. He came halfway out of his chair to pat me on the back—which did nothing except knock my breath away each time I almost caught it. When I could breathe again, I waved him back into his chair and picked up as if I hadn't spent the past five minutes coughing and sputtering. "What did you find out?"

"He was renting a room from a woman named Corelle Davies. She runs a Laundromat over on the north side."

"Have you talked to her?"

He nodded. "We have. She didn't have a lot to add, except that Hobbs had been living there for about two months."

That fit with what I'd already learned. "If he was here that long, why didn't anybody notice him around town?"

"I'm sure some people did," Jawarski said, leaning back to avoid hitting our server as he slid a plate of egg rolls in front of us. "It was just never an issue until he turned up dead."

I opened a package of disposable chopsticks and spent a few seconds thinking about that while I rubbed the sticks together to get rid of loose splinters. "Did his landlady say whether he had friends?"

"We asked. She didn't notice anyone hanging around."

"So Hobbs just rented a room from her and then lived there in seclusion until the night he fell onto the highway in front of my car?"

Jawarski picked up a piece of egg roll and dipped it in the fish sauce. "That seems to be the story so far."

"Yeah, well, I don't believe it. In fact, I think Hobbs was a very busy boy from the time he came to Paradise until the night he died." I leaned in close to make sure I wasn't overheard. "I talked to a couple of kids who work at Walgreens. One of them saw Hobbs talking to Quentin Ingersol just a few minutes before he turned up dead."

Jawarski's brows knit. "My men interviewed those employees—"

"Yeah, I know, but the checkout girl wasn't allowed to talk to the police. Her manager did all the talking." I gave him Britnee's name and added Chase's for good measure. "I don't know how much they'll be willing to tell you. They're both under the impression that they can be fired for talking to you, so you might want to find them when they're not working."

Jawarski nodded and nudged the last piece of egg roll toward me. "Did she happen to hear what Hobbs and Ingersol were talking about?"

I polished off the egg roll and drained my tea. "Britnee said that Quentin told Hobbs to back off. What do you suppose that meant?"

"I have no idea, but I plan to find out."

"I also overheard Quentin having an argument with someone tonight at the recreation center. I couldn't hear everything, but they were talking about a woman who supposedly has proof of something."

"Oh?" Jawarski looked up, obviously interested. "How did you manage to overhear them?"

"I was in the ladies' room. They were right outside."

"You were eavesdropping."

"Not intentionally. Not at first, anyway. But when I realized they were having an argument, I wasn't going to walk out into the middle of it."

He grinned and picked up a piece of pickled carrot with his chopsticks. "Good plan. Any idea who Ingersol was arguing with?"

"None. Sorry."

We ate in silence for a few seconds, but something was still bothering me, and I had to ask, "Why are you discussing the case with me?"

"You object?"

"No, but it's definitely a change of pace. Usually, you do that whole cop thing. You know, the 'stay out of the investigation' bit?"

Jawarski chuckled. "And you always do exactly what I say."

"Well, of course I don't. Don't be ridiculous."

"Look," Jawarski said, his smile fading slightly, "it's not that big a deal. It just occurred to me that the more information I withhold from you, the more eager you seem to investigate on your own. I thought it couldn't hurt to see what you'd do if I gave a bit more."

"Ah, I see. It's just a ploy."

"I wouldn't call it that," Jawarski protested mildly. "I'd say it's more of a strategy."

I made a face. "Same thing. And what if I don't change my evil ways?"

He shrugged and took my hand again. "I guess we'll have to cross that bridge when we come to it, won't we?"

Chapter 30

Jawarski and I stayed late, eating, talking, laughing—
both of us apparently reluctant to end the evening, neither of
us willing to take that next step and suggest we go home together. I'm just old-fashioned enough to believe that once
you take that step, there's no turning back. You're in it all the
way, whether you want to be or not.

When the restaurant closed, we walked through the parking lot together, arms linked around each other's waists.
Again, the longing to have someone permanent in my life
rose up strong and hot. I'd missed this—dinners together,
long walks in the moonlight, intimate conversations about
absolutely nothing—but I needed a bit longer before I could
let myself trust it.

After a long time, Jawarski settled me in the Jetta and
walked to his truck on the other side of the parking lot. I could
have watched him walk forever, but I knew he wouldn't leave
until he saw me drive off, so I started the car and pulled out
onto the nearly deserted street, heading home. Jawarski
pulled out behind me and turned in the opposite direction,
and his taillights disappeared before I reached my first turn.

For the first time in days, I didn't think about the murder.
It had been too wonderful an evening to spoil with thoughts
of dead bodies and knife wounds. I wound along the curving
two-lane road that separated the Lotus Blossom from the
west end of town, slowing as I came around the curve near the
recreation center.

I was surprised to see the beam from someone's headlights on the grassy slope between the center and the base-

ball/soccer fields. Wondering who was at the center this late, I slowed and glanced into the parking lot as I drove past. When I spotted Coach Hendrix's familiar Ford truck, I tapped the brakes to slow the car even more.

In the gleam of the headlights, I saw someone moving around. A few feet farther down the road, I realized there were two people there. One was Kerry Hendrix, the other the increasingly lumpy figure of Dwayne Escott.

So the two of them were still friends. Or at least on speaking terms. I pulled to the side of the road and turned out my headlights, hoping they wouldn't notice me there. They talked for a few minutes, their breath forming thick clouds in the cold November air. The conversation looked so normal at first, I wasn't sure whether I was disappointed or relieved.

After a while, Kerry turned toward the truck as if the conversation was over, but Dwayne had other ideas. In a move swifter than I would have imagined for such a large man, he grabbed Kerry's shoulder and jerked him back around so they were facing each other again. Dwayne leaned toward Kerry aggressively, his arms waving wildly in broad, agitated gestures.

Kerry jerked away from him, shoving Dwayne in the chest with both hands. The shove caught Dwayne off guard, and his arms windmilled wildly as he tried to regain his balance. Kerry took advantage of the moment and jumped into the cab of his truck and, with one last parting shout out his open window, drove off.

I stayed where I was until Dwayne calmed down and walked around to the front of the recreation center. When I was relatively certain that neither of them would see me, I pulled away from the curb and headed for home.

I called Jawarski the minute I found a signal again, but the call went straight to his voice mail. I left a message and drove home, where I poured a Pepsi over ice and turned on the TV for the background noise. Within minutes I was caught up in a list of questions that seemed to be growing by the day.

What *had* Kerry and Dwayne been arguing about? And

who had been in the hall of the recreation center with Quentin? What did Lou Hobbs, Kerry Hendrix, Quentin Ingersol, and Dwayne Escott have in common? There must be something. What were Hobbs and Ingersol arguing about—excuse me, *discussing*—right before the murder? And what really happened the night I thought I'd seen Hobbs shot out at Hammond Junction?

I spent the next morning taking a quick inventory of supplies, but by noon I'd decided that I had a batch of laundry upstairs that desperately needed to be put through the washer and dryer—and there was only one place with the equipment to do the job right.

Old maps of Paradise divide the town into distinct sections, with Chinatown running along the creek bed and Swede Alley just above that. If you follow Swede Alley half a mile north, you'll find yourself surrounded by modest single-family houses and apartment buildings, schools, and the less glamorous businesses no town can survive without.

I pulled up in front of the Laundromat and climbed out into the brilliant autumn sunshine. Someone had propped open the Laundromat's door with a plastic carton, and the clean scents of laundry soap and fabric softener drifted out into the morning. I could see a couple of people milling around inside the building, one heavily pregnant woman sitting with her feet up and flipping idly through a magazine, and a couple of dark-haired, dark-eyed kids darting amid the carts and chairs as they played.

I rolled down the windows for Max, grabbed the laundry basket from my backseat, and carried the load into the building. It had been a while since I'd done my laundry in public, and all the reasons why I didn't came rushing back the moment I stepped through the door. Personally, I think there *is* a hell—and it's a Laundromat.

I took a few seconds to get my bearings, then gritted my teeth and found an empty machine close to the "office"—a corner separated from the rest of the Laundromat by a long table—where a slight woman with white hair was folding towels. She wore a pair of knit blue pants and a turtleneck sweater with a snowflake design. Over it all, she wore a lime-green smock with huge pockets.

After stuffing my clothes into the washer, I sprinkled soap powder over the mound and fed a handful of quarters into the machine. When the washer started filling, I wandered over to the office.

The woman glanced up as I approached. Her small, wrinkled hands stilled in the act of smoothing the towel she'd just folded. "Yeah? Do you need something?" Her voice was a surprise. Rough—probably from years of smoking—and far deeper than I would've expected to hear coming out of a woman her size.

I jerked a thumb toward the metal box on the wall. "I didn't see any fabric softener. Do you have any I could buy?"

She nodded toward a wall that housed a bank of dryers and cut partway through the large room. "Fabric softener's in the vending machine on the other side of that wall."

"Oh. Thanks." I turned away, then glanced back. "Is your name Corelle Davies?"

She glanced up, her eyes narrowed with wariness. "Who wants to know?"

"My name is Abby Shaw. I own a business here in town—"

Corelle began shaking her head before I'd finished talking. "Whatever it is you're selling, we don't want any." She jerked her thumb toward a sign on the wall behind her. "No soliciting, or can't you read?"

"I'm not selling anything," I assured her quickly. "I'm just trying to find someone who knew an acquaintance of mine. His name was Hobbs, and I heard that he might have rented a room from you."

Corelle squinted up at me. "Where did you hear that?"

Jawarski might have been willing to talk about the case with me, but I didn't think he'd appreciate my dropping his name, so I evaded the question. "I don't know. Around. Would you mind if I ask you just a couple of questions? It won't take long."

"I already answered all the questions I'm gonna. You want to know what I said to the police, you can ask them."

"Thanks, I'll do that. Did you know Hobbs before you rented the room to him?"

Corelle grabbed another towel from the basket at her side. "Nope."

"So he just found you through a newspaper ad or something?"

"Or something. How should I know?"

"He didn't tell you?"

She snapped the towel in the air and folded it in half. "He didn't tell, I didn't ask. Now, if you'll excuse me, I'm busy."

"Sure. Just one more thing before I go. Did he tell you *anything* about himself? Where he came from? What he was doing here in town? How long he planned to stay?"

Corelle finished folding the towel and put it on top of the stack. "We didn't talk much. He came and went. I rarely saw him." She eyeballed me for a minute and asked, "You with the police or something?"

"Not exactly. So Hobbs didn't tell you why he was here?"

Corelle picked up the stack of towels and carried them to the other side of the office area. "You tell me why you're asking first."

"It's personal."

"Yeah? Well, so are my answers." She fished a pack of cigarettes from a pocket of her smock and turned toward the open door. I guess she thought the conversation was over.

Not being one to let a little thing like that stop me, I followed her outside. "So he didn't tell you why he was here?"

She lit a cigarette and inhaled until her cheeks caved in. "If you leave now, I won't call the cops on you."

"If I leave now, I won't find out what I want to know. Come on, Corelle. What's the harm in answering a few questions—unless you have something to hide?"

She glared at me, her eyes hard and pebbly. "You don't give up, do you?"

"Afraid not."

"Who did you say you were again?"

"My name's Abby Shaw. I own a candy shop downtown."

"Yeah? I knew a lady owned a candy shop once. Name of Grace Something."

"Grace was my great-aunt." I'm not above name dropping when it might do me some good.

Corelle looked interested. "No kidding? You Tuck and Elaine's girl?" I nodded, and she exhaled a thick plume of smoke. "Well, I'll be. Why didn't you just say so? What do you want to know?"

Who could have guessed it would be so simple? "Did Lou Hobbs tell you why he was in Paradise?"

"He told me he was here on business, but I don't think he was telling the truth."

"Oh? Why not?"

"Because he mentioned a couple of places that haven't been around here in a while, like the roller rink over on Fairmont and Ray's Drive-In. If you want my opinion, he's been here before, but not for ten, fifteen years."

That set me back a couple of paces. The places she'd mentioned had been popular teen hangouts for years, but they'd both gone out of business while I was living in California. Did that mean that Hobbs was from Paradise? That might explain his connections to Ingersol and Hendrix, but if he'd lived here, why hadn't anyone else come forward to say that they recognized him?

"Did he tell you what kind of business he had here in town?"

Corelle watched the smoke drifting up from the end of her cigarette. "If he did, I've forgotten. He was a quiet one, I can tell you that. Didn't talk much at all. I tried making friendly conversation when he first moved in, but I guess he wasn't interested in talking to an old lady."

"What about visitors? Did he ever have any?"

"None that I ever saw, except the first day he came to look at the place. Had a friend with him that day."

Interesting. I wondered why she hadn't mentioned that to the police. "Do you know who it was?"

She shook her head. "Don't know his name, but I've seen him around. Big fella, kind of balding. Blond hair."

Quentin Ingersol? He was tall and blond, and looking more suspicious by the minute. Or—Marshall? The thought made me almost sick. Or could it have been Dwayne? "And

Hobbs? Did you run a background check on him before you rented the room to him?"

Corelle gave a sharp laugh. "Now, how would I go about doing that? I don't have that kind of money. Most of the time, I barely get from one end of the month to the other." She took her last drag and crushed out the cigarette beneath her foot. "Besides, he seemed all right."

"Why do you say that?"

"I asked for a deposit, but he said he didn't have enough money. He'd been down on his luck, and he was here to get back on his feet. That's when his friend popped up and guaranteed that the rent would be paid."

"The blond man."

Corelle nodded.

"And you believed him."

"I didn't have any reason not to."

I could think of a few, but I kept them to myself. "Did you happen to notice what kind of car they were in that day?"

"Sure. I may not know the driver, but I'd know that car anywhere." Corelle turned toward the door and grinned at me over her shoulder. "They were driving Marion Escott's Cadillac."

Chapter 31

"Abby! You remembered!" Beaming with delight, Marion Escott pushed open her screen door and ushered me into the cool, dark interior of her house. I held out the box of caramels I'd gone back to the shop to pick up, and glanced around to see if Dwayne was lurking nearby. I couldn't see him, but I hadn't noticed him immediately last time I was here either.

"I put in all your favorites, plus a couple of new varieties," I told Marion as I sat on the sofa. "I hope you like them."

"I know I will." Marion set the box aside and looked at me expectantly. "You look worried, dear. Is something wrong?"

"I'm not sure," I said, trying to ease into the conversation. "Is Dwayne around today?"

"Dwayne?" Marion scowled in confusion. "Do you need to talk to him?"

"I'm not sure," I said again. The fact that she hadn't actually answered my question wasn't lost on me, but Marion has always been notoriously protective of her babies. "Maybe I misunderstood what he said last time I was here, but I thought he told me he hadn't seen a man with a limp around town."

Marion's spine straightened almost imperceptibly, but I knew she sensed a threat. "If you're talking about the man who was murdered in town, I'm sure that's what he said. Dwayne wouldn't know anyone like that."

Yeah. He was obviously too classy to know any murdered people. "Has he been driving your car while he's here?"

"Sometimes, why?"

"I'm afraid somebody saw him in town with Lou Hobbs, the murder victim, a couple of weeks before the murder."

"That's ridiculous. Whoever told you that is lying."

I didn't want to put Corelle in the hot seat, so I left her name out of it. "The person I talked to said that Dwayne was driving your car."

Marion shook her head firmly. "Impossible. Dwayne told you he didn't know that man. If he says he didn't, then he didn't."

I wondered what kind of mother and grandmother I would have made. Would I have been able to look at my offspring honestly, or would I have put blinders on and refused to see them as they really were? "Has he ever mentioned the name Lou Hobbs to you before?"

"Was that the murdered man? Of course not."

"What about Kerry Hendrix or Quentin Ingersol? Are either of them friends of his?"

Clearly angry, Marion got to her feet and shoved the box of caramels at me. "I don't know why you're asking all of these ridiculous questions, Abby, but I don't like it. Dwayne is a good boy. He hasn't done anything wrong, and he doesn't know the man who was murdered. Now, I'll thank you to leave."

Disappointed but not surprised, I stood. I couldn't think of any argument for staying, so I let her usher me outside again. The door slammed behind me, and I stood on the porch trying to decide what to do next. I was halfway down the driveway when I heard a loud bang coming from the garage and realized that Dwayne must be hard at work out there.

Without giving myself a chance to think twice, I hurried down the driveway. The rolling door on the garage was closed, but the side door stood partway open, and another loud bang told me I'd been right. Dwayne was inside.

I knocked lightly on the door and stepped inside the garage at the same time. Large pieces of furniture lined the walls, blocked the windows, and threw the whole garage into shadow. I could see a single bare bulb hanging from the rafters at the back of the garage, but the place was so crammed full of furniture I wasn't sure how to get back there. "Dwayne? Are you in here?"

Something metal clanged loudly, and an instant later

Dwayne materialized out of the clutter. He held something in his hand, but I couldn't get a good look at it. I was too busy looking at the unwelcome scowl on his face. "What in the hell do you want?"

That was a good question. I wanted answers, but it seemed like a good idea to be cautious about how I went after them. I decided to act as if our encounter at the bank had never happened. "I was just talking to your grandmother. She said you were out here, and I thought I'd come out and see what it is you do."

He darted a rapid glance at something behind him. "This isn't a good time. Come back later."

That glance made my internal radar go off, and I'd have bet the farm he was hiding something back there. In fact, the whole setup felt funny to me. A row of carefully cut wooden decorations stretched away on the floor in front of me. They were beautifully crafted and intricate, but they were obviously new. In that instant, I understood that this wasn't an ordinary workshop, and Dwayne wasn't restoring old tables and chairs.

"Sure. That's cool," I said, trying to look as if I meant it. "I don't want to intrude. I'm just curious, that's all. Your grandmother can't say enough about the work you're doing."

"Yeah? Well. Whatever." Dwayne shifted his weight, and the part of him that had still been in shadow moved into the light. He was holding a massive wrench in both hands, and the sight of it made my stomach turn over. "What did you need to talk to Grandma about?"

I wasn't planning on provoking him, but I calculated my chances of outrunning him just in case. Considering his bulk and the way his pants hung low on his hips, I figured the odds were slightly in my favor. "I didn't need to talk to her about anything. I brought her that box of caramels I've been promising her."

"That so?" He cocked a look at the box in my hands. "Then why do *you* still have it?"

That was another good question. I held out the box impulsively. "I brought this one for you."

He didn't look convinced, but he took the box from me,

and I considered that a step in the right direction. He put the wrench down on an unfinished two-drawer dresser with a deep scar running up the side and pawed through the first layer of caramels. I breathed a sigh of relief that I wasn't in imminent danger of having my head broken. If he'd been on the verge of attacking, he'd still be holding the wrench.

The candy didn't relax him, though. He was definitely worried about me seeing something. Every glance into a corner, every shift of his beady little eyes, only convinced me more.

"I think I may have misunderstood something you told me the other day," I said as he shoved a piece of candy into his mouth. "Didn't you say you hadn't seen the guy with the limp?"

Dwayne's eyes flicked away from the candy and landed on my face. "That's right."

"Was that before or after you guaranteed to pay the rent on his apartment if he couldn't?"

"Who said I did that?"

"I happened to run into his landlady today. She mentioned that you were with him when he rented the room from her."

Dwayne swallowed the caramel and growled, "Bitch."

"Are you saying you weren't with him?"

He glowered at me from beneath a thick line of sandy-colored eyebrow and shoved the box of candy at me. "I'm not saying nothin'. Why don't you take your candy and get out?"

After he'd had his dirty fingers all over the box? Was he nuts? I shook my head and pressed the box back at him. "Keep it. Throw it away. Whatever. Why did you lie about knowing Lou Hobbs?"

Dwayne jammed the lid on the box and tossed it onto a table. "I don't have to answer your questions."

I kept one eye on the wrench, just in case. "No, but you will have to talk to the police when they get here."

"You gonna rat me out?"

"They're going to find out you knew Hobbs sooner or later," I said with a shrug. "If you didn't kill him, why don't you just admit it?"

He snatched the wrench again and whipped around to glare at me. "Don't you dare try to pin that on me. I didn't touch that sonofabitch."

I felt myself flinch, but I forced myself to hold my ground. He wasn't out of control yet, but he *was* trying to intimidate me. "Can you prove that?"

"I don't have to. Not to you."

"No, but you might have to prove it to the police. Where were you last Monday night, Dwayne?"

"Go to hell."

"Does that mean you *don't* have an alibi?"

"Not that it's any of your business, but I was right here, working."

"What time?"

"All evening. Whatever time Lou Hobbs got himself whacked." He stared at me, hard. "I didn't kill him, so get the hell out of here, and let me get back to work."

That sounded like good advice, but I still had a couple of questions, and I might not get another chance to ask them. "How did you know him?"

"That's none of your business."

"Did you know him when he used to live here?"

In the blink of an eye, the anger left his face, and nervousness replaced it. "Where did you hear that?"

"Around. Is that how you know him?"

"Lou Hobbs never lived here," he said, leaning in so close I could smell something sour on his breath. "You got that?"

An uncomfortable warning darted up my spine, and this time I *did* draw back. "I don't believe you. I think Hobbs did live somewhere around here, and I think that's how you and Quentin and Kerry know him."

Dwayne straightened sharply. "You think you're so smart, don't you? You think you have it all figured out, but you don't know shit."

The look in his eyes stopped me cold, and suddenly I understood the reason for his edginess. "You know who killed him, don't you?"

"I don't know anything."

"I think you do. I think you know exactly what happened, and I think you know why. So why haven't you gone to the police?"

In one quick movement, Dwayne took me by the shoulders, spun me around, and propelled me toward the door. "I don't know anything," he said again, "especially not who killed Lou Hobbs." He shoved me out onto the lawn with such force, I nearly lost my balance. "Now go away and leave me alone."

He slammed the door between us, I heard the lock turn, and reluctantly I admitted that our conversation was over. I could see Marion watching me from her kitchen window, and I knew I'd just lost a friend and Divinity had lost a long-time customer. But I consoled myself with the knowledge that she was in serious denial. Dwayne was lying. I could feel that in every cell of my body. He *knew* who the murderer was. All I had to do now was get him to tell the police.

Chapter 32

I tried to call Jawarski on my way back to Divinity, but ended up having to leave a message. The delay in telling him what I knew chafed, but there was nothing I could do. I'd see him that night for Richie and Dylan's party, but I didn't want to talk about the murder there.

He'd apologized, Jawarski style, for the comment he'd made while we were in his office, and I was no longer hurt by it, but I couldn't forget it. I wanted to show him that I wasn't only interested in him for his connections, and the best way I knew to do that was to avoid talking about the murder.

I went straight back to work. Karen had been pulling so much of the weight around Divinity lately, I gave her the afternoon off and spent the rest of the day catching up on all of the things I should have been doing in the shop.

By the time we locked the doors, Liberty and I had polished most of the glass, mopped the black-and-white checked floors, and given the wrought-iron chairs and tables a thorough cleaning. We'd restocked the shelves Karen hadn't been able to get to, and even spent a few minutes brainstorming next month's window display.

At seven, I raced upstairs, changed into a new pair of black pants and a suede tunic in a shade the online catalog had called "bark." Satisfied that the color really didn't wash out my skin tone or make me look ready to pass out, I slipped on a pair of low heels (I am *so* not a stiletto gal) and gave my appearance a final once-over.

Jawarski and I had agreed to meet at the party, so I opened a jar of peanut butter so Max would have something to do besides chew my shoes and take inventory of the bathroom garbage. Once I was satisfied that Max was content, I headed out.

Parking near the Silver River Inn is impossible under normal circumstances. When Richie and Dylan entertain, it's a nightmare. I circled the inn forever before I finally found a spot wide enough to wedge the Jetta into. Slipping my keys into my pocket, I resisted the urge to rush up the stairs. Making a good entrance into a room isn't my strong point, but I do try not to barge in red-faced and out of breath.

Richie spotted me the instant I came inside and swept down on me like a hawk. "Don't you look *fabulous*? Where did you find that gorgeous blouse?"

I started to tell him, and he put a finger to my lips and stared at me, horrified. "Darling, *never* tell where you got your clothes. Never, ever, ever. Be flattered that someone asks, but don't give away your secrets."

"It's not much of a secret," I told him.

He waved me off with a flick of his wrist and a purse of his lips. "And that's part of your problem, if you don't mind me saying." He weaved a little on his feet, and I caught a whiff of alcohol on his breath, which is how I knew we were in for a long night filled with lots of gossip. Richie loves hanging over the back fence any time, but especially after he's had a drink or two.

I linked my arm through his and strolled into the room with him in tow. Since my last visit, the place had been transformed. Hundreds of tiny white lights twinkled from the rock around the fireplace, the support pillars that held up the loft overhead, and every other surface that could possibly be lit. The cornucopia centerpieces spilled their bounty onto tables set with sparkling crystal and gleaming silver. The china looked old and exquisite, each piece rimmed by a single gold band that blended perfectly with the centerpieces.

Guests milled about, most holding a glass and taking care not to bump into the tables. "This is beautiful," I told Richie. "Did you do this?"

He shook his head and grinned. "Dylan did most of it. Isn't he incredible?"

"That's almost an understatement," I agreed. "Have you seen Jawarski yet? I'm supposed to meet him here."

"Not yet." Richie waved to someone across the room and nudged me farther into the room. "Rachel's here somewhere, though, and Ginger—the owner of the antique shop I was telling you about—?" He paused and waited for me to indicate that I remembered. "She's right over there. See the tall blond guy by the window?"

I spotted Ginger talking to a tall man with wheat-blond hair and a superior smile. A few feet away, Marshall stood by himself, watching Richie and me. His gaze made me uncomfortable, and the memory of that stupid kiss came rushing back. I shoved it away and focused on Ginger's companion. "You invited Quentin Ingersol?"

"Yes. Do you know him?"

"We've met."

Richie pulled his gaze away from whatever he'd been watching and settled it on me. "Is there a problem there I should know about?"

I shook my head. "Not really. I went to his office to ask him some questions. Let's just say he was pretty creative with his answers."

"Quentin? That surprises me. Dylan really likes him. Me?" Richie held out a hand and wiggled it from side to side. "Not so much. So what were you asking him about?"

At the risk of getting creative with my own answers, I decided that telling Richie the truth in his current condition would be only slightly less public than putting my response on a billboard. "I don't even remember. It wasn't important."

Richie seemed to accept that, but about ten seconds later he whipped around, mouth open, and wagged a hand at me. "I know what it was. You were talking to him about the murder, weren't you?"

A movement in the hallway behind me caught my eye, and I saw Jawarski coming toward me. Richie had announced his guess so loudly, several people standing nearby turned to look at us. I motioned for Richie to be quiet and lowered my own voice as far as I could and still be heard. "I really don't want to talk about that tonight, okay?"

"But it was, wasn't it?"

I tugged Richie toward the kitchen and whispered urgently, "Listen, Richie, this is important. I really don't want to talk about the murder while Jawarski is here. So will you drop it, please?"

He nodded solemnly. "Well, of course, Abs. Anything for you." Before I could seal the deal, his face brightened, and he surged forward, arms wide. "Here he is now, the man of the hour. We were just talking about you, Jawarski. Was your nose itching?"

Jawarski tossed a smile in his direction and leaned in to kiss my cheek. I lifted my face and took a breath of the air around him, mentally listing each part of his unique scent before I realized what I was doing. Like it or not, he was becoming important to me.

"How was your day?" he asked as he drew away.

It was an innocent question, but in light of my conversations with Corelle, Marion, and Dwayne, I felt heat creeping into my face. This would be the ideal time to tell him what I'd learned if I hadn't vowed to avoid the subject.

I smiled and walked slowly toward the makeshift bar Richie and Dylan had set up near the cash register. Dylan stood behind the counter, entertaining a couple of guests. "My day was fine," I said. "How was yours?"

"Fine. Busy." He stiffened noticeably, and I realized he'd spotted Marshall. He put his hand on the small of my back, one of those protective gestures I like—unless the guy's being possessive. I didn't know how to interpret Jawarski's move.

He guided me around a couple who'd stopped walking abruptly. "The boys have gone all out tonight, haven't they?"

I glanced around again and noticed with relief that Marshall had joined a conversation with a couple of other guests. "And they said it was just a casual dinner party."

"Maybe this *is* casual for Richie."

We reached the bar. Jawarski asked for a Heineken, Dylan poured me a Chardonnay, and we wandered back through the crowded room making small talk until the crowd and the alcohol made us both long for fresh air. Since neither Richie nor Dylan had made any noises about dinner, Jawarski and I wandered out onto the front porch and stood in the chilly evening breeze looking out at the city.

"Do you ever regret moving here?" I asked after a few minutes.

Jawarski shook his head. "Nope. It's a good place. It seems to fit me."

"You don't regret living so far away from your kids?"

He slanted a look at me. "I miss 'em. No doubt about that. But I think they do better when their mom and I aren't in the same place."

"You wouldn't have to live in the same town. Even if you lived across the state, you'd be closer than you are now."

Jawarski turned so he could look at me better. "What's going on, Shaw? Are you trying to get rid of me?"

I grinned and shook my head. "No, of course not. I'm starting to like having you around." I let my gaze travel down to the street, where a truck rattled past. "I don't know. Maybe I'm just trying to make sure you're not going anywhere before I let myself get too close."

We fell silent for a few minutes, listening to the sounds of the town around us and the party through the open doors. A flash of headlights swept the street, and another truck appeared on the road. It rolled past the inn slowly, its bed filled with a tarp-covered load. I started to look away, but something about it made me hesitate.

Jawarski followed my gaze. "Something wrong?"

The truck turned slowly off the street and pulled into the parking strip next to the antique shop. I watched to see if it was going to back out again, but the taillights blinked out, and the truck's door opened. "A delivery? This late?"

Jawarski's posture stiffened. "Seems a bit odd, doesn't it?"

Before I could answer, Ginger Ames came into view two floors below at street level. She must have seen the truck coming and let herself out a service door in the basement. "Must not be anything to worry about," I said to Jawarski. "She's the shop's owner."

He let out a heavy breath, and his shoulders relaxed again. "Good. I'm not in the mood to work tonight."

I heard Richie call everyone to dinner and turned away just as the truck's driver hopped from the cab. This time I knew exactly what made me stop. "That's Dwayne Escott," I said, and all the suspicions I'd entertained while I was in his garage turned into reality. I wondered if Ginger knew what he was doing and hoped like hell she didn't.

"Who's Dwayne Escott?"

Still determined not to talk about the murder, I said only, "I've known him since we were kids. His grandmother and my mother knew each other. I haven't seen him in years, but he's back in town and living with his grandmother about two miles out of town on Motherlode."

I wondered if Jawarski would make the connection with Hammond Junction, but he didn't say anything, so neither did I. "According to Marion, he's refurbishing secondhand furniture and selling it to bring in a few extra dollars, but I was out there this afternoon, and I think he's creating phony antiques. I think his grandmother is so used to protecting him, she can't even see what he's up to."

I didn't want Dwayne to see me, so I moved a couple of steps to the right, behind a cluster of scrub oak. When a second door slammed and Kerry Hendrix came around the back of the truck, I was very glad I'd followed my instincts.

Jawarski looked away from Dwayne, Kerry, and Ginger long enough to glance at me. "You were out there this afternoon?"

"I promised to take Marion some caramels."

"And you took advantage of the opportunity to check out Dwayne's operation?"

"I talked to him for a few minutes."

"Because you thought he was creating fake antiques, or because you thought he had a connection to Lou Hobbs's murder?"

I hesitated, torn between my vow not to discuss the murder tonight and the urge to tell Jawarski what I knew. I liked to think I was a woman of my word, but I'd made that promise to myself before Dwayne Escott came rolling down the street, bold as brass, with a truck full of phony goods.

"Because I knew he had a connection to Lou Hobbs," I

said with a sigh. "I don't know if he's connected to the murder."

Jawarski wagged his head from side to side. "Apparently, feeding you information isn't a real deterrent to this compulsion of yours." He watched as Dwayne began unhooking the clamps keeping the tarp in place. "All right. What's his connection to Hobbs, and when were you planning to tell me about it?"

"I was going to tell you in the morning—and the only reason I planned to wait that long is that I didn't want you thinking that I only like you for your murders."

Jawarski took a second to digest that before asking, "And his connection to Hobbs?"

"He was with Hobbs when Hobbs rented the room from Corelle Davies. According to Corelle, Dwayne guaranteed that Hobbs's rent would be paid."

"She told you all of this?"

"Only after she found out that I'm related to Aunt Grace." Across the street, Dwayne pulled the tarp off the load in his truck. We weren't close enough to see the furniture in detail, but I could tell that he'd stuck a couple of small pieces in with one large highboy dresser.

"And I suppose you asked Dwayne about the rent arrangement while you were touring his workshop."

"Yes, but he denied it. And he didn't take me on a tour. In fact, he did everything he could to keep me from seeing what he was doing." Dwayne lowered the truck's tailgate, and I frowned. "Do you think Ginger knows what Dwayne's up to?"

"She's meeting him after hours to accept a shipment of furniture," Jawarski pointed out. "I'd say it's a safe bet to say that she does."

"So are you going to do anything?"

"About what? Right now, neither of them is doing anything illegal. As a matter of fact, you don't *know* that Dwayne is actually faking antiques, so what I have right now is a great big pile of nothing." He held up a hand to stem the protest he must have sensed coming. "And yes, I'll check into it. If they're scamming the public, we'll take care of it."

"But—"

"If the antiques are fake, and she tries to pass them off on the public, we'll get her," he said again. "Now come on, let's go eat. I'm starving."

His reassurances should have made me relax, but they didn't. Trying to figure out who killed Lou Hobbs was starting to feel like a game of Six Degrees. I was becoming convinced that everything going on in Paradise was connected; I just didn't know how. But somewhere out there was a piece of the puzzle that would link Lou Hobbs, Ginger Ames, Quentin Ingersol, Kerry Hendrix, and Dwayne Escott together.

All I had to do was find it.

Chapter 33

"The two of you certainly seem to be getting along well," Richie said a couple of hours later. As if I couldn't figure out what he meant, he grinned suggestively and nudged me with his shoulder.

I was standing over a sink of hot, soapy water, up to my elbows in bubbles, but the heat that crept into my face had nothing to do with the crystal I was washing. In the other room, Jawarski was helping Dylan clean away the dinner mess and get the dining area ready for the breakfast crowd. I glanced over my shoulder to make sure he wasn't going to come in and catch us gossiping like a couple of teenagers before I nodded. "Yeah, I think we are."

"Well, I, for one, couldn't be happier." Richie carried a tray filled with dirty glasses across the kitchen and slid it onto the counter beside me. "It's about time we saw you smile."

I gaped at him. "I smile."

"Not like this, you don't. And don't go getting all embarrassed and everything," he warned. "You've been such a loner since you came back to Paradise. It's about time you came out to play with the rest of us."

The urge to argue with him rose up inside of me, but it was an old habit I was trying to break—especially when the other person happened to be right.

"You know," Richie said as he went after another cluster of glasses, "if the two of you ever want to stay here, Dylan and I would give you a terrific deal. I know you probably don't want to spend the money on a place right here in town, and I understand that. But the offer's there, just in case."

"That's really generous, but I don't think that's going to happen—at least not for a while yet."

Richie stopped walking and spun around to gape at me. "You don't mean to tell me that the two of you haven't—"

"I don't *mean* to tell you anything," I said with a laugh. I was growing more comfortable with having friends to confide in, but I hadn't quite reached the point of talking about my sex life—or lack thereof.

"Are you serious?" Richie came closer and leaned on the island that stood between us. "What are you doing hanging around here then? Go on. Get out of here. Drag that handsome hunk of a policeman home and have my way with him."

I laughed and shook my head. "When the time is right—and it's not right yet—I'll have *my* way with him, not yours. And *that's* the end of that discussion."

Richie made a face and dumped a handful of trash into the can. "All right. Fine. What do *you* want to talk about?"

I didn't hesitate to ask the question that had been on my mind all through dinner. "How much do you know about Ginger?"

"Ginger? From the antique store?" Richie came around the island and picked up a towel, waiting for a glass to dry. "Not much. Why?"

"Do you think there's any chance she could be connected to the guy who was murdered the other night?"

"Is that a serious question? I want to talk about sex, and you want to talk about murder. Girl, you have some real issues."

Grinning, I handed him a dripping crystal goblet. "That's old news, I'm afraid. And yes, it's a serious question."

"I have no idea if she's connected to him. Why?"

"I don't know. Just a hunch, I guess. Do you remember seeing a man with a limp hanging around her store?"

Richie thought about that for a second, then shook his head. "Not while I was there, but that doesn't mean much. I don't care what Dylan tries to tell you, I haven't been at the shop *that* much."

I smiled and washed another glass. "I believe you. It's just that there have been several strange things going on in Paradise lately, and I'm starting to think they're all connected. I just can't figure out how."

Richie's smile faded slowly. "What things?"

I shook soap and water from my hands and slid two more glasses into the sink. "I thought I saw the dead guy get shot, out by Dwayne Escott's house a few nights before he was actually killed. And in between, I saw him hanging around Kerry Hendrix's truck. And someone else saw him getting into a car with Quentin Ingersol. I saw Kerry and Dwayne arguing the other night, and tonight they're working together to unload a truck. There's a connection between all four of them; I just don't know what it is."

"Have you asked any of them?"

"Everybody denies knowing the dead guy. Believe me, none of them are going to tell me anything, especially not about the murder."

Richie's entire face lit up with victory. "So you *do* think Quentin has something to do with the murder."

"Maybe. I heard that the dead guy, using the name Lou Hobbs, met with him several times, and they had some kind of conversation just minutes before he was found dead. Of course, Quentin denies everything."

Richie hooked a glass onto the rack overhead and frowned thoughtfully. "That's odd."

"Why do you say that?"

"Well, I think I saw them together."

"Where? When?"

"It was at O'Schucks in a booth near the back of the bar."

"You're sure it was Quentin and Lou Hobbs?"

"Well no, but Quentin was with someone I'd never seen before, and I know just about everyone in paradise, at least by sight. Ask Dylan. He saw them, too. And they were *way* into whatever conversation they were having. Dylan and I wondered if maybe Quentin had switched teams . . . if you know what I mean."

"I don't suppose you heard what they were talking about?"

Richie shook his head. "Sorry. They were way in the back, like I said."

"Can you remember who was sitting near them? Anyone who might have overheard their conversation?"

"I wasn't paying that much attention. They weren't there long, though. I can remember that."

"How long?"

"Maybe ten minutes."

I rinsed a glass and handed it to him. "Did they leave together?"

"I think so. They were both there one minute and both gone the next. I didn't notice them leaving, though."

I chewed my bottom lip and tried to shove this new piece of the puzzle into the jumbled picture I already had. It had to fit somewhere, but I sure didn't know where. The only thing it did was to back up Elena Whitehorse's claims that Quentin spent time doing something with Lou Hobbs.

Growling in frustration, I tackled the next goblet in line. "This is making me crazy. Nothing seems to bring me any closer to figuring out what's going on."

Richie swept crumbs from the island into the trash. "Maybe you're trying too hard."

"Or maybe I'm not trying hard enough."

"I doubt that. What do you have so far?" I opened my mouth to answer, but he held up a hand to stop me. "What you have is a murdered guy who everybody knew but nobody admits to knowing. Why do you think that is? I mean, I can understand the murderer lying about knowing him, but according to what you've told me, *nobody* claims this guy as a friend."

I stopped working and turned to look at him, dismayed that I hadn't made that connection for myself. "Why would they do that? To protect themselves from something?"

Richie nodded. "Probably."

I could feel something dancing just out of my reach, but I couldn't wrap my mind around it. "Yeah, but what? Why would admitting that they knew Hobbs be dangerous to anybody?"

"Maybe they're afraid that the killer will come after them."

"Just for admitting they knew him?" I shook my head. "That doesn't make sense."

"It would if he's the one thing that could link them all together."

My hand stilled as Richie's suggestion sank in. "You mean that Hobbs isn't the key to finding the next clue, he *is* the clue?"

"Yeah, I guess." Richie found an open bottle of wine and poured what was left into two clean glasses. He handed one to me and perched on a barstool in front of the island. "Maybe you'd find out something horrible about all of these people if you could just connect them, and maybe the only thing that *can* connect them was Hobbs."

I smiled slowly. "Hobbs came back to town and threatened to expose whatever they're hiding—"

"So one of them killed him."

I laughed softly, warming to the idea a little more with every word. "Because they assumed that if he was dead, that would be the end of it. The police would write him off as some homeless derelict who didn't matter to anyone, and they'd all go on about their business as if nothing had ever happened."

Richie held up his glass and touched his rim to mine. "Instead of focusing on Hobbs, maybe you should be trying to tie the suspects together."

It sounded so simple standing there in the kitchen of the bed and breakfast after a scrumptious dinner and an evening spent with friends. All I had to do was expose what someone had already killed once to keep hidden.

It should be a piece of cake.

Chapter 34

Thick, dark clouds moved into the valley overnight, and as I opened the doors to Divinity the next morning, I suspected we'd have snow before nightfall. The prospect of another storm filled the whole town with restless energy, and a steady stream of customers kept all three of us busy all morning.

About one o'clock, the stream slowed to a trickle and finally dried up altogether. As the first flakes of snow drifted lazily past the shop windows, we collapsed at one of the wrought-iron tables to catch our breath.

Karen let out an exhausted sigh and put her feet on an empty chair. She ran a glance across the nearly empty display cases and shook her head in wonder. "Do we have *any* fudge left?"

"Not much," I said. "I'm going to be busy tomorrow trying to replace what we sold today."

Liberty sat with her elbows on the table, her chin in her hands. "I can help, if you want. I'd love to learn how to make the candy."

My first instinct was to refuse the offer, but I swallowed the words and smiled. In spite of my original reservations, she'd turned out to be a good employee, and I knew I should lower some of the defensive walls I'd put up between us. "I'm afraid Karen's ahead of you in that line, but we can talk about working on some easy recipes one day soon."

Karen rotated her feet on her ankles, alternately flexing and pointing as she did. "We won't have much time between now and spring. When the skiers hit Aspen and Vail, we're usually busy all the time."

"Wow. No wonder you needed me. I had no idea."

"Too much for you?" I asked.

Liberty shook her head quickly. "Absolutely not. I'd much rather be busy than bored."

"Good answer." I slid down on my tailbone and made myself more comfortable. "Since we have a minute, can I ask you a few questions about some of the people you went to school with?"

Karen stopped rotating and put her feet on the floor. "What's this about? The murder?"

I nodded and said to Liberty, "I've managed to connect Lou Hobbs to Quentin Ingersol, Kerry Hendrix, and Dwayne Escott. Do you remember if they were all in your class at school?"

"The last three were. I don't remember Lou Hobbs."

"You remember them all?"

She grinned sheepishly. "I decided to look through my old yearbooks the other night. I didn't know any of them very well, but they were all friends."

"Thanks. That's what I figured. Are you sure Lou Hobbs wasn't in your class? How about Arthur Hobbs?"

"I don't think so. I can bring in the yearbooks if you want to be sure."

"Thanks," I said again. "I might ask you to do that." I stood slowly and slipped behind the counter, filling a cup with ice and Coke. "What do you remember about that group of kids? I understand Kerry Hendrix was popular."

"Oh, he was. He always had kids around him. Boys *and* girls."

"Do you remember any of the girls?"

She closed her eyes and kneaded her forehead gently. "I can just *see* one of them," she said when she looked at me again. "Pretty girl with red hair. Oh, what *was* her name? She wasn't in the yearbook, or I'd remember."

"Take your time," Karen said gently.

"I remember thinking the name fit because of her hair, but I can't—" She cut herself off with a shake of her head.

"Was it Ginger?"

"Ginger! Yes, that's it!"

"Ginger Ames?" Karen's eyes grew wide. "She was one of them?"

"Are you sure?" I asked. "Her brother told me the other day that Ginger had a huge crush on Kerry, but that he never gave her the time of day."

"He's wrong. She and Kerry had a thing for a while, but I'll bet her brother didn't know about it. Kerry didn't really care about her. I don't think he really cared about anyone. But Ginger was mad over him for a while." She rolled her eyes at the memory. "Kerry was like that. The girls in that crowd would have done anything he asked them."

I'd seen that happen before. It made me want to lock up Dana and Danielle and bury the key until they were thirty or so. "Ginger came back to town at the same time Lou Hobbs showed up. I'm betting that's no coincidence."

"Unfortunately," Karen said, her expression grim, "I think you're right."

I don't know how long we sat there in silence, digesting information, but Karen finally broke the silence. "So the fake antique scam is also connected to the murder?"

I nodded reluctantly. "I'm starting to think it must be. Are you sure there wasn't anyone else in that group? Anyone who might be in town now?"

Liberty tilted her head to one side. "Well, there was Davey."

"Davey? Do you know his last name?"

"Mendoza."

I sat up a little straighter, convinced that she'd handed me the missing piece of the puzzle at last. "Do you think Davey Mendoza could be Lou Hobbs?"

Liberty shook her head without even taking time to think about it. "Impossible."

"How do you know?"

"Because Davey Mendoza is dead," Liberty said with an apologetic smile. "He died right after graduation in a car accident."

My flame of excitement sputtered and died away. "He's dead?"

"And has been for the past nine years. There's no way he could have come back to Paradise as Lou Hobbs."

"Slow down, slugger. Start again, and this time talk a little slower so I can understand you."

We sat in Jawarski's cramped office, staring at each other over the lamp on his desk. Outside, the storm clouds had darkened, making it look more like twilight than early afternoon.

"Listen faster," I snapped. "I was talking to Liberty a few minutes ago, and she told me about something that I'm *sure* is important."

Jawarski perched on the corner of his desk, putting my face level with his stomach. "Something about a kid named Davey Mendoza."

Admirable as his flat stomach is for a man in his early forties, I lifted my eyes to meet his. "Yes. He was killed in a car accident shortly after that whole group graduated from high school."

"And you're sure this is related to Hobbs's murder because . . . ?"

"It's a gut feeling."

"That's what I thought."

"Don't dismiss me without even hearing me out," I complained. "First, you have a whole group of kids centering around Kerry Hendrix. Quentin Ingersol and Dwayne Escott are with him everywhere he goes. They're practically inseparable. There's a fourth kid in the group: Davey Mendoza."

"Okay." Jawarski folded his arms across his chest. "Go on."

"Then you've got the girls—girls who'd do just about anything for these guys. You know how some young girls can be. One of them is Ginger Ames—the same Ginger Ames who showed up back in Paradise a couple of months ago and opened an antique shop that we both know is selling phony antiques."

Jawarski inclined his head slightly. "We don't *know* anything."

"All right, we *suspect* that she's selling phony antiques. Probably just enough phony stuff mixed in with real pieces so people don't get suspicious right away. I have no idea why she's doing this, except that she's still insecure enough to do what people ask her to."

"Who would ask her to do this?"

"I don't know. Apparently, she was head over heels for Kerry Hendrix back in high school. Maybe she's still trying to please him."

"Or maybe Hendrix knows something about her she doesn't want anyone else to know."

I thought about that for a second, then shook my head. "I don't think so. Those men I heard arguing at the recreation center were talking about a woman and the proof *she* had. I think they were talking about Ginger." I hadn't forgotten that Liberty could have been the mystery woman, but an unexpected surge of loyalty kept me from saying so. I just hoped that loyalty wasn't misplaced.

Jawarski stood and walked around his desk slowly. "But why do that? If you're right, and Davey Mendoza's death is somehow at the heart of all this, why is it suddenly an issue now?"

"I think Hobbs was blackmailing the others."

Jawarski's gaze shot to mine. "You think what? Why?"

"I was at the bank the other day. Dwayne Escott was trying to cash a check, but the teller couldn't do it. His account was overdrawn."

"That doesn't mean he was being blackmailed."

"It doesn't *prove* that he was being blackmailed," I corrected him. "But I have a hunch that he was. The teller said that this wasn't the first time he'd been overdrawn, and Hobbs always made deposits of cash."

"Well, hell, if that's the case, half the population's being blackmailed. Come on, Abby." Jawarski dropped heavily into the chair behind his desk and picked up a file folder. "I've gone through the report on the kid's death twice. It was an accident, that's all. He was driving under the influence, and he lost control."

"You're sure?"

"I knew the cop who had the lead in the investigation. He was a good man, and an even better cop. If there was anything to find, he'd have found it."

Disappointed, I sank back in my chair and racked my brain for answers. Liberty had filled me in on the details she could remember about Mendoza's accident. He'd gone off a cliff a few miles northwest of town, halfway between Paradise and Aspen. The road was narrow and winding, much of it running along steep cliffs that fell away to a narrow river valley far below. By the time they'd recovered the car and body, there wasn't much left of either.

"What about suicide?"

"I don't think so. Everything in this file indicates that Mendoza had an accident. According to McMillan's notes, there were skid marks all over the road going up that hill. Mendoza might have been drunk, but he was working the brakes, trying to stop the car. If Davey Mendoza had been intent on driving himself off that cliff, he'd have aimed straight."

"You don't know that," I argued without conviction.

"The evidence doesn't support any other answer—not well enough to take to court. And that's what I have to think of, Abby. You were a lawyer—you know that. I can suspect someone all I want, but unless I can find evidence that will stand up in court, I've got nothing."

"I know," I said, suddenly weary. "Go on."

"The testimony of witnesses—several kids at the party heard Mendoza making plans for the following day. Nobody mentioned him being despondent, worried, or acting strangely, and it seems unlikely that he'd make plans with friends if he planned to leave the party and drive himself off a cliff."

"So you think the accelerator got stuck?"

Jawarski nodded. "That's what the investigators on the case believed."

"And what physical evidence was there to support that theory?"

"There wasn't much. You saw the photos." Jawarski flipped open the folder and studied the report again. "I'll admit this part is odd," he said after a minute. "The crime scene investigators recorded the first skid marks at the base of the hill."

"Which means what?"

"That he deliberately sped up that hill. They estimated his speed at over seventy miles an hour."

"Seventy?" I gaped at him. "And they're *sure* it wasn't suicide?"

"We probably won't ever be one hundred percent certain, but they called it an accident, and we have to go with that. He was eighteen and drunk. He probably thought he was invincible."

Maybe he did, but I wasn't bound by the same rules and regulations. "Is there any chance someone else was there? Maybe someone who rigged the accelerator at the bottom of the hill and then sent Davey Mendoza to his death?"

Jawarski looked up from the file wearing a deep scowl. "Murder?"

"Why not?"

"You want me to list all the reasons, or just the top three?"

I smiled at his attempt at humor. "Give me the top three."

"Okay, how's this for starters? How could Mendoza have been alert enough to try to stop the car, but so out of it he let someone put him in that position in the first place?"

"What if it was more than one person? What if three guys overpowered him or something?"

"Such as Hendrix, Ingersol, and Escott?"

I grinned. "If you insist, we can use them for argument's sake."

"Okay, what's the motive? And how did they force him to drive?"

He had me there. Everything fit perfectly—at least in my head it did—except for the motive. There didn't seem to be any reason for anyone to want Davey Mendoza dead. "We'll have to work on that," I admitted. "What about opportunity? I know they were all at the party together, but maybe Mendoza wasn't the only one who left early."

"Maybe not. Why don't you ask Hendrix about that when you see him tonight?" Jawarski teased.

I called his bluff. "Good idea. I'll do that."

His expression sobered immediately. "I don't want you talking to Hendrix about this case again, Abby. I don't want you talking to Ingersol or Escott, either. Or to Ginger Ames. From here on out, you leave this investigation to the department."

"Come on, Jawarski. I'm the best person you've got working on this case, and you know it."

"I won't deny that you've gathered some information that may turn out to be valuable, but you haven't brought one scrap of proof. There's nothing here I can use."

Chapter 35

"Abby, call K Hendrix."

I found the note taped to my front door when I got home from Jawarski's office. It was only a few minutes after seven, but Divinity's windows were dark and the parking lot empty. Jawarski and I had gone round and round over the evidence—or lack thereof—for hours. Much as I hated to admit it, there really wasn't a single shred of evidence to support my theory, but I still believed I was on the right track.

The storm had rolled into the valley while I was at the police station, and as I unlocked the front door, thick flakes drifted from the sky. The snow was falling so fast it had already covered my footsteps in the parking lot.

I ripped the note from the door and crumpled it in my fist. The sky itself could have been falling, but I still wouldn't have been in the mood to talk to Kerry Hendrix. I checked my watch, saw that I had an hour until practice, and groaned aloud. Maybe I'd get lucky, and the coach would cancel because of the storm. It couldn't hurt to wish.

I fed Max a couple of Beggin' Strips and filled his dish with kibble, then found a can of Coke in the fridge and carried it into the living room. My conversation with Jawarski had left me exhausted and disheartened, and the only thing I wanted to do was watch a little mindless, empty entertainment and go to bed early.

I pulled my emergency stash of toffee from the end table and munched a couple of pieces. Half a can of Coke later, I felt revived enough to face the world again—at least for a couple of minutes. Yes, Aunt Grace's toffee is that good.

Since I couldn't put it off any longer, I steeled myself for the miserable experience of talking to Coach Hendrix, smoothed out Karen's note, and dialed the number. As I punched in the last four, I became dimly aware of something niggling at the back of my mind. A moment of déjà vu, maybe. That strange, unsettling feeling that you've been somewhere and done something before. The phone rang twice before I realized that the moment was more than déjà vu.

I stabbed at the Off button and shot up from the couch, almost tripping over Max as I raced to my bedroom. I threw open the closet and tore through the laundry hamper, trying to find the jeans I'd been wearing the day Elena gave me the phone number Hobbs had used when he was alive. I found three sweaters, four pairs of panties, socks, towels, and the black pants I'd worn to Richie and Dylan's dinner party, but the jeans weren't there.

Frustrated, I searched the bathroom, the floor of my closet, and finally lifted the bed skirt so I could check under there. When I spotted a denim leg, I yanked the jeans out from under the bed and shoved my hand into the pocket. There, deep in the bottom of the pocket, I found a crumpled piece of paper. Hands shaking, I smoothed it out and compared the numbers. The first time through, I thought I'd dreamed the match. After the second, the air left my lungs in a *whoosh*, and I sat back against the headboard.

So there it was. Proof that Lou Hobbs had used Kerry Hendrix's phone. I dialed Jawarski's number, got his voice mail, and left a message. I thought about walking back to the police station, but with the snow coming down so fast and thick, Jawarski was probably out dealing with fender benders and slide-offs. I'd have to wait until morning to tell him.

I called Kerry, got his voice mail, and left a message.

I tucked the number and message away into a dresser drawer, changed into clothes for practice, and put milk on the stove to heat. If I had to go out in the storm again, I wanted something warm and soothing to take with me.

The temptation to curl up with a good book was almost painfully strong, but every instinct I had was screaming that Kerry was involved in Lou Hobbs's death, and I didn't want to do anything that might make him more suspicious.

I tossed Max a rawhide bone and was just pouring the cocoa into a travel mug when someone knocked on the door. "It's about time," I said as I threw open the door. "Do you know how many times I've tried calling you?"

"You've called me?" Marshall looked both surprised and pleased.

"Oh. Sorry. No, I thought you were someone else." I stood there uncertainly for a minute, unsure whether to invite him in or turn him away.

"You're worried about why I'm here. Well, don't be. I'm not here for . . . you and me. I need to talk to you about Ginger."

My hesitation vanished immediately. I stepped aside to let him enter. "I have practice in about forty minutes, but I have a few minutes. I was just making homemade cocoa. Would you like some?"

He nodded and blew on his hands to warm them. "I'd love some, thanks."

"Make yourself comfortable. I'll be right back."

"I can come in there if you want. I don't mind the kitchen."

"Whichever you want," I called back. "It won't take long."

He came to the door and watched me while I poured the milk and measured the cocoa. "Ginger's in trouble," he said softly, "and I need some advice. She's gotten herself involved with the wrong people, and they've pulled her into a scheme that's going to send her to prison if she gets caught."

I glanced over my shoulder. "Selling fake antiques?"

Marshall's face fell. "You know?"

"I figured it out."

"Have you . . . have you told anyone else?"

"Have I told the police?" I nodded. "Jawarski and I both witnessed a delivery, so it's safe to say the police are aware of what she's doing. I don't know how they'll catch her, or when, but they will. If you want to help her, convince her to turn herself in and testify against the others. That might get her a lesser sentence."

Marshall sank into one of the chairs at my chipped old table and buried his face in his hands. "I had no idea what she was doing until tonight," he said when he could speak again.

I wasn't sure I believed that, but I pretended to.

"Ginger's not a strong woman, you know. She never has been. She's easily persuaded." He rubbed the back of his neck and let out a thin laugh. "She was an easy mark for those guys back in high school, and nothing's changed."

"Why did she decide to come back to Paradise?"

"Kerry talked her into coming back. He could always get her to do anything he wanted. Dwayne had taken these antiquing classes, and Kerry got the bright idea about having him fake some antiques to make some quick cash. They needed someone to front the business for them."

"But why Ginger? I'm sure she wasn't the only woman who would have gone along with Kerry's scheme."

Marshall lifted one shoulder. "I don't know why they wanted her, but I know why she agreed. She's had a rough time the past few years: a couple of divorces and a bankruptcy, and she lost her job just a few weeks before Kerry called her. She was feeling desperate."

"Out of curiosity, what kind of car does Ginger drive?"

"A black Tahoe. Why?"

"With a broken light on the side?"

A confused scowl creased Marshall's face. "I don't know. Is it important?"

"Not right now. Don't worry about it." I thought about that while I stirred the cocoa into the milk and watched it dissolve. "I understand being desperate," I said, "but if you want me to feel sorry for her, forget it."

"No, I—"

Marshall pulled off his glasses and cleaned them with his shirttail. "I came here to ask you not to go to the authorities. I know it's too late, but she's promised to stop what she's doing. She knows it was wrong." He put his glasses on again and blinked to adjust his eyes. "She's not a bad person, Abby. She's just . . ." his shoulders slumped, and his voice dropped. "She's just weak."

The cocoa began to steam, so I filled our cups and carried them to the table. "I understand how you feel, Marshall, but she's been cheating people. Stealing their money and giving them something worthless in return. She's not a child. She knew what she was doing when she agreed to go along with the idea."

"I know." Marshall wrapped both hands around his mug and stared at it for a long time. "It's not just the antique scam," he said so softly I almost missed it. "She's pregnant."

Okay *that* surprised me. "I didn't realize she was seeing anyone." *Oh God,* I thought. *Is Kerry Hendrix the father?*

"She's not seeing anyone now. The guy who was killed? Apparently he's the baby's father."

Well, that put a new spin on things.

Marshall lifted the cup to his lips. "She swears she wants to start over, Abby. She begged me to help her. If she goes to jail, they'll take the baby away when it's born. And there's no guarantee they'd let me be the baby's guardian. With my schedule at the restaurant, I'm never home. I think it would kill her if the baby was given to strangers."

I'd been wrong; there *was* a part of me that felt sorry for her. It was the part that longed for children of my own and knew I'd probably never have them. I couldn't imagine being pregnant and knowing that the baby would be taken away.

"It won't kill her," I said, more to myself than to Marshall. "It'll be tough, but she'll get through it, and she can always petition the court to get the baby back once she's out of jail."

Marshall shook his head and rolled his eyes. "You have more faith in the system than I do."

"If she cleans up her act, there's no reason the court won't grant her request." I realized that my cocoa had been sitting untouched, so I worked my spoon through it for a few seconds. "Did she tell you who Hobbs really was?"

Marshall looked genuinely confused. "What do you mean?"

"I'm pretty sure Hobbs wasn't his real name, but I'm also ninety-nine percent convinced that he went to school with Ginger and the others."

"I suppose it's possible, but why would he use a fake name?" Marshall thought for a second, then gave his head a firm shake. "No, it's *not* possible. Ginger would have told me."

Just like Marion Escott, the poor guy was in serious denial. "And you didn't recognize Ginger's boyfriend?"

Marshall started to shake his head but stopped himself. "I never actually saw him close up. He was always waiting in the car or in the house while I was outside. We were always going to get together for this or that, but it never happened. The closest I ever came, I guess, whas when I found his body, and I didn't recognize him at all."

"Do you remember a kid who used to hang out with the rest of that group? Davey Mendoza?"

Marshall's gaze flew to mine. "Sure. Yeah. I haven't thought about him in years. What makes you ask about him?"

"Do you remember how he died?"

A pained grimace stretched across his face. "Car accident. He'd been drinking at a party and went off the road on a hairpin curve. Why? What does that have to do with any of this?"

"I don't know that it does," I said with a sigh. "I'm just trying to figure out something that connects Kerry, Dwayne, and Quentin to Lou Hobbs. They all knew him, but they all claim they didn't. Why do you think that is?"

"With those people?" Marshall shrugged. "It could be anything."

"Was Davey alone when he died?"

Marshall nodded. "I remember Ginger saying that some of the kids felt bad, because they didn't insist on going with him, but they said he'd wanted to leave before the rest of them were ready. They said he was upset over some girl. Got into it a little bit with one of the other guys. You know how that goes."

"Which other guy?"

"What? Oh. I think it was Kerry Hendrix."

My heart beat a little faster. "Kerry and Davey fought?"

"I don't think they actually fought. I think it was just a bit of chest thumping, and then Mendoza decided to take off."

I put my chin in my hand and sighed again. "Okay. Fine. So we know Hobbs wasn't Davey Mendoza. Is there anyone else from that crowd that he could have been? Maybe someone who hung mostly on the fringes?"

Marshall thought for what felt like forever. *"Maybe,"* he said at last. "There was a guy named Rusty Hogan who took off for New York about that time. He didn't have a limp, though."

"Anything could have happened between then and now," I pointed out. "Is that the only reason you think it might be him?"

Marshall shook his head. "He was kind of a loner. Didn't have a lot of family. I think he was living with an aunt and uncle, but they didn't pay a lot of attention to what he did. My mom used to fuss about it. You know how moms are: Somebody ought to talk to his aunt. Somebody ought to take him under their wing."

He smiled at the memory. "Anyway, I remember him because we were working at the same restaurant. He was a busboy there, and one day he just didn't show up for work. I never saw him again. He was the kind of kid who could have disappeared, and nobody would have noticed."

I nodded as I mulled over what he'd said. "I guess the next question is whether he was the kind of guy who came back the same way."

Chapter 36

Between piles of snow and parked cars, the roads were almost too narrow for the Jetta. I drove slowly, alternately telling myself I was doing the right thing and muttering at myself for being too stupid to live. I should just tell Jawarski what I knew and let him handle it tomorrow, but something—either curiosity or pure stubbornness—kept me from driving straight to the recreation center.

Before leaving home, I'd called Jawarski again and left a message telling him what I knew and what I planned to do. Hopefully, he'd check in soon. I couldn't let myself think about what might happen if he didn't.

Half a block from the Ivy Attic, I slid into a parking spot on the side of the road. Five minutes, I promised myself as I hiked through shin-deep snow along the unshoveled walk. I'd just ask Ginger a couple of questions and then be on my way.

I let myself into the antique shop, grateful for the warmth that rushed out to wrap itself around me. Ginger was sitting in an antique chair, a paperback novel open on her lap, the cat lounging on the back cushion.

She stood uncertainly when she noticed me, and I saw fear in her eyes before she pulled herself together and turned on her smile.

"Good grief, Abby. What are you doing out in this weather? Are you nuts?"

"I might be," I said with a halfhearted smile. "If you're driving home tonight, you might want to leave early. The roads are really slick."

"Thanks." Ginger set aside her book and shooed the cat

away. "Well, now that you've come all this way, what can I do for you?"

I waved her back into her chair. "I'm not here to buy anything. I'd like to ask you a couple of questions, if that's all right."

"I suppose it's okay. What's up?"

"I'd like you to tell me what you can about Davey Mendoza."

Ginger's head snapped up so quickly I almost felt the muscles pull in my neck. "That's a blast from the past," she said with a tight laugh. "What do you want to know about him?"

"I want to know about the night he died."

"I don't know anything about the night he died."

"That's not true," I said. "I know you were at the same party that night, and I know that Davey left the party because he was upset over a girl. What I want to know is whether that girl was you."

Ginger's chin shot out stubbornly. "Of course not. What a question."

"Then what does Kerry Hendrix know about you that makes you jump when he tells you to?"

"He doesn't know anything."

"What do you know about him? What proof would he and Quentin Ingersol be trying to get from you?"

Her eyes flew wide, and fear shot across her expression again. "I don't know what you're talking about."

"I think you do," I said. "I think somebody killed Lou Hobbs—or was it Rusty Hogan?—because he knew something they didn't want anyone else to find out. If you know what it was, you could be in serious danger."

At the mention of Rusty's name, Ginger's shoulders sagged and her head drooped.

"I'm right, aren't I? Lou Hobbs *was* Rusty Hogan."

She covered her face with both hands, and a sob racked her body. "Yes."

I gave her a moment to pull herself together. Then I said, "You're carrying his baby, aren't you?"

She lifted her head, and I saw tears shimmering in her eyes. "Marshall told you."

"Yeah." I sat on a nearby ottoman and leaned closer. "Why did Davey Mendoza and Kerry Hendrix get into it the night of the party?"

Ginger shuddered and wrapped her arms around herself. "I went out with Davey a couple of times. I was supposed to be at the party with him."

"But you went with Kerry?"

She nodded miserably.

"Why?"

"I was young and stupid, okay?" Ginger stood up so fast, the rocking chair banged into the wall behind her. "I thought Kerry Hendrix was *it*. The finest thing in pants. It wasn't just me, either. All the girls thought he was the best thing that ever happened to Paradise. The guys, too. Dwayne and Quentin would have done almost anything for him."

The cat jumped onto a table a few feet away, and a cup dropped to the floor, shattering on impact. I jumped halfway out of my skin. Ginger let out a tiny yelp as the cat bounded away to someplace safer. "What *did* they do for him?"

"I don't know what you mean."

But she did. I could see the horrible knowledge and the pain of holding onto something she'd rather have never known reflected in her eyes. "What happened, Ginger? You can't keep this a secret any longer. It could cost your life and the life of your baby."

She walked a few feet away, rubbing her arms and staring out the window at the storm. "Davey found me and Kerry together. He freaked out. I mean, *completely* freaked out. He went after Kerry like a maniac."

"They fought?"

She nodded slowly. "It was horrible. I thought Davey was going to kill Kerry. Some of the guys finally separated them and convinced Davey to take off."

"And that was it?"

She turned back to face me. "No."

"Kerry and the others followed him, didn't they?"

She nodded again.

"If you knew they'd gone after him, why didn't you let someone know?"

"I couldn't! Kerry made me go with them. He wasn't about to leave anyone behind."

That didn't surprise me.

"Kerry couldn't stand losing, especially in front of witnesses."

"Who else saw the fight?"

"Just the four of us."

"You, Quentin, Dwayne, and—"

Ginger's eyes locked on mine. "Rusty. He was in the car with Davey."

That *did* surprise me. "He was in the car when it went off the road?"

"No. Davey had been drinking—a lot. He was in no condition to drive. Rusty knew he had to get Davey out of there, or Kerry would kill him once he got his breath again. I think we all knew what Kerry was capable of, even if we didn't want to admit it." She held her head in her hands and massaged her temples lightly. "We caught up with them at the bottom of that hill. Kerry was driving, and he forced their car off the road. They dragged Davey out of the car and—" She broke off, unable to say more, and for a few minutes the sound of her sobbing filled the shop.

I waited in silence for her to go on.

"They killed him," she said, wiping her eyes with her sleeve. "They just kept hitting and hitting until he was finally gone. When they realized what they'd done, Quentin wanted to call the police, but Kerry told us all that we'd get the same treatment if we ever breathed a word to anybody."

"And you believed him," I said.

"Wouldn't you?"

"If you'd gone to the authorities," I said, "they could have protected you. They could have made sure that the kids responsible for Davey's death went to prison, and the rest of you would have been protected."

Ginger laughed bitterly. "For how long? Ten years? Fifteen? Kerry has a long memory. He never forgives, and he never forgets."

There was no sense arguing. She'd made her decision a

long time ago, and nothing could be changed now. "What about Rusty?"

"He took a beating, too, but not nearly as bad as Davey. They messed up his leg, but that was about it. The guys loaded Davey into the car and rigged it so that it would look like he'd had an accident, and they left Rusty there. I guess they thought he'd die, too, since he couldn't walk." She looked up at me and took a ragged breath. "I got the hell out of Paradise as soon as I could, and I vowed I'd never come back."

"And yet, here you are. Why?"

"I ran into Rusty about six months ago. We were both in a bad place, and I think we felt a connection. Anyway, we hooked up. We needed money, bad, and he got this idea to blackmail the others. I didn't realize what he was doing at first, but I put it together eventually. I mean, he never went to work, and he always had money."

"He was getting it from Kerry, Quentin, and Dwayne?"

She nodded. "One of my old girlfiends tracked me down on the Internet, and I told her about Rusty. She must have told Kerry, because then *he* tracked me down and told me he needed me to come back and front this phony antiques scheme. We knew it was just a scam to get Rusty back here, and I didn't want to come, but Rusty talked me into it. He said we could finally see justice done."

An incredible sadness sat on my chest like a weight. "So you came back to Paradise." My throat tightened at the irony.

She caught back a sob. "We were right to be afraid of Kerry all those years ago. He meant what he said. He killed Rusty. I know he did."

I leaned forward eagerly. "Did you actually *see* Hendrix stab Rusty?"

She shook her head sadly. "No, but I know what he's capable of, and I'm sure it was him. Dwayne and Quentin aren't cold enough."

I realized suddenly who Quentin had been arguing with that night at the recreation center. Dwayne might be a big lump of a guy, but he was probably the most squeamish of the lot and the most likely to try talking the others out of their plan.

There was just one question left, and I had to ask it. "What about that night out at Hammond Junction? Do you know what happened then?"

Ginger dabbed at her eyes with the cuff of her blouse. "Rusty got a call from Dwayne asking him to stop by. Said there was something he wanted to discuss and made it sound like he was going to roll over on the others. Like an idiot, Rusty went out there and found all three of them waiting for him. It was an ambush. They would have killed him that night if you hadn't come along when you did. You gave him a chance to get away."

"But I know he was shot. I heard the gun go off and I saw him fall."

"It was Rusty's gun," Ginger said, taking another swipe at her eyes. "He'd loaded it with blanks. He knew Kerry was dangerous, but he didn't want to hurt anyone. He just wanted them to take him seriously. The guys jumped him, and Kerry wrestled the gun away. At some point, Rusty managed to get free. I think the others were glad, but Kerry chased him."

"And 'shot' him with the blanks?"

Ginger nodded. "Rusty heard that first pop, and he knew what he had to do. They thought they'd killed him."

But he'd risen from the dead for a second time. I guess the third time was the charm. This time, he wouldn't be coming back.

Chapter 37

With fewer than ten minutes until practice started, I left the Ivy Attic and hurried through the icy temperatures to my car. Thankfully, the recreation center was less than two miles away. Awful possibilities raced through my head as I drove. I hated thinking of any child in danger, but I was self-ishly glad that Wyatt and Elizabeth had pulled Brody and Caleb from the team. At least I didn't have to worry about them.

I reached the center in record time and parked as close to the door as I could. Praying silently, I half ran, half slid across the parking lot and along the icy sidewalk to the front door.

I moved quickly toward the gym, where the sounds of sneakers on the lacquered floor and bouncing balls took a weight off my mind. It sounded like business as usual.

Squaring my shoulders, I pulled open the gym door and stepped inside. Eight boys were lined up in front of the foul line practicing foul shots. Hendrix was bent over the ball cart picking up the lone remaining basketball on the bottom row.

A short boy with sandy hair stood next to him, his skinny legs sticking out from his uniform shorts like pieces of straw.

"Caleb?"

He looked away pointedly.

My heart shot into my throat, and I swear it stopped beating. What was he doing here? I glanced around for Brody, but it looked like Caleb was here on his own.

Kerry growled, "It's about damn time, Shaw. Where the hell have you been?"

Knowing that he'd committed at least one murder and possibly two made me reluctant to get snarky with him, but I didn't want to behave so differently that he wondered what I was up to. "That's great, Kerry. You want to watch your language in front of the kids?"

He snorted a laugh and tossed a basketball to one of the boys. "I wasn't talking to the kids, I was talking to you. You got a problem with showing up on time?"

I shrugged and hoped I looked casual doing it. "No problem at all. I just ran into a little weather. I got your message and tried to call. What did you need?"

"Ryan needed a ride, but I took care of it. Next time, leave home earlier."

"I'll make a note." I tossed my coat and gloves onto the bleachers and prepared to take my usual spot on the sidelines. I wondered if Jawarski had listened to his messages yet, and what he'd do when he heard mine. Would he follow the trail I'd left, or decide he could wait until morning to talk to me? I wasn't even sure which one I wanted him to do. All I had to do was be careful not to let Kerry see that I knew about Davey Mendoza's murder. If I could do that, we'd all get through practice without incident, and Jawarski could arrest Kerry where the boys wouldn't have to see their coach led away in handcuffs.

The boys lined up to practice the pick and roll, and I tried to work up an expression of patient boredom while I watched. But seeing Hendrix interact with the boys made me nervous, and waiting for Jawarski to show up made me want to crawl out of my skin. Kerry had committed a horrific murder, yet he walked around as if nothing unusual had ever happened in his life. I envied his unflappable attitude. I wasn't nearly so calm.

Keeping one eye on Caleb, who sat on the bleachers across the gym, I filled the cooler with sports drinks and laid out towels. I thought about trying to talk to him again, but the dirty looks he lobbed across court at me convinced me to wait a while longer.

Frankly, I was surprised that Caleb wasn't on the floor with the others. Then again, Hendrix hadn't gotten away with murder, twice, by being stupid. Since Wyatt and Elizabeth had pulled Caleb from the team, the team's insurance would no longer apply, and Kerry could have been held liable if anything happened to Caleb during practice.

While Kerry barked instructions, I started worrying that my voice mail to Jawarski had gone astray. It happened sometimes with the department's outdated phone system. Twenty minutes into practice, I decided the risk was too great. Maybe I'd slip out while Hendrix and the boys were busy and call Jawarski one more time from the receptionist's desk. It couldn't hurt, anyway. I'd also ask Wyatt and Elizabeth if they knew Caleb was here.

Setting the stack of unused towels on the bottom row of bleachers, I walked quickly toward the door.

"*Now* where are you going, Shaw?"

I stopped halfway out the door. "To the ladies' room, if that's all right with you."

Kerry cocked an eyebrow at the sarcasm in my tone, and a cool smile curved his lips. "Of course. Hurry back."

Heart pounding, I turned away. I was certain I could feel him watching me, but I didn't dare check to be sure. Instead of going straight to the receptionist's desk, I crossed the hall to the restroom. I even locked myself in a stall, flushed, and washed my hands to make sure anyone listening at the door would hear all the expected sounds.

I stood in front of the mirror, staring into my own eyes and giving myself a silent pep talk for courage, then walked to the door and pulled it open as quietly as I could. If the boys had gone back to practicing, I'd make a quick phone call before going back inside.

I had the door halfway open when a dark shadow loomed right in front of me. Startled, I let go of the door and stumbled back a step. Kerry caught my arm and hauled me roughly out of the restroom.

My heart shot into my throat, but I tried not to let him smell my fear. "What the hell are you doing?" I demanded. "Let go of me."

"I don't think so." His voice sounded low and ominous, right next to my ear. An involuntary shudder racked my body, and he chuckled at my response. "Not so tough now, are you, Shaw?"

"Are you crazy? Don't do this in front of the boys."

Kerry grinned and yanked me toward the gym. "Oh, they're not here anymore. I sent them downstairs to the exercise room. All except this one, that is." He glanced down, and for the first time I realized he held Caleb's arm with his other hand.

The poor kid's eyes were huge in his small face, and his lip quivered. "I'm sorry, Aunt Abby. I—"

Kerry shook him roughly. "Not now, Caleb. Why don't we all go back inside and have a little chat?"

All at once, my focus shifted. It didn't matter any longer whether I was safe. The only thing I cared about was getting Caleb out of there. Kerry started to walk, and in desperation I tried to make myself a dead weight so he couldn't move me. "I'm not going anywhere until you let Caleb go."

"Sorry. I can't do that. But hey, if you don't want to come with Caleb and me, you don't have to."

He loosened his grip on my arm, and I fell to the floor in a heap. I had two options, neither of which appealed to me. I could let them go and call for help, or I could stay with Caleb and do my best to protect him. He looked so frightened, the choice wasn't difficult to make.

"No, that's all right," I said as I scrambled to my feet. "I'll come."

Kerry didn't say a word, but the sick smile that spread across his face made my blood run cold. "I thought you might see things my way." He turned Caleb toward the gym and shoved him in front of us. I followed, hating myself for passively going along with his insane plan. But Caleb was here, and I couldn't leave him. Wyatt and Elizabeth would never forgive me if anything happened to him. I'd never forgive myself.

Inside the gym, Kerry shut the doors to keep anyone from looking in as they passed. "Caleb and I had an interesting chat earlier," Kerry said. "Why don't you tell your Aunt Abby what you told me, kid?"

Caleb swallowed convulsively, then blurted, "I didn't mean to. I didn't know."

"Shut up," Kerry growled, cuffing Caleb on the shoulder. "Just tell her what you told me."

Caleb's gaze dropped to the floor, and when he spoke again, I could barely hear him. "I told him that you think maybe he killed that guy. That's why Mom and Dad pulled us off the team."

Oh, Caleb. My heart dropped with a *thunk*. "That's okay," I said, hoping to reassure him. "You didn't know."

Kerry put an arm around Caleb's narrow shoulders. "Now, see, that wasn't so hard, was it? The big question now is, what on earth gave you a crazy idea like that?"

"Let Caleb go," I bargained, "and I'll tell you everything you want to know."

Kerry laughed low in his throat. "That's funny, but I don't think so. I think Caleb's going to stay with me until I'm sure I don't need his help any longer. So how about it, Abby? What gives you the right to go around slandering a guy like that?"

My heart was pounding so hard, I could barely hear myself think. I tried telling myself that Kerry wouldn't hurt someone so young, but it didn't help. Kerry was capable of almost anything, and we both knew it.

"I don't think what *I* know is important," I said, trying not to let him see how terrified I was. "Don't you care more about what the police know?"

"If they knew anything, they'd be here instead of you."

Again I was faced with a choice—whether to pretend I didn't know anything, or to admit everything—but I had no idea which would be best for Caleb. If I could rattle Hendrix, maybe I could distract him long enough for Caleb to get away. It was a risk, but one worth taking.

"They know what really happened the night Davey Mendoza died," I said. "They know about the fight, and about the car, and they know about Rusty Hogan. They know that Rusty and Lou Hobbs were one and the same, and they know that Rusty was blackmailing you, Quentin, and Dwayne with what he knew."

Kerry's expression changed from smug and self-assured to wild-eyed and furious. "You're lying."

"They know you and Davey fought over Ginger Ames, and they know that Davey would have been the one standing here tonight if the other guys hadn't pulled him off of you. It's only a matter of time, Kerry. The police are probably on their way right now."

He turned and wiped his face with one hand. I grabbed Caleb's hand and pulled him free before Kerry knew what hit him. "Run, Caleb!" I shouted, giving the boy a shove toward the doors. "Get out of here!"

Kerry whipped back toward me, saw that Caleb was already halfway across the gym, and backhanded me. His knuckles grazed my cheekbone, and pain exploded in my head. I tasted blood and nearly lost my balance, but if it meant that Caleb was safe, I didn't care.

"This is *your* fault," Kerry snarled. He was so angry, spittle formed in the corners of his mouth, and I could see the veins in his neck bulging. "Everything was under control until you stuck your nose in where it didn't belong."

Now that Caleb was safe, I realized how much danger I was in. Kerry could have killed me right there. It wouldn't have taken much to push him over the edge. But showing weakness wasn't an option, either. I tried to take stock of my surroundings without letting him see what I was doing. The only things I could reach without running halfway across the gym were a stack of towels and a cooler full of sports drinks. Neither was going to offer much in the way of self-defense.

"I'm not the one who murdered two people," I said.

"Shut up."

"Give it up, Kerry. The police know everything. You're through."

"Shut up!"

I prayed silently for Caleb to think rationally enough to call for help, for Jawarski to listen to his messages and find me, for any kind of miracle at all. "If you turn yourself in, the DA might go easier on you," I said.

"I *said*, shut up!" In one swift move, Kerry grabbed my throat in one huge hand. "Or I swear to God, I'll kill you."

I gasped for breath and struggled to stay upright under the force of his grip. Fear pumped through my veins, but so did an intense hatred of the man in front of me. "You can kill me, but that won't help," I croaked. "They'll just get you for three murders instead of two."

"I guess that means I have nothing to lose, doesn't it?" Spinning me like a rag doll, he released my throat and wrapped an arm around my waist. "We'll see how quick that cop boyfriend of yours is to move in while you're with me."

He propelled me across the floor toward the locker room. While one part of my mind screamed that I shouldn't let him move me to a second location, the other part reasoned that I might find something to use as a weapon in the other room. We reached the heavy wooden door a moment later, and Kerry used me to push it open. Pain shot through me in all directions as I hit the door, and my knees buckled.

"Keep moving," Kerry warned, "or you're no good to me."

I knew what that would mean. Somehow, in spite of my fear and the pain, I had to make sure he needed me. "I could talk to the police for you. Explain—" My words cut off as he backed me hard into a row of metal lockers.

He leaned in close, his face contorted and ugly. "You say another word, and I'll break your neck right now."

I nodded mutely, knowing I'd pushed him as far as I could. We were alone in the darkened locker room, and my options were closing off quickly.

I felt behind me, trying to find something—anything—I could use to defend myself. Nothing. Absolutely nothing.

Without warning, Kerry jerked me forward again and pushed me toward the outside door. I had one chance to save myself, and I had to take it. I took two steps, then let myself go limp, focusing all my attention on making myself as heavy as I could. This hadn't worked the first time, but it had to work now. It *had* to. Just long enough for me to break his grip on me.

This time, I caught him off guard. He held on as long as he could, but his grip finally loosened, and his footing shifted slightly. I took advantage of that misstep, pulling on his arm as hard as I could to bring him to the floor.

He fell hard, and I scrambled to my feet at the same time. The outside door was no more than twenty feet away, but it felt like miles. I hurried toward it as fast as I could, but I was no more than halfway when Kerry's hand snaked out and caught me by the ankle.

He gave a sharp twist. Pain shot through my leg, and I collapsed against the bench in front of the lockers. With pain searing my ankle and thigh, I battled tears of frustration and anguish. I caught my breath and lashed out at Kerry's face with my free foot.

He let out a roar and lunged for me. I hit the floor and crawled backward, kicking at him with both legs and ignoring the fiery heat that shot into my hip with every move. I kicked out over and over, hitting him wherever I could, until he collapsed on the floor, his breath a harsh rasp in his throat.

I staggered to my feet, putting as much distance between the two of us as I could. I was ready to do anything, whatever it took to make sure I survived and Caleb got home safely to his parents. Spotting a hand weight at the far end of a bench, I lunged for it and lifted it above Kerry's head just as Jawarski burst through the door.

Chapter 38

"Come on, Caleb. Pass the ball." While ten little boys raced up and down the court, I limped up and down the sidelines and watched the Miners' score slowly creep up on that of the Grizzlies. The wounds from my battle with Kerry Hendrix had been healing for weeks, but I still ached in places I hadn't even known I had.

After Jawarski led Hendrix away in handcuffs, I'd been promoted to the chief volunteer position on the Miners. Without Kerry Hendrix and his ego in the way, I found that I enjoyed coaching the team more than I'd thought I could.

I glanced at the scoreboard again, but faster than the score could change, the time clock wound inexorably toward zero. The bleachers weren't exactly packed, but everybody who mattered had come to the game to cheer the boys (and their coach) on.

Someone whistled. Someone else shouted out one of the boys' names. The ball left Caleb's hands and met Brody's with an accuracy that both pleased and startled me. "Great job, Caleb. Way to pass."

Brody dribbled, searching for an opening into the key where Nathan Whitehorse, the Miners' center, battled the Grizzlies center for position.

"Shoot it," I heard Wyatt shout from the stands.

Wyatt's not an easy man to ignore, but Brody did it. "When you're ready," I whispered. "Not until you're ready." We'd gone over this drill a hundred times in the past two weeks, slowly and surely building his ability to retain focus. It was a common problem for all the boys, but they were getting better.

One minute thirty seconds. Brody found his opening and lobbed the ball to Nathan. Nathan backed into the opposing center, ducked, and then quickly jumped over the other boy and shot the ball.

It arched delicately toward the basket, and a collective gasp came from every onlooker in the stands. The ball seemed to hover over the basket, then it dropped, hit the rim, and bounced off the backboard into the waiting hands of the Grizzlies' center.

Both teams raced to the other end of the court, but the Miners were no match for the Grizzlies, and as the time clock ran out, the score read 37 to 34.

"Good job, Miners," I said as the boys wandered dejectedly off the court. "Great effort. Good hustle. You did good, Brody. Your focus was incredible. Caleb, that pass was right on the money. Terrific play."

My encouragement didn't do much to soothe their battered egos, and they straggled off the court with their shoulders slumped and their heads down. They'd been struggling since the news of Coach Hendrix's arrest hit the grapevine. It had to be unsettling to realize that the coach they'd all admired had killed two people in cold blood.

Someone jumped to the floor behind me, and a second later Wyatt put a hand on my shoulder. "They *almost* did it this time."

"One of these days, we're going to surprise you," I predicted.

"I have no doubt," Wyatt said. "Listen, I heard they set a trial date for Ingersol and Escott. Are you really going to testify?"

"I have to," I said, meeting my brother's concerned gaze. "My testimony alone won't be enough to put them away, but maybe it will help."

Wyatt shook his head in exasperation, but he didn't argue with me. "What about Ginger? Are you testifying against her, too?"

I shook my head. "I don't actually know anything."

"You know what she was doing. You're the one who figured it out."

"But I never bought anything from her. She never actually scammed me. Jawarski thinks she'll probably strike a deal with the DA, anyway. Just having phony pieces in her store isn't actually a crime."

Wyatt shook his head slowly. "What a mess." We watched the kids for a moment, and when he spoke again, his mood had lightened. "You still coming by the house after? Elizabeth says that she bought all the stuff you told her you needed. What are you making, anyway?"

I grinned, anticipating his reaction. "You remember Aunt Grace's Candy Bar–Stuffed Baked Apples?"

Wyatt's eyes grew wide, and he looked about six years old. "With ice cream?"

I laughed and stuffed dirty towels into a bag. "Of course with ice cream. What do you think?"

With a whoop of excitement, my big, bad brother hurried off to find his wife, and I turned around to look for my assistant coach. I found him serving sports drink to a couple of players who'd spent most of the game on the bench.

He straightened when he saw me coming, and his blue eyes sparkled with appreciation. What can I say? I think it's the whistle I now wear around my neck. A powerful woman drives him crazy. Who knew?

"Good game, Coach."

"Yeah. I was proud of them. I wish for their sakes they could have won, but I think they felt good about the effort. I hope they did, anyway."

Jawarski wrapped his arms around me, and I realized that my head fit snugly under his chin. "You win some and you lose some," he said softly.

Yeah.

I'd done a little bit of both in the past few years, but as long as I kept winning the ones that mattered, I knew I'd be okay.

Chocolate Raisin Rum Drops

Yields about 48, depending on how big you make them

3 cups seedless raisins
1 cup light or dark rum
12 ounces semisweet chocolate pieces or bittersweet chocolate
1 tablespoon light corn syrup

Place the raisins in a large bowl. Add rum and cover with plastic wrap.

Let the raisins soak for 3 hours.

Drain raisins by putting them in a strainer, but *don't press on them*! Drain the liquid into a bowl to use later. It's terrific for fruit compote or over ice cream.

Combine the chocolate pieces and corn syrup in the top of a double boiler. Place over hot simmering water until the chocolate melts and is smooth, stirring occasionally.

Remove from heat.

Fold raisins into melted chocolate, making sure they're coated well. Drop by teaspoonful onto waxed or parchment paper.

Chill until firm, and store in the refrigerator.

(When packing for gift giving, layer the mounds between two pieces of waxed paper to prevent sticking. Alternately, you can place them into mini paper liners.)

Old-Fashioned Molasses Candy

Yields 12 servings

> 3 tablespoons butter (do not use margarine or other substitute),
>   softened and divided
> 1 cup sugar
> 3/4 cup light corn syrup
> 2 teaspoons cider vinegar
> 3/4 cup molasses
> 1/4 teaspoon baking soda

Grease a 15 × 10 × 1 inch pan with 1 tablespoon butter. Set aside.

Combine sugar, corn syrup, and vinegar in a heavy saucepan and cook over low heat until sugar is dissolved. Stir frequently.

Increase heat to medium and cook until a candy thermometer reaches 245°F (firm-ball stage). Stir occasionally while cooking.

Add molasses and the remaining butter, and cook uncovered, until a candy thermometer reaches 260°F (hard-ball stage). Stir occasionally.

Remove from the heat and add baking soda. Beat well.

Pour into the prepared pan. Let stand for 5 minutes or until cool enough to handle. Butter your fingers well and quickly pull the candy until firm but pliable (the color will change to a light tan).

When the candy is ready for cutting, pull it into a 1/2-inch rope and cut into 1-inch pieces.

Wrap each piece in waxed paper or colored candy wrappers.

Candy Bar–Stuffed Baked Apples

Serves 4

4 medium apples
1/4 cup toffee candy bar, chopped into medium-sized pieces
1/4 cup chocolate-covered nougat nut candy bar, cut into medium-
   sized pieces
2 tablespoons unsalted butter
1/4 cup toffee candy bar, chopped into fine pieces.
1/4 cup chocolate-covered nougat candy bar, chopped into fine
   pieces
3/4 cup soft apple cider
1 tablespoon sugar
Vanilla ice cream

Preheat oven to 350°F.

Scoop out the stems, cores, and seeds from the apples. Use an apple corer and small melon baller to make the job easier. Leave the apple bottoms intact.

Cut off the top 1/2 inch of each apple, then stand the hollow apples in a baking dish.

Stuff the apples with the medium-sized pieces of chopped candy bars. You'll use about 2 tablespoons total for each apple.

Place 1 1/2 teaspoons butter in each apple on top of the candy.

Stuff the apples with the finely chopped candy. You'll use about 2 total tablespoons of candy per apple.

Whisk together the cider and sugar in a bowl and pour over the apples. Bake uncovered until the apples are tender, about 1 hour and 20 minutes.

Remove from the oven and let sit for 5 minutes.

Place the apples on plates and top each with a scoop of ice cream. Spoon the pan juices over the ice cream and serve immediately.

Candy Corn Suckers

Serves 20

> *lollipop collar molds*
> *silicone baking mat*
> *6- or 8-inch lollipop sticks (as needed)*
> *candy corns (as needed)*
> *2 cups sugar*
> *2/3 cup light corn syrup*
> *2/3 cup water*
> *1/4 teaspoon lemon or orange extract*
> *yellow or orange food coloring*
> *small plastic bags (one for each lollipop)*
> *plastic toy rings (spider, turkey, etc.)*

Lay lollipop collar molds on sheet pan lined with silicone baking mat. Fit the molds with sticks and place 1 piece of candy corn inside each collar. (If you don't have collar molds, just lay out the sticks in rows on a Silpat mat. Leave about 3 inches of space between each stick and place a piece of candy corn above the stick.)

Combine the sugar, corn syrup, and water in a small saucepan (preferably one with a spout for pouring). Fit the pan with a candy thermometer, and bring mixture to boil over high heat.

Without stirring, cook the mixture until the candy thermometer reaches 305°F (hard-crack stage). (While the syrup cooks, occasionally wash down the sides of the pan with a clean brush dipped in water to prevent crystallization.)

Remove pot from heat and dip it into an ice bath for 15 seconds to stop the cooking. Add a few drops of extract (to taste) and food coloring as desired, and stir very gently with a wooden skewer until the color is evenly distributed. (To avoid those pesky air bubbles in the finished lollipops, stir gently in both directions, but be careful not to overmix.)

Pour or carefully spoon the syrup into the molds (or over the sticks and candy corns to make a quarter-sized disk).

Cool the lollipops until hard, at least 20 minutes.

Lift the suckers off the mat and remove from the molds. Slip plastic bags over the lollipops and gather the bag shut with a plastic finger ring.

Store in an airtight container for up to 2 days.

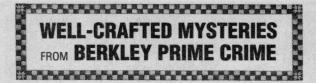